J.C.

*To Kather
Enjoy ~
Lona*

Where There's Smoke

Leanne Leonard

© L. Leanne Leonard 2002 (updated 2014)

Cover Art © Mya Bainbridge Photography

This book is dedicated to my parents, Barb and Ozzie who taught me that I could be or do anything I wanted and to trust in myself. And to the L's — Laura, Laurie and Laurel — who encouraged and sweat with me through all the hard bits. Thank you.

Chapter one

Fred Hennessy had been the most crotchety man Casey Michaelson had ever met.

Until now.

Her surly neighbor's grandson came wrapped in a better package than the cantankerous old coot, but Kieran Hennessy was just as crazy if he thought he could slip his architectural abomination past the committee by blinding them.

He paced before a bank of tall, narrow windows, back and forth between the podium and an easel displaying an artist's rendering of a late Nineteenth Century brick-front morphed into neo-modern glass and steel. Casey blinked tears away, uncertain whether the offending proposal or the blazing sun outside the windows were to blame. The glare strobed on and off with Hennessy's every pass. On. Off. On. Off.

"The façade stays exactly as is." He selected a drawing from the easel and slid it across the table under her nose. He loomed over her and ran a finger across the decorative supports near the roofline. "Right down to the last corbel."

"You're scalping the building." Casey shifted back, away from his warm body and the tanned skin below the unbuttoned collar eight inches from her nose, but couldn't ignore the scent that wafted to her. What cologne smelled of cinnamon and...chocolate? She grabbed her glass and gulped her water. "There are guidelines..." she sputtered.

"Guidelines?" He snatched the drawing back and stuffed his presentation boards into their leather case. "More like old-fashioned, out-dated restrictions." He slammed his portfolio shut and zipped it closed. One side of his lip and jaw worked against unspoken words. Muscles pushed against the fabric of his tailored shirt as he stuffed the portfolio up under an arm and snatched up his jacket, knocking his easel over with the motion.

Charcoal grey trousers wrapped his bottom as he stooped to retrieve the wooden rack and her gaze followed the long legs to the floor.

A cough brought her back to the room and she flushed.

"It's not polite to stare," the woman beside her whispered.

"I wasn't staring." A little too quick. A little too high.

"What would you call it?"

"Processing," Casey said.

"Processing what?" She winked. "His butt?"

Kieran stood in a hallway outside the meeting room rearranging his possessions and steadying his emotions. The narrow-minded association view was going to put him out of business before he even got started. If he hadn't already sunk so much money into the place he might cut bait and run.

Now it was too late. Everything he had was tied up in this venture and with the renovations half-done, he couldn't shake free without finishing the project or at the very least, undoing what he'd started. That top floor view—unobstructed by crumbling brick and thick wooden casings—should be the perfect accompaniment for his culinary vision. But without these renovations, Tethys would just be another seafood restaurant in a sea of seafood restaurants.

He massaged the back of his neck. Committees and guidelines were going to put him in the poorhouse, his business would be done before he even got it off the ground.

Off the ground? He laughed aloud.

What was the matter with that

woman anyway? Was her pretty little head simply used for holding her hair? Couldn't those brilliant blue eyes see that anything had to be better than the dilapidated state of his building at the moment? His grandfather had done nothing on the place in the last twenty years, maybe longer. He hadn't spent a penny on anything beyond canned spaghetti and tomato soup.

"Still, all I get is flack," he grumbled.

He set his items down and slipped his arms back into his jacket. Maybe he should have sold the place when he had the chance. That developer had offered him good dollar for the building. He could have taken that and built what he wanted somewhere else for half the money and less hassle.

So why hadn't he?

Memories, that's why. Sentimental horse crap.

He grabbed his portfolio and turned on his heel, nearly colliding with the woman standing behind him. He took a step back. Where had she come from?

"Hello." She smiled and extended a hand. "My name is Cynthia Lenoch."

He hesitated a moment before shaking the offered hand. "Kieran Hennessy."

"I know who you are. I own a building a few blocks from yours." She leaned in conspiratorially. "They think they can control everyone and everything down here. Especially that Casey Michaelson. Even her ex-husband—"

He raised a hand up to stop her. "I'm not interested in talking about committee members—"

"No. No. Of course not." Her smile faltered, but she continued. "I just meant if we could get rid of her, the committee might see the light."

"There are seven committee members," he sighed. "I don't think one member would change policy."

"If we got the right member or..." she glanced over her shoulder and lowered her voice. "If we could disband the committee."

No committee—no bylaw? "And how do you propose to do that?"

"We've formed our own committee."

God. No.

"Look, Mrs...?" He shifted his items readying to leave.

"Miss," she corrected. "Miss Lenoch. Please, call me Cynthia."

"I'm not looking to join a committee."

She touched his elbow, leaned

in closer and smiled up at him. "We thought you might be our spokesperson."

"Why me?"

"You handled yourself well in there."

Right. That's why he still didn't have committee approval.

"And our other spokesperson quit."

"Why'd he quit?"

"Oh, his place burned down a few weeks ago."

"That's too bad."

"Too bad?" She spat the words and laughed. "Luckiest man in the world. Insured to the max and the guidelines for new construction aren't nearly as restrictive." A dreamy glaze captured her eyes. "If only I could be so—unfortunate." She winked and handed him a card. "Give me a call if you're interested."

"I will."

He picked up his briefcase and smiled for the first time all evening.

A piercing squeal drew Casey out of a dead sleep.

"What the—"

Acrid smoke rolled out from

under the master bathroom door, burning her throat and eyes. Her thundering heart shook her out of bed and she cast her gaze about for anything to tuck under the door to stem the tide of smoke flowing under the door. She grabbed her robe off the end of the bed and kicked it into place at the bottom of the door before hurrying across to the window. She flipped the latch at the top of the old sash and tugged. No movement. She pulled her t-shirt up over her mouth. Tugged again. Nothing.

What the hell? She'd had it open a few days ago. Why wouldn't it open now?

Another deficiency to add to the ever-growing list that included the flooring repairs keeping her out of her penthouse one floor up. Why had she ever agreed to let her ex-husband's construction company carry out the renovations? She drew an angry breath, regretted it as the smoke ripped her throat raw and she launched into a coughing fit that nearly dislodged a lung.

Sirens whined in the distance and she squinted through teary eyes toward the street. Another fit of coughing doubled her over. She skinned a case from a pillow and covered her nose and mouth. Casey hammered the sash. Yanked again.

Nothing moved.

"Help!" the screech that emerged was nothing like her voice

and she stuffed her face back into the pillow case.

Noxious fumes stabbed at her lungs and sliced her throat. She yanked her bedside lamp free and swung it toward the window. Dizziness pulled her off balance and she stumbled left, righted herself and swung again. Her knees buckled as the lamp went through the glass and the hole brought a cool rush of night air into the room. She gulped greedily at it. Coughed. Gulped some more.

She had to move. Had to stand. Had to get out. Had to survive to kill her ex-husband.

She fisted the lamp and put her other hand on the window sill to pull herself upward as more glass showered her. Vise-like hands grabbed her upper arms and lifted her through the window. Cool night air enveloped her and her lungs fought to drink its freshness. Arms reached under her knees and back to lift her off the cool metal slats. Her protests were lost in a coughing fit and she leaned into the strong chest.

Who? She tried to look up, to see his face, but her eyes burned and her head spun.

Something familiar but her burned nostrils couldn't place it.

"It's all right. I've got you." Low. Soothing. He pulled her tighter. "Relax."

She couldn't think right now. Couldn't focus. She gave in, rested her head against his bare shoulder.

His shoes scraped and squeaked against the metal slats of the fire escape as he turned each corner descending ever closer to the ground. Casey closed her eyes against the pounding in her head, but opened them when the circular motion of following the flights downward made her nauseous.

She inhaled, coughed, inhaled again. She crinkled her nose against the kaleidoscope of fire smells. The toxic mix of burning finishes and building materials swirled into the sky above. Had everyone gotten out?

Casey shifted her gaze toward the ground, regretted it and tucked her head back against her rescuer's chest. Her sharp intake of breath brought new spasms to her airways and her body shook.

A gentle hand caressed her hair. "It's all right." He pulled her closer and started down another flight. "We're almost there."

His arms wrapped her securely against him, cushioning her from the movements and her own fear. His scent drew her to him, her nose following the mixture of soap and spice into his neck. She closed her eyes and reveled in the warmth that spread down her face, over her shoulders and along her body to pool where his arms supported her lower back and legs. The contrast of his fiery skin against her cool bare legs was—

Bare legs. Panties. What the hell was she doing? She jerked her head up into something hard and her rescuer cursed. He stumbled, nearly dropping her. She tightened her grip.

"Sorry," she croaked, her raw voice foreign even to her.

He adjusted his grip and said nothing, but there was a distinct shift in his gait.

She should tell him to put her down. She was a big girl, tough, independent. She held a third degree black belt in Goju Ryu Karate, for Christ's sake. She could stand on her own two feet. Yet the thought of putting those two feet on the slatted fire escape so far above the ground made her insides churn.

Stupid. Irrational. Aggr—

"I've got her." A firefighter slipped an oxygen mask over her mouth and nose.

They were on the ground.

Her cheeks blazed as the second man carried her across the debris between her building and the next. He set her down on the bumper of the rescue truck, tucking an emergency blanket around her shoulders. An ambulance silenced its whine and pulled up to the curb behind it.

"Casey!" Kate West called.

"Thank God you're safe." Her neighbor moved over to meet her. "We were so worried."

A weak smile spread across Casey's lips and she shook her head. She tugged the mask away from her face. "I'm all right," she croaked and touched her neighbor's arm.

"Your ex-husband was going to go in after you."

"Jim?" What was he doing here?

Casey leaned around the end of the rescue truck and searched the crowd for her ex-husband. She didn't see him.

"Yeah, but someone else was already bringing you down the fire escape."

Casey waved at the ragtag group gathered away from the action on the far sidewalk. Were they all there? One. Two. Her head ached. She couldn't concentrate.

"We're all fine," Kate said.

The paramedic urged Casey's attention back to him and settled the oxygen mask back over her nose and mouth, then helped her onto the gurney he and his partner had wheeled behind the truck.

Thank God. Everyone was out and fine. That's all that mattered. The building could be fixed. Her dojo. She closed her eyes and sank back against the thin gurney mattress. Her business took up most of the ground level of the building and she'd only recently finished updating the floors and changing rooms. She took as deep a breath as her lungs allowed and shifted to catch a view of the building.

Smoke billowed from some of the ground floor windows and from her temporary digs six floors up, but the rest of the building appeared largely unaffected. Thank God for fire doors.

Firefighters adjusted hoses and streams of water created black sooty clouds that poured out the shattered windows of the basement level antique shop. Persistent flames licked out at the brick exterior. The amber glow played against the muscular figure of her rescuer like the sun dipping behind a tree and Casey pulled her mask away. Darkness and shadow obscured the face that was turned toward her, but when he stepped into the light of a streetlamp Casey nearly choked on her sharp intake of breath.

Kieran Hennessy.

Soot streaked from hairline to chin and he stood with his legs slightly apart, arms crossed over a bare chest that narrowed to his waist. Untied shoes protected otherwise bare feet. He ran a hand through messy blond hair and moved toward her. Plaid boxers rested on his narrow hips and he reminded her of one of those highland warriors from the historical novels she hid under her bed. She settled herself back against the gurney and took a few deep draws of oxygen.

Why did it have to be him?

Chapter two

The strong odor of burnt furniture wafted out the empty window opening and across the sidewalk. Engine brakes echoed down the corridor created by the three story parking structure that straddled Front Street and the truck narrowly missed a rubbernecker pausing to gawk at the burned out storefront.

A light breeze flapped the yellow tape that barred entrance and Casey shuddered. Just two days earlier she'd nearly met her demise a mere six floors up. Shattered glass still littered the edge of the sidewalk closest to the building and large plywood planks rested against the wall.

What the hell had happened?

The building had been retrofitted with sprinklers and fire doors as per code and yet here Casey was standing in front of a blackened mess. Had her tenant left an old appliance turned on? Or had it been the construction crew renovating the antique shop?

She glanced up the façade to the main floor that housed her Karate dojo. Soot blackened the bricks and plywood blocked the now empty panes. Further up little evidence of fire could be seen. And yet the condo she'd been staying in had been filled with smoke. She worried her lip between her teeth. Why was that? She stepped sideways and scanned the side of the building. Aside from the lowest floor and hers, there was little evidence of anything amiss. Strange.

Her gaze zigzagged back down the fire escape and she shuddered. Had she really come down that? She wrapped her arms around her body. What if those arms hadn't managed to haul her out onto that metal platform? Her throat ached at the memory and she turned away from the building. There was no sense going back over it again. She'd already been over it a hundred or more times. The call had been close and that was sufficient. It was time to move on.

Her gaze snuck back to the basement storefront. What if her building was declared unsafe and she and her tenants couldn't move back in? She'd sunk everything into the building, its design and renovations. Her business. Her home. Her tenants. Everything would be lost—

She dropped a barrier on those

thoughts. Not everything. It was simply a building. Everyone had gotten out safely and that was what was important. Everything else could be fixed. At least she hoped it could.

Casey turned away from both building and thoughts toward the now empty wharf across the road near the river. Demolition that removed remnants of three old structures from the once thriving dock left an unobstructed view of the river. A tug slugged its way atop the churning current of the Fraser River toward the Patullo Bridge while vehicles whipped along the commercial bypass route right in front of her.

She closed her eyes, forcing her breathing into time with the movement. She employed the meditation techniques she'd learned from her Japanese sense to exhale her worries on the wind. Inhale, visualize, breathe in, breathe out.

"Casey?"

The voice pulled her back to the basement antique shop. Charlie Griffin, a local firefighter and one of her karate students, stood on the other side of the empty window frame. His stark white firefighter's shirt provided an odd contrast to the soot-black background. He skirted some debris and stepped up to the opening.

"What are you doing here?" he asked.

She shrugged. "I don't know. Where else was I going to go?"

"I thought you'd still be in the hospital."

"Not this kid." Two days had been more than enough. "Any idea on cause?"

He shook his head. "Nothing definitive." He hedged a moment, glanced back over his shoulder. "I can't really discuss it."

What did that mean?

"What's going on Charlie?"

"Nothing. We're just investigating."

"Just standard practice, right?" she said.

Another hedge. A stampede rushed her chest and she coughed as she drew a deep breath.

"Arson?" she sputtered.

He cast a glance back over his shoulder as if he might confide in her, but his lips simply thinned into a line. "We won't finish our investigation for days."

A shudder chased up her neck, standing the little hairs on end. She pressed the palm of her hand against her suddenly throbbing temple and swallowed.

"How bad?" she asked.

Charlie shook his head. "The

shop's a write-off, but most of the rest of the building is intact. The main floor has some damage at the back, mostly smoke and water, but it's localized to the rear elevator lobby and dojo changing rooms." He glanced back over his shoulder. "Your apartment suffered some damage, but all in all, it's is fairly minor. You were lucky."

Lucky. She tucked her lower lip under her teeth and nodded. She had been lucky. "Any idea when I can get in?"

Another white shirted firefighter floated across the back part of the store, black pants camouflaging the second investigator's lower body.

"Structural engineer should be here sometime this afternoon, but there are no guarantees."

"Maybe I'll go grab a coffee, hang around a bit. You want anything?"

"Nah, I'm good."

She sighed, headed past the lone tenant in Kieran Hennessy's building—Pete's antiques. The shop, part of the area pandering to the vintage crowd, was run by a strange little man with an eye for junk. She rounded the corner and started up the hill, but paused halfway up. The block's steep grade left her damaged lungs burning and she wheezed. She glanced back down toward the river, took a draw on the puffer they'd provided at the hospital and continue upward. At the corner, she crossed the street to the coffee shop and glanced back over her shoulder at the cordoned off front entrance of her building.

She'd sunk everything into the property. Her divorce settlement came in the form of the red brick building and its renovations. A small book shop took up a corner of the first floor while her karate school took up the rest. The building had been strata titled, though she maintained ownership of three floors of condos including the penthouse along with the main and basement floors. Her karate school and the building provided her only sources of income. If the building failed inspection—

She turned away, entered the coffee shop and joined the line at the counter. She couldn't think about that. She couldn't leave here. It was home. The only one she'd know since—

"How—"

Caught daydreaming, she spun round ready for anything.

Hennessy raised a brow. "...are you feeling?"

She flushed and dropped her hands to her sides. "A little edgy."

"Apparently." He nodded toward the menu board behind the counter. "What'll you have?"

Her protest died on her lips as he reached round her waist to slide his prepaid card across the counter to the clerk. The quick contact with her middle conjured images of bare chests and plaid boxers and she suddenly found it hard to breathe.

He ordered some complicated concoction and turned expectantly to her.

"Breakfast blend, black," she managed.

He smiled and walked to the far pick up counter where she joined him a few moments later.

"Traditional," he said.

The barista spouted something about a caramel, half-something.

Casey shook her head and raised her cup. "*Coffee.*"

Hennessy laughed, stuffed a lid over his whipped cream and followed her out onto the sidewalk. "Any news yet?"

The hot coffee burnt her tongue and she drew air to cool it. She shook her head not wanting to draw any more attention to her wagging tongue.

"The fire inspectors are there now. I'm not sure how long it'll take."

"What are you going to do if you can't go back in?"

"She's going to stay with me." The familiar voice turned her around.

Jim.

"You okay?" her ex-husband asked.

"Yes, thanks," she said.

Jim drew his gaze up her neighbor's six feet and down again then turned to her. His eyes narrowed and her chest tightened. He turned back to Hennessy.

"Jim Taylor—husb—"

"*Ex*-husband," she corrected.

Her ex nodded and offered a smile, one that had gotten her in trouble all those years ago. What had happened along the way to push them so far apart?

"Kieran Hennessy." He shifted slightly, coming closer to Casey as he extended a hand in greeting.

Jim's stance widened and his fists balled. The smell of alcohol wafted the short distance to her. She sighed. That's what had happened. Hennessy shifted closer, his soft cotton shirt brushing her elbow. Jim shifted too.

Great. Just what she needed. Casey drew a tired breath. "What are you doing here, Jim?"

"I heard about the fire and I wanted to make sure you were all right." His gaze shifted away from her to the sidewalk and flitted off into the distance.

"Thank you for your concern, but I'm fine."

"You'll need a place to stay." He reached toward her, but she shifted away.

"I'm sorted, thanks." She raised her cup toward Hennessy. "I have to get back. Thanks for the coffee—and last night."

"Last night?" Jim's voice tightened. His eyes burned into her.

"I don't owe you an explanation."

Jim's knuckles whitened. His respiration came in short spurts. Kieran touched her shoulder and smiled.

"I hope we're still on for this morning. I could use a work out."

She blinked a few times, but picked up on his cue.

"If we're allowed in, I'm going to do a light training session today, but you're still welcome to join me."

He nodded. "Well, it was good to meet you."

Jim looked from Casey to Hennessy and back again. His eyes narrowed and she could almost picture the ridge he bit inside his cheek. His mouth twitched with words he itched to speak, but he remained silent and walked the short distance to his pickup.

"I'm glad you weren't hurt," Jim mumbled before he climbed behind the wheel and slammed the truck's door.

"Sorry," she said as she turned back toward Kieran.

"You have nothing to be sorry about."

They waited for the cuckoo that signaled the walk and crossed to the south side of the street. A squeal of tires behind them signaled Jim's departure and Casey kept her gaze steadfastly focused on the signal.

Hennessy frowned. "Are you going to be all right?"

She bit down at the renewed embarrassment the quiet question evoked. Regret followed. Regret for the loss of her marriage—not for what it was, but for what it might have been.

"Yes. Thanks again, Mr. Hennessy."

Kieran waved her off. "No need. And it's Kieran." He leaned against the brick corner of his building. "You *do* have a place to stay, right?"

She nodded and followed his movements as he rolled a sleeve up to his elbow. His worn work shirt, while not tight, did little to hide the muscular chest she'd become too familiar with.

"I'm staying with a friend."

"I have to get back. We're putting the finishing touches on the dining room."

She smiled. "You still plan to open at the end of the month?"

He nodded. "The main floor."

"Good."

"It'd be better—" He hesitated.

She steeled herself against the rest of the statement but it didn't come. She surveyed the length of legs to scuffed work boots then back up. He shifted his coffee to the other hand and started on the other sleeve.

"Come to the opening. It should be a good party. I know the chef." He winked.

"Maybe I will."

He rolled his sleeve up over a gauze bandage that encircled his right forearm.

She drew in a breath. "What happened?"

He glanced at the bandage and laughed. "Stupidity."

"Looks serious."

"Nah, mere flesh wound." He

thumbed over his shoulder. "I'd best get back."

She watched him move along the sidewalk a few steps then started down the hill toward Antique Alley. A yawn tensed her body and she blinked the fatigue away. Charlie and his partner were deep in conversation when she rounded the corner. She sipped at her coffee, but the caffeine did little to stifle the yawn. Maybe she'd head back to Tory's for a nap.

A nap. She hadn't napped since she was a kid and even then, she hadn't gone down without a fight. She and her younger brother had given new meaning to the words 'hide and seek'. A smile crossed her lips then faded. That had been a world ago. A different time, a different life.

Casey shook herself away from the memories and half-ran across the two lanes of traffic to her car. She leaned on the trunk a moment to recover from the spate of coughing that overtook her then pulled the driver's door open. She set her cup in the holder and stuffed the key in the ignition. The engine caught with one twist and she grabbed the gear shift before catching the flutter of paper under her windshield wiper.

She freed a folded rectangle of newsprint from under the wiper and smoothed the article across the hood of her car. A crude red X had been drawn through the picture that accompanied the article about the fire at her building.

The picture was of her. Casey fisted the article to her chest and searched the surrounding area for the culprit.

Who?

Better yet, why?

Chapter three

Her movements played like a scene from a movie and the long stick she swung whistled through the air with alarming speed. Her focus didn't waver as she waged a battle against an opponent only she could see. Kieran shifted right and leaned against the wall to watch.

The crisp white uniform did little to accentuate the body hidden underneath, but his arms tingled with her remembered form despite the weeks since they'd touched. He could still feel the long muscular legs and the heat of her breath against his neck. She'd shuddered at her meager attempt to walk herself down the stairwell. So pale. So fragile. He hadn't wanted to relinquish his hold, even to the firefighter.

Casey spun and whipped the six foot staff around. It snapped and vibrated with the force. He straightened.

Perhaps he shouldn't judge this book by its cover.

"Mr. Hennessy." She smiled and

crossed to the cherry wood trimmed doorway. She turned away from him, bowed and stepped out into the lobby.

"Ms. Michaelson." He dipped his head slightly. "Where'd you learn to handle such a big stick?"

She sized it up, then turned to him. "A little more than you're used to?"

"Maybe a little." He closed the distance between them. "Perhaps you could show me what to do with it."

Her smile told him he was in trouble and he was on the floor with the pointy end of the staff at his throat in an instant. She spun it back out of the way and offered a hand.

Not exactly what he'd been hoping for.

"What can I do for you, Mr. Hennessy?" she asked when he was upright.

He held out a small takeout container. "I'm afraid it might be a little disheveled."

She set her weapon against the wall and popped the white container open. "Chocolate cake?"

"I call it a Turtle Torte. Chocolate, caramel, pecans."

"Are you trying to bribe me?"

"Would it work?"

"Probably not."

"All right, then. Consider it a neighborly gesture." He smiled.

"Turning over a new leaf?"

He laughed. "Can't beat 'em and all."

"That mean you're giving up?"

She crossed and rummaged for something under the counter. Rice paper wall hangings boasting Asian characters fluttered with the breeze of her movements. The white fabric covering her heart-shaped bottom contrasted against the polished wall panels behind her. He sidestepped slightly and enjoyed the view before she shifted into a crouch.

"What would I do with my Tuesday nights then?" he asked.

"Bake cookies?"

"I don't bake cookies." He crossed to the opposite side of the counter rested his elbows on it, leaned forward and looked over the countertop at her. "Besides, someone has to keep you out of trouble."

"Does it always have to be you?" She slid the torte onto the counter and leaned beside it.

"Apparently."

She swiped her finger against the side of the container and stuck it in her mouth. Her eyes narrowed and sparkled.

"Oh my God. I take it back."

"What?"

"Bribery is a distinct possibility."

He waggled his eyebrows and smiled. "I'll be back later with the whole cake then."

Her laughter reverberated through his body.

"This is more than enough."

"You sure?"

A nod.

"If you change your mind, you know where I am." He crossed to the door and tugged it open. "I better get back."

She followed him to the doorway, seemed to hesitate a minute before she continued out onto the sidewalk behind him.

"I was just going to take a break. My coffee stinks, but you're welcome to join me." She held up the container and nodded toward the back of the dojo. "We can share this."

"Thought you'd never ask."

He took five long strides back through the door and followed her across the foyer toward the training floor. Rectangles divided the expansive wooden floor bordered by racks of traditional weapons. Her restraining arm kept him from passing through the open entry.

"You'll have to take off your shoes."

He lifted a brow, but sat on the bench to the right of the doorway. "All right, but I don't usually do this on a second date."

"Second? Wouldn't that imply a first?"

He untied his first boot and slipped it off.

"You've forgotten already? Fire escape. Moonlight. Nuzzling."

"Nuzzling? Ha!" She picked up her weapon. "More like groping." Her voice was serious, but she was smiling.

His pulse quickened at the remembered contact. Her bare thighs were warm and smooth to the touch. Her golden blond hair, silky against his shoulder and fingers when he'd tried to reassure her she'd be fine.

"Honey, when I grope you, you'll know it." He yanked his second boot off and stood.

Casey pushed open the fire door at the rear of the dojo, the curling damp floorboards cool on her bare feet as she stepped through into the rear elevator lobby. Drying fans blew from both directions and a few gaping holes where firefighters had checked for damage decorated the back wall.

"Private elevator?" Hennessy nodded appreciatively.

"Freight elevator, but I use it to access my suite from the dojo."

What was she doing? This was her world, her private space. She rarely brought anyone into it and yet here she was opening it up to the man who'd caused her nothing but trouble over the last few months. The man who wanted to change the face of her neighborhood, to obliterate the history and traditions she'd fallen in love with.

"Remind me not to ask what to do with this." He indicated the ceremonial sword that rested below a single portrait on the wall in the small elevator lobby.

"Are you sure? It seems you could use a shave." She reached up and stroked his chin.

She pulled back and turned away. Why had she done that?

His grin widened into a toothy smile. "I do, do I?"

Brain damage. That was it.

Inhaling all that smoke had turned the logic center of her brain to mush. Now she was using that reptilian thing psychologists were always talking about, the part that was the size of a walnut or pea or something.

She ushered him into the

elevator, yarded the accordion lattice gate across and twisted a key in an out-of-place security panel. The smell of chocolate filled the small box and she drank it in greedily before realizing what she was doing. She clenched her jaw.

What the hell was the matter with her? Some man brings her a bit of chocolate, pays her a little attention and she becomes a...girl.

Casey cranked the old-style brass lever across to seven and the elevator lurched into action. Thanking him for saving her life was the polite thing to do. Her grandmother would be proud. Still as soon as he finished his coffee, she'd get rid of him. That shouldn't take too much—no one ever asked for seconds of her coffee.

"I didn't think there were any elevators like this left." Hennessy's knuckles were white around the brass rails.

"I had to fight to keep it."

"Oh?"

"Yeah, I think they only gave in to shut me up."

"So, if I keep coming back and bugging, the committee will give in?"

"Probably not. And it wasn't *the* committee anyway."

"But being a pain worked for you."

She flashed him a look. "I wouldn't say I was a pain. Just...persistent."

"I can be persistent."

"But I still had to cough up the ten grand for upgrades to meet the—"

"Guidelines."

She bit her tongue as he followed her out into the five foot square foyer that boasted an exposed brick accent wall, black and white prints and dark brown upholstered bench. He trailed his fingers over the rough surface before following her through the back door to her suite.

"Nice," he said.

She had to agree. Tory had helped her arrange her things over the week since the engineers had certified the building. She'd had to buy new bedroom furniture and replace the few miscellaneous items she'd actually moved into the lower floor condo from storage, but she'd escaped relatively unscathed.

Casey smiled. She'd been lucky that the fire doors had been solid and that Jim's 'it'll be ready next week' replies had kept her from moving more of her stuff in.

She'd been even luckier that her neighbor had reached her in time.

"I'll take those." She took his

boots and started into the condo. "Come on in."

She dropped his boots near the door leading to the front elevator lobby and led him into the open living area that took up the entire river side of the building. Tall narrow sash windows brought in light and glimpses of the Fraser River. Dark hardwood flooring contrasted the light furniture and old brick ran down the west wall. Each room on that side enjoyed the same rustic accent.

"You mind?" He thumbed toward the windows.

"Not at all, make yourself at home. I'll start the coffee."

Casey set the take-out box down on the island that divided the kitchen from the rest of the living space and headed for the back counter. She grabbed the coffee carafe, filled it, dumped some coffee in the basket and clicked the machine on. Plates clattered on the granite counter top and Hennessy turned her way.

Morning sun blazed round his body where he leaned against the wooden window frame and gazed toward her. He rested one foot on the frame and his leg triangled across the window. Powerful arms rested over his chest while the line of his back tapered gently to his waist. Sunlight accentuated the angles of his face and she could just make out the relaxed lines.

"Gorgeous."

She flushed and her heart galloped.

A quick smile flitted across her face when he turned back toward the river.

He was talking about the view.

She halved the dessert onto two plates and let her face cool. "Soup's on."

He slipped onto the stool across from her, cocked his head to one side and reached toward her. His hand brushed her cheek and Casey leaned into it, caught herself and straightened. He retrieved something from her hair and held it up for inspection. Chocolate cream.

His grin widened.

She turned on her heel and retreated to the coffee maker. What was she? Fourteen? She couldn't remember the last time she'd been such easy prey for a pair of beautiful eyes and a bit of flirtatious nonsense.

Definitely brain damage.

She filled two cups with questionable brown liquid and turned back. She slid a cup his way.

"Thanks," he said.

"You might want to hold off on that until you've actually tasted it."

"It can't be that bad."

She shrugged.

He sipped and winced. "I saw your picture in the paper. Interesting article."

Article? Had he—

She lifted her gaze to his, but she noted only interest.

"Hometown girl?"

"Close enough. It's the only place I'd call home." She slid a stool around the kitchen side of the counter and seated herself across from him. "My grandmother grew up here, just down the road actually. She'd tell me stories about what it used to be like."

"You spent a lot of time together?"

A nod. "I came to live with her when I was thirteen." And angry. "She passed away just last year." Her gaze instinctively sought four charcoal sketches arranged on the wall at the end of the counter.

Kieran's gaze followed. "Nice. Is that one this building?"

"Yes. She sketched it as an anniversary gift."

"Talented." He forked a bit of chocolate into his mouth and reached for the cup, but seemed to think better of drinking. "Talented."

"Thanks."

"How long have you been living here?" he asked.

"I've been staying downstairs while they were finishing this place up. I guess it's about six months, but we bought the building almost ten years ago."

"Good timing."

"Definitely, before property values went through the roof. It was an office building then."

"How come it took so long to do the renos?"

"I don't know. It took us a while to agree on what we were going to do with the place. Jim resisted the loft thing for a long time thinking he could buy your building too, knock everything down and do some big project."

"Imagine that."

She flashed him a look. "Your grandfather wouldn't sell and the city wouldn't allow it anyway. With the divorce, I got the building and most of the renovations."

"Nice settlement."

True. But it hadn't been without its costs. "He got the business and a couple of current projects." She glanced around. "It's taken a long time, but I think it was worth it."

He glanced back at the view. "You've done a wonderful job..."

She could feel the 'but', waited for it.

"Don't you think it would have been better if you could have turned this into a wall of windows?"

Here it was. The real reason for his visit.

"Or better yet, incorporate an open terrace?"

She worked her jaw then forced herself to relax. "I have a roof."

"Not the same."

"True enough, but we're in the process of turning into a common garden for the building."

"Must be nice."

She wasn't sure she liked his tone. "What must be nice?"

"Having the committee in your pocket like that."

"What are you talking about?"

"They wouldn't allow my roof top deck."

"That's because you wanted to rip your top floor off at the same time."

"That was two proposals ago. My—"

She held up a hand to cut him off and dumped the contents of her plate and his back into the takeout box.

"Did you really think you could win me over this easily?"

Who the hell did he think he was?

Better yet, how simple did he think she was?

A bit of flirting and chocolate and she'd miraculously change her mind. Never mind that it wasn't up to her.

Men.

What the hell was the matter with them?

The forkful of turtle torte suspended en-route to Hennessy's mouth spilled onto the counter as she grabbed his elbow and extracted the fork from his grasp. She led him to front foyer, pressed his boots and dessert box into his abdomen and opened the door.

"Just take your cookie and leave."

Charlie Griffin stood in the doorway, hand suspended as if he were about to knock. Confusion gnarled Hennessy's features as he sidestepped the firefighter into the elevator lobby.

"It's." He shoved one foot into a boot. "Not." Then the other. "A cookie." He jabbed the elevator button.

Charlie burst into laughter as she closed her door behind him.

"Just what is so damned funny?" If he didn't stop laughing she was going to show him her latest takedown technique.

"Take your cookie and leave?"

Casey stopped. Had she really said that?

"What can I do for you, Charlie?" She breezed by him toward the kitchen.

He followed her around the corner. "You're not going to like this."

"Just spit it out, Charlie." Casey stacked one chocolate marred plate atop the other.

He flattened the papers he carried on the countertop. "It's arson," he said.

"Arson?"

Casey grabbed the counter for support. The suggestion had come up in their earlier conversation, but the confirmation still turned her knees weak. Her mouth opened but she couldn't find words. Why?

She lifted her eyes to Charlie.

"Yes." He sighed. "I can't give you the details but it's definitely arson and your insurance company has requested the findings."

"My insurance company?"

"It's pretty standard in these things, but they'll withhold payment until—"

"Until what?"

He swallowed and his eyes shifted away.

Good God. "They think I did it?"

"You're definitely on the list. You have the most to gain."

"And lose," she said. She crossed the room to a small desk and tugged the article she'd found on her car window out of the drawer. She slid it onto the counter. "I found this on my car."

Charlie's jaw worked against unspoken words and he inhaled a noisy breath. "When did you get this?"

"Last week when I stopped by."

"Why didn't you say something then?"

Casey opened her mouth, but she just shook her head. Why hadn't she?

Chapter four

Casey put one foot out onto the rain dampened metal platform and froze straddling the sill. Her brain knew the fire escape was safe and that she wasn't likely to plummet to her death, but that didn't stop her endorphins from arguing.

"Are you sure you don't have the measurements?" her voice shook.

"Sorry. No. The guy's new. I could send someone else out..." She started back in. "But, that would take another two days and we'll miss the order. If we miss the order..."

The price break would disappear. She sighed. "You're sure you can't—"

"Nope."

Was that amusement she heard in his voice?

She didn't really need a new sash, did she? Surely the plastic cover she'd been using since the fire would suffice. Or maybe a plywood plank like they'd secured over the opening downstairs would do.

She swallowed hard. "I'll call you back."

Casey tossed the phone onto the bed, touched the measuring tape she'd clipped to the waistband of her pants and stuffed paper and pencil into her back pocket. She gripped the brick edges of the window opening.

Breathe. Focus.

"You can do it."

What was her problem? She faced and overcame challenges all the time. She leaned to the left, caught a glimpse of the ground through the open slats and pulled back.

Challenges that were firmly rooted on the ground.

Fresh beads of perspiration sprung across her brow and she leaned her head back against the empty window frame. Where the hell was Charlie? He'd promised he'd be there a half-hour earlier to help, but when she'd phoned to see where he was, his wife hadn't known.

Casey pulled the second leg through the opening and sat a moment on the sill, both feet resting on the metal platform. She tried to straighten, but her legs rebelled shaking her back onto her bottom. Her fingers ached from gripping the weather worn wood so hard, but she couldn't seem to force herself to relax.

"You can do this." If she repeated the mantra a million times, she might believe it.

She took a few deep breaths willing her heart to slow down, closed her eyes and visualized standing and measuring the outside sash area, pictured every movement needed to complete the task. She breathed in and out, let go of the sill and opened her eyes.

Casey straightened, steadied her still-shaky legs, turned and unclipped the measuring tape. She lined up one end with the left side frame and stretched the metal casing on her right. She sidestepped to eye the measurement, but couldn't quite reach. A click locked the tape in place and she slid right, hooked the end of the tape over the far edge then released the lock.

The measuring tape recoiled with a snap and she lost her grip. She juggled right, left then right again, stretched in an effort to grab the tool. Black metal stairs descended sharply in front of her and she pulled back too quickly, lost her footing and slid down four steps before coming to a stop. Her fingers gripped vise-like on the rail and she pulled herself to it.

The ground spun below her and she squeezed her eyes shut.

If she didn't stop shaking

soon, her body would rattle right off into the abyss.

Now what was she going to do?

Through the open window, the double ring of the enter-phone signaled a visitor at her front door. She glanced back over her shoulder and scowled.

Charlie.

Maybe if she yelled, he'd come round the back to help.

She chewed on the thought a moment. Charlie *would* help—provided he could hear her calls—but then what? Would he ever let her forget?

Jim hadn't. Remembered mistakes flashed out at her unbidden, replaying like scenes from a movie. She shook away the memories. Charlie wasn't Jim, but she couldn't bring herself to yell.

Casey cast a quick glance over her shoulder. Visualization had helped her out onto the platform, visualization could help her back inside. She closed her eyes. Three stairs. The platform. And—

A window rattled open to her right and she snapped her head round.

"Morning Ms. Michaelson."

Why did it always have to be him?

She stared off toward the

river. "Morning, Mr. Hennessy."

"Kieran."

"Right. Kieran."

"What ya doing?"

"Oh, just hanging around."

He sat on the sill, inhaled deeply. "Fine morning for it now that the rain has stopped."

"Don't you have some cookies to bake or something?"

Men. Never around when you wanted them, always around when you didn't.

"I don't bake cookies." He hooked one leg out the window and let it dangle.

She glanced down at the ground below him, regretted it and closed her eyes. Stupid. All she had to do was stand up, walk to her window and climb in.

"Maybe I should petition your committee to put decks out here."

"Decks?" What was he talking about?

"Yeah, those glass panels would be perfect, don't you think?"

Glass panels? The ones with the metal tubing? Who was he trying to kid?

"No, I don't." She stood and stepped up toward him.

"Why? The glass would provide an unobstructed view of your precious brick."

"*My* brick?" She hated the way he glanced down his nose at everything she valued. Locking eyes, she climbed up even with him. "It's a community, Mr. Hennessy. We decide things together."

"Only when it works in your favor."

"If you want balconies, you could probably do something like ours here."

"And what if I don't want that kind?"

She stepped close to the railing. "If you don't like it, move." She spun round and shoved one leg through the open window into her bedroom.

Of all the condescending, overbearing, dimwitted, destructive jerks she'd met, Hennessy had to take the cake. Hell, he was a chef, he probably made the damned cake.

"Ms. Michaelson?"

"Yes, Mr. Hennessy?" She caught his smile over her shoulder and narrowed her gaze.

"Have a great day."

She yarded her other leg into the room before it dawned on her where she was and she turned back to the window.

Hennessy was already gone.

Damn. She owed him another one.

Casey cinched her black belt around her waist as she walked down the hall from the bathroom.

"You just about done?"

Charlie stared at her for a moment then tucked his hand inside the open flap of his gi top, straightened it and stepped back through the window opening into her bedroom.

"Yeah." He set the tape measure back into the toolbox on the floor.

"Thanks for your help, Charlie."

"Anytime. At least now you can order the new sash."

He turned to close and latch the window. Why didn't you just measure one of the dojo windows? Aren't they all the same size?"

Damn. Why hadn't she thought of that?

She stared past him at the fire escape, shook her head.

"What?"

"Nothing."

"Something."

His eyes twinkled with

amusement at her retelling, but he didn't laugh.

"Why didn't you wait for me?"

"I called Dina and she didn't know where you were."

"Oh. Uh..." He shifted his weight and a corner of something peeked out at her from the flap of his karate uniform top. He shoved it back in. "I had to do something after work."

"What's going on Charlie?"

"Nothing. I just had to be somewhere." His abrupt turn halted the conversation. "Come on, we're going to be late."

She grabbed the paper with the measurements off the nightstand and headed after him. Evasion. She'd not seen that trait since the early days when a grief-stricken and lost Charlie had been dragged to the dojo by a friend. In the two years since he started training, he'd found something to hold onto, something to pull himself up with. He wasn't falling down that hole again, was he?

Casey followed him into the elevator and cranked the dial for Main. The motor clunked into action and they moved slowly downward.

"You can talk to me, Charlie."

"There's nothing to talk about," he snapped.

The elevator doors opened and Charlie cast a quick glance backward. "Sorry," he said in a low voice before she lost him in the crowded dojo.

Kieran found himself awash in a sea of white; traditional karate uniforms broken only by colored belts. He raised a brow and shook his head. This wasn't really his thing. But he'd been drawn by the continual stream of white passing his door and the promise of staring into those cold blue eyes again.

Hell, maybe he could warm them up.

He slipped off his shoes and slid onto an open spectator's bench to the left of the training room door. The *Battle of the Dojos* was small as far as tournaments went—or at least how Kieran expected they went.

The two rows of karate students lining the walls of the large training area were focused on the demonstration in the middle. Two of the rings were occupied by black belts, but only one held his attention. Casey bowed, placed her hands in front of her and closed her eyes. Her breathing was so controlled and rhythmic that his fell in time with hers until her yell nearly sent him off the seat.

A man wearing a karate uniform temporarily blocked his view and

Kieran slid over to allow him to sit the bench. Familiarity niggled, but Kieran couldn't quite place him.

The man glanced out at the floor then turned back. "You're the cookie guy."

Cookie guy? Great. Tethys served seafood and fancy desserts. Cookies were *not* on the menu.

"Charlie Griffin. Assistant Fire Chief, friend and student."

"Kieran Hennessy." He shook the extended hand. "And I don't bake cookies."

Another yell startled him back to the floor.

"Ki-ai," Charlie smiled. "Takes an opponent off guard, too."

Casey moved with remarkable swiftness, her motions crisp and strong. She snapped her head around began a new combination and she yelled again.

"I can see that."

"In forms, it helps with breathing, improving rhythm and focusing power."

Casey's every movement captured the black belt's attention and he tensed and relaxed with her. The man was a firefighter in every sense of the word. Fit. Strong. Muscular. Kieran's six-pack suddenly felt like a keg and he tightened his abs.

"Nice, Sensei." Charlie grinned.

"I'll take your word for it."

"You don't think so?"

"I wouldn't know."

His stomach burned and Kieran relaxed. Who was he trying to impress anyway? He leaned forward, elbows on knees. He drew a sharp breath as pain snaked up from his forearm. He shifted the sleeve away from his arm.

"You all right?" Griffin asked.

Kieran nodded.

"What'd ya do?"

"Stupid, really." He shrugged. "Burnt myself."

Griffin's eyes narrowed. "How'd you do that?"

"Occupational hazard. I got too close to an open flame."

"You should have it checked out." The second black belt finished and Griffin stood. "I have to help score-keep, so enjoy yourself."

"Thanks."

Kieran watched a few more black belt demonstrations, some board breaking and weapons but nothing could hold his attention quite like the blue eyes he caught staring at him every few minutes.

So in control, so poised, so professional.

It was hard to believe that just a couple of hours earlier, she'd had a death grip on the metal rail of her fire escape, unable to move up or down for fear that one false move would send her tumbling to her death. He smiled at the contradiction.

She smiled back and walked toward him. Halfway across the room she stopped to talk with a young student, helped the child tie her yellow belt and ran a caressing hand over the child's head. Casey winked and smiled at the youngster who seemed to beam in response.

"Sensei?" Griffin slid up beside her.

He spoke in a voice too quiet to overhear, but given Casey's change in expression, there was no doubt it had something to do with Kieran. She cast her gaze to the floor, seemed to steady herself and turned back him, her smile firmly back in place.

"We're going to have to quit meeting like this or people are going to start talking."

"Looks like they already are."

"Who, Charlie?" She shook her head. "Yeah, he thinks I should stay away from you."

"Why?"

"You tell me." She fixed an assessing glance on him then broke into a smile. "Nah, he just didn't want me to take too long." She leaned in closer. "He thinks I'm trying to get out of judging white belts."

Yeah, right. "Something wrong with white belts."

"No. It's just that the divisions are big and everyone does the same kata." There was a loud yell from a ring in the far corner. A young white belt turned and punched for all he was worth. "They do have enthusiasm, though."

Kieran laughed.

"Thanks for your, uh...help earlier."

He waved her off. "Don't know what you're talking about."

"I better go."

She walked back across the dojo toward Charlie Griffin. The firefighter glared Kieran's way then turned back to the ring.

What the hell was that about?

"I'm serious. He has a burn on his arm." Charlie spoke under his breath.

"So." She glanced at Kieran. "He's a cook."

"You need to be careful."

"Come on, Charlie, why would he do such a thing?"

"You're the chair of the committee that's holding up his renovations, you've been fighting him for months."

"Yeah, but it won't matter if I'm not there, the committee is still going to do what it has to. It would be pointless for him to do something like that."

"Maybe it's become personal. Or maybe he just wants you distracted long enough to get his stuff passed."

A cough silenced their conversation and Casey called the next competitor to the line. The nervous child in front of her bowed and Casey smiled at the memory of the first time she performed kata in tournament. She tried to bolster the child's confidence, but he burned through his moves and sat down with the speed of someone wanting to be done. She called him back to the line for his scores.

"Judges," she called. "Scores up." The five ring judges lifted the score cards.

The large group drained her energy as each of the twenty-five children came forward. While she watched for the telltale signs of practice and power, Casey's mind wandered. Was Charlie right? Was her neighbor up to something? He did have a knack for being in the right place at the right time.

Or was that the wrong place at the wrong time?

If it hadn't been for him, she'd have likely died the other night in that bedroom. He'd retrieved her in the nick of time. Had that been because he had the inside track?

She didn't think he had the burn then, but—

"Scores up." She held up her cards and waved another black belt over. "I need a break."

Casey wandered into the back room for a moment, waited for the washroom to clear and went in to splash some water on her face. What if Charlie were right? What if it were Kieran Hennessy who'd torched her building the other night?

Memories of her near-naked savior rushed her like a waterfall. Had he been in such a state of undress because he'd been in bed when he heard the alarm or had he shed his clothing to hide the telltale signs of his part in the arson? Both were possibilities.

And the burn. She paused.

She'd assumed he'd burnt himself on an oven or pan, but come to think of it, he never actually said what had happened. And what about the article? Had he simply mentioned it in passing? Certainly the free local paper arrived on every doorstep in the city and other people had mentioned it too. Was everything as it seemed or were those emerald green eyes and easy smile hiding something?

She splashed more cold water on her face and gave herself a mental shake.

Perhaps Charlie had a point.

Chapter five

Casey walked across her living room to the windows. The last rays of sunlight danced on the river and she could see a few pedestrians dotting the footbridge over the train tracks and down toward the boardwalk. Maybe she should change and visit the Quay's Paddle Wheeler Pub to celebrate the tournament's success.

She glanced toward her neighbor's windows. Maybe he'd—

No. She needed to stay away from him at least until she discovered his motives—ulterior and otherwise. She started down the hall to her bedroom. His shift in attitude seemed genuine, something that might naturally happen after yanking a neighbor out of harm's way.

She tossed her gi in the laundry basket, slipped into her robe and slid the window up. Fresh air wafted into the room and she drank it in. She sat on the window ledge, pulled one foot up onto the sill with her and wrapped her arms around her leg.

Why was she such a lousy judge of character when it came to men?

Stop it.

Casey pushed up off the ledge. She wasn't going to do this today. Everything went perfectly. She'd hosted her first tournament in her own dojo and it had come off without a hitch—so long as you didn't count the looky-loos that tried to get a peek at her charcoal basement. Her dojo had even managed to glean the spoils of victory, a shiny little karate guy perched atop a large plastic trophy.

What else could she want or need?

She glanced at the apartment across the way then forced herself across the room. He'd rescued her all right, but the man wasn't some fairytale prince come to save her. He was out for himself. He wanted to get his way with the committee and if he could have his way with her in the process, so much the better.

Metal rattled as she freed a blouse from a hanger on the closet rail. She wasn't being fair. The man had risked his own life to make sure she got out of her building. She had no evidence that of any wrong-doing other than Charlie's suspicions and Kieran had been nothing but cordial to her since the fire.

Maybe that was it. Why was he being so nice?

Steam filled the small shower stall as Casey adjusted the temperature of the water. A quick rinse and—

Tory's familiar ringtone pulled Casey back into the other room and she flopped across her bed to grab her cell.

"Hey roomie! What ya up to?"

"Uh, answering my phone."

"Funny."

"What's up?" Casey rolled off her bed toward the window.

"So, who's the guy?"

"What guy?"

"The one Charlie's jealous of."

"Charlie's married."

"He's still jealous."

"We're friends."

"Doesn't mean he's not jealous. And don't change the subject."

"What was the subject?"

"The guy."

"What guy?"

"You're not going to tell me, are you?"

"Probably not."

"How about I pick you up and we go for dinner so you can *not* tell me in person?"

"There's nothing to tell."

"Right, that's why you were so focused during the judging."

"I was focused."

"Maybe, but not on the white belts."

Casey flushed. "Focus is overrated."

A laugh. "I'll be there in ten."

Casey hung up, stepped into the shower and rinsed. Her nose tingled as she returned to the bedroom. She adjusted her towel and stepped closer to the window. Sniffed.

Was that smoke?

Not again.

Outside the window, darkening smoke curled from behind Hennessy's building and sirens whined to a stop nearby. She closed and secured her window, dressed and headed for the street.

A quick glanced at her bedroom doorway reassured Casey that the events of the other night were not replaying, but her pulse rolled like drums in a tattoo.

Emergency vehicles lined the street; the spinning lights pulled colored patterns across the sides of nearby buildings as she pushed out of her main entrance. Blue, red, and white patches mixed with the amber glow of the flames. Artificial darkness fell over the street as smoke obscured the late afternoon sun. Goose bumps prickled Casey's arms.

Which place was it?

She rushed west, but had only just crossed the intersection when a barricade stopped her progress. A block or so down the street storefront windows shattered and glass flew onto the sidewalk. An excited murmur rumbled through the small crowd and Casey's stomach tightened.

"Was there anyone inside?" someone asked the cop keeping watch over the crowd.

He shook his head and shrugged. "I can't comment at this time."

What did that mean? Casey shuddered and followed a group of people across the street where pedestrian traffic still moved along the sidewalk. She skirted the people gathered outside the coffee shop and continued down the block a few yards. Across the street flames licked through the windows of the first three floors despite the steady flow of water.

If *someone* was in there—

"Hey, babe."

Casey closed her eyes. Babe?

"Hi, Jim."

He pulled his head back as if trying to focus. "Don't say it like that." His growl brought the aroma of alcohol and she turned away.

Why wouldn't he just go away?

"You'd think being this close to the Police Station would ensure your safety."

Casey glanced down the road to the converted century-old post office building that housed the Police Station.

"They patrol here, same as anywhere."

"But you must be worried. A woman alone—with all of this happening?" She ducked away from the hand he attempted to wrap around her shoulder.

"I can take care of myself." Tory pulled up to the curb and honked. "I've got to go."

He grabbed her arm to stop her retreat. "Where you gotta go?"

She glanced down at his hand. "Take your hand off me."

"I just want to talk." He gripped harder.

Casey twisted her arm out of his grasp and stepped back ready.

"Hi-ya!" He wind-milled his

arms in the air.

"You're making a fool of yourself."

"I'm the fool? You're the—"

"Go home, Jim."

He swung her round and put both hands on her shoulders. She went with the momentum, broke from his grasp and sidestepped out of his way. His eyes widened and he shifted toward her but hesitated.

"Don't bother." Hennessy's voice was a hard, cold contrast to the warm hand he placed at the base of Casey's back. "Why don't you just go sleep it off?"

Hennessy brushed past her.

"You again!" Jim railed and jerked an unsteady thumb toward Kieran. "You sleeping with him?"

Casey made to protest, but Hennessy cut her off.

"What if she is?"

Jim took a swing at Hennessy who stepped out of the way letting the drunk tumble to the sidewalk.

"What did you do that for?" Jim looked up at Kieran in confusion.

"I didn't do anything."

Jim's unsteady second attempt was even less successful than the first and he glanced off the metal table near the window of the coffee shop. Blood spurted from his nose. Hennessy grabbed a stack of white paper napkins from the dispenser, shoved them at Jim's chest.

"Clean yourself up and catch a cab." He turned to Casey, ushering her toward Tory's car.

"I don't need a cab," Jim yelled and pushed himself up off the sidewalk. He grabbed Hennessy's shoulder. "You'll regret this. She's a bitch. She'll use you all up then leave you."

Hennessy whirled around and punched Jim square in the jaw sending him sprawling back onto the sidewalk. Hennessy grabbed Casey's hand and tugged her toward the corner where Tory had abandoned her car. He tucked Casey into the front seat, closed the door and stood guard.

Her cheeks burned hotter than the fire across the street and she suddenly wished the firefighters would turn their hoses this way. Then again, that would just draw more attention. She chewed at her thumb.

Who the hell did he think he was?

Her protector?

She didn't need protecting, she could handle herself—had handled herself on many occasions. She heaved at the door, but Hennessy's big body was in the way. She shifted directions toward the driver's seat. Tory yanked her door open and slid in.

"You okay?"

"Yeah."

Hennessy's butt pushed up against the passenger window.

"Nice ass."

"Nice ass for a nice ass," Casey grumbled.

"What?"

"I said he's an ass." She crossed her arms over her chest.

"I can't believe you."

"Me? I was doing just fine until Dudley Do-Right stepped in. He turned it into a three ring circus."

"Whatever." Tory's green eyes narrowed and her shaggy blond hair swayed with the movement of her head.

"What does that mean?"

"Don't take this the wrong way. You're my friend and I love you, but..." she took a breath. "You're an idiot."

"How could I possibly take that the wrong way?"

"Look. Jim's the problem here, not this guy."

"Jim's just—."

"Jim's just having trouble trying to adjust. Jim's just stressed about work." She fixed Casey with a stare. "Jim's just a jerk and it's about time you noticed it."

"Divorce! Hello!"

"And yet, he's still here."

"It's not like I invited him."

"You do. Every time you help him find a cab or pick him up or make an excuse for him."

"He—" She stopped herself.

Tory's tone softened. "He's an ass, hon'. He's trying to keep you down." She nodded to the butt in the window. "Now this backside—"

Hennessy crouched beside the passenger door, his smile broadening at the women's laughter. Tory flicked the switch for the passenger window and leaned across Casey to her neighbor.

"What are you doing for dinner?"

"Why did you do that?" Casey moved the ice round her glass with her straw.

"What?"

"Invite *him*."

"Cause I thought it was time for you to move on." She scanned the surrounding area.

Move on? With him?

Her gaze found Hennessy near the bar talking with another patron. He leaned in intent on what was said then shook his head and pushed back in his chair. His teal green shirt was open at the collar, the long sleeves rolled to just below the elbows and his discarded suit jacket hung on the back of the chair beside Casey. Slate gray slacks followed the curve of his leg to the black leather shoe resting on the rung of the chair.

"Or for me to," Tory added.

Casey choked on her drink. "You?"

"Something wrong with that? Mr. Forgettable has been gone for months." Tory played with her straw.

What's-his-name's final fling had cost him a wonderful woman and saved Tory years of heartache.

"I just didn't think you'd be interested."

"What's not to be interested in?" She took another sip and leaned closer. "Tell me about the boxers again."

"Boxers?" Hennessy grinned.

Tory's grin matched his. "Are you of Scottish decent?"

Casey flushed and glared at

Tory.

"So tell us about the restaurant, Mr. Hennessy," Tory scooped some salsa onto a chip and crunched it between her teeth.

"Kieran," he corrected. "And nope. No shop talk." He extracted some cholesterol-on-a-chip from the plate and wrapped the stringy cheese around a crispy tortilla. "Good company, good food." He stuffed the chip in his mouth and winced. "Like I said, good company."

Tory's eyes sparkled as she sipped at her drink. "I know the bartender. I'm sure I could get you the recipe."

"What would you have to do?" He reached for another chip and raised his brows. "And can I watch?"

Tory's laugh earned another glare from Casey and she lifted her shoulders in question. Casey stuffed her straw in her mouth and slumped back against her chair.

"So what do you do, Tory?"

Casey worked the straw with her teeth as Tory flashed a toothy grin, brushed Kieran's forearm with her finger tips and selected an unadorned chip from the bottom of the pile. "I'm an assistant manager at a courier company downtown."

"Assistant manager?" He leaned forward, one elbow on the table, the other lifting his sleeve of amber ale.

"Yep. Moving up in the world." She leaned in, her shoulder contacting his. "Get to do more work for less money."

His gaze lingered a moment, his smile broadening. Casey fiddled with her straw some more, took a long sip and looked away.

How was it she became a third wheel at her own celebration?

"Actually, I'm just finishing my degree."

"What in?"

"Psychology."

"Really?"

Kieran's face softened with interest. His attentive gaze surveyed Tory's face. Casey wanted to do something—anything—to bring those green eyes her way. She opened her mouth—

"What made you take that route?"

—filled it with a chip.

"Just look at the company I keep." Tory waved a hand around the table.

Casey crunched hard at Kieran's throaty laughter. He leaned forward, attentive, interested. Casey shifted in her chair and shook some more ice cubes into her mouth.

"Actually, I got a job at a kids' camp a few years ago and one thing led to another."

"So your specialty is children?"

"That's the plan. Educational psychology."

"What about you, Ms. Michaelson?" He turned his gaze on Casey.

"Oh, call her Casey for Christ's sake. You practically made a baby on that fire escape."

"Tory!"

Her friend giggled and sipped her drink dry. "Look at that. Empty." She headed for the bar.

Kieran's green eyes sparkled as he followed Tory's progress to the bar where she leaned on the polished surface. She slid her glass across the bar and said something to the bartender. He laughed and Casey turned back to the table.

"Where'd you find her?"

"Karate."

"Bet she's a fighter." His gaze wandered back to Tory.

Casey crunched a piece of ice. "She'll knock you on your ass."

He turned back to her, eyes narrowed. "And what about you?"

"You want to go a few rounds?"

she snapped.

His smile faded. "Seems I already am."

He crossed his arms on the table behind his glass and surveyed her a moment, then turned his attention to Tory. She'd settled herself on a stool near the bar and was laughing at something the bartender had said.

Casey stirred her drink. What the hell was the matter with her?

Kieran Hennessy. That was the matter. His cinnamon and chocolate scent so close to her and yet, those green eyes focused on another. Damn.

Ridiculous.

They were incompatible. They had different goals, different desires. Tradition, so much a part of her life and living, played no part in his. He wanted progress at all costs, worshiping the here and now, the modern. He had no regard for the history of that lovely building he wanted to lop the top off of.

Ludicrous.

It shouldn't matter that his gaze followed Tory; that he smiled when she did. Casey wasn't interested in him. She *wasn't*.

"Maybe I should go," she said.

His gaze drifted back to her.

So why did her heart speed up when his eyes probed hers?

She set her glass on the table. "Tell Tory, I'll call her tomorrow."

Chapter six

Casey hesitated a moment, staring at the far end of the overpass that took pedestrians up over the railway tracks and across to downtown. At one time, she'd been frozen with panic at the top of the open stairs, unable to climb down without a person in front of her and a lot of encouragement. Now she barely paused.

Brickwork patterns decorated Columbia Square on the other side and the design seemed to fit with the old rail station on her left. The building had been converted to a restaurant some years earlier and other than the sign on the side of the building, the original structure remained intact. The designers had embraced the building's heritage. Why couldn't Kieran?

His first name rattled around her brain. She'd worked hard to maintain the distance between them. Familiarity increased the chances for conflict of interest—and heartache. She clenched her jaw against the thoughts. She'd mistaken casual flirting for honest interest and—

Sneakers pounded on the pavement, coming up quickly on her right. She sidestepped, turned and stepped back—ready. A jogger cast a confused glance her way and continued past. Casey smiled uneasily, allowed herself a wary laugh.

In self-defense, she taught women to walk with their heads up, a confident stride; to be aware. Now she was letting thoughts of her neighbor distract her.

He'd been playing to her feminine side, trying to whittle away at her defenses. And she'd been an easy target. He'd rescued her from a burning building, certainly that would have some psychological effect. There must be a syndrome or something she could blame. She'd have to ask Tory.

Casey inhaled deeply at the thought of the two of them together. She should be happy for Tory. She deserved a nice guy for a change; God knew Mr-two-timing-jerk hadn't been one. But Tory had simply picked up her heart and carried on.

Maybe that was the difference? Tory still accepted everyone, trusted. How did she do that?

A bottle rattled across the sidewalk and Casey shifted away from it. She caught the silhouette of a crumpled man sitting in a doorway. A flame illuminated the grimy face and he sucked a cigarette to life. She blew a sigh and continued down the block.

Be aware.

But was Kieran the good guy he appeared to be? Charlie didn't think so. She pulled her cell phone out and called Tory. What if Charlie was right? She hadn't mentioned anything to Tory. The phone rang four times. No answer, then voice mail. Where was she?

Casey turned back, dialed again.

"Come on, pick up," Casey mumbled under her breath.

What if something happened? She'd never—

"Thanks a lot," Tory said by way of greeting.

Had to love call display. "For what?"

She started back on her path, caught a hint of movement further down the block. She inched forward stretching her neck for a view. Nothing.

"Abandoning me. I go over to talk to Kevin and you take off."

"I didn't think you'd miss me." She shifted left to the edge of the sidewalk.

"Why wouldn't I miss you?"

"You seemed to be having a good time with—"

"Kieran?"

Casey flushed, but said nothing.

"Are you jealous?"

"No." Too quick, too high pitched. She swallowed. "I'm happy that you've hit it off so well. Charlie doesn't trust him though. That's why I was calling. He thinks he has something to do with these fires."

"Why's that?" Her voice lowered conspiratorially.

Casey kept an eye on the nooks and crannies of the old buildings. "He's got a burn on his arm."

"And he's a cook. He could have just brushed up against something."

"That's what *I* said."

"But Charlie doesn't think so?"

"Uh-uh."

Clink-click.

What was that? She stopped, looked around. Nothing.

"Charlie's paranoid."

"Maybe, but be careful anyway."

Clink-click. Closer. She checked over her shoulder, surveyed the visible doorways.

"Well, there's no need to worry."

"Uh. Why's that?" Casey narrowed her eyes picked up her pace.

Clink-click. Further down. Spark.

"He left right after you did." Keys jangled, before an engine started and the familiar ding, ding of a seatbelt reminder. "Blue tooth isn't working. Gotta go. I'll call you tomorrow."

"Tory?" She'd hung up.

Casey pressed end. Hard heels hit the pavement in front of her as the metallic clink sounded again. Flames shot from a lighter and cupped hands shielded the cigarette he drew on. Orange flame glowed under the brim of a ball cap illuminating the whiskered face. A deliberate lift of his head brought dark eyes to hers and his smile knifed through her.

He stepped toward her, but she maneuvered to keep her escape route free. He continued past her, blew smoke back over his shoulder. She let out a breath she hadn't realized she'd been holding when he rounded the corner out of view.

The pedestrian button beeped under her touch and she took another quick glance over her shoulder. Gooseflesh trailed down her neck and down her shoulders. She wrapped her arms around her ribs and started across the street. She was sure she'd never seen him before, but the way he stared...what the hell had that been about?

Casey stepped up onto the sidewalk in front of Hennessy's building. Paper still lined the front windows, but etched glass depicted the restaurant's namesake, hair billowing in great waves. Casey studied the lines a long moment before continuing on. Another backward glance brought nothing but empty sidewalk and she tried to shake her fear away.

Transformation of the neighborhood remained incomplete. While upgrades and new builds brought a new class of people, strange souls still inhabited the area and dominated at night. She should know better than to walk alone. She continued past Hennessy's building to her own.

Next time!

Scrawling spray painted letters splashed across her dojo windows came into focus for a short moment before something flew through the window of the neighboring bookshop. She turned away as the window exploded. Glass bit into her scalp as she and she threw up an arm to shield her face.

Squealing tires and the smell of burnt rubber assaulted her senses but by the time she lifted her gaze toward the street only the trail of black smoke and blackened strips of pavement remained. The heat washing over the side of her face drew her attention back to the building in front of her. Flames snaked out the gaping hole in the glass and the unmistakable smell of gasoline replaced burning rubber.

Good God. Al!

Casey slid into her reading chair, two hands wrapped around a warm cup of tea. The open window beside her brought in fresh cool air while her flannel sleeping pants and oversized long sleeved shirt kept her warm. She couldn't shake the smell of singed hair from her nostrils despite the long shower.

She'd tried to push into the bookshop, to get to Al, but had been turned back by the heat of fire fueled by piles of paper. She absently picked at heat curled locks that touched her shoulder as she closed her eyes to the memory of Al's lifeless body being pulled from the structure.

The old man had been sleeping on a couch in the back of the shop when the firebomb had been thrown through the front window. He'd had no chance of escape. A tear snaked down her cheek.

None of this made any sense. First the antique shop, now the bookshop. Why? Was she the target? And if so, why not just come through the front door?

Was all of this her fault? Had she done something to someone and this was payback?

Was that what *Next time* meant?

Next time...what?

Next time he'd do more damage? Or next time he'd kill her?

A sip of tea did little to stop the shudder moving up from the pit of her stomach. Were the two things connected? They had to be, didn't they? But what did it mean? What was next?

Casey shook her head to stop that line of thought and switched off the light. The flashing blue message beacon drew her to her phone and she flipped it over, checked the incoming calls.

Jim.

She dialed voicemail. "You bit—" Deleted. Just what she needed. A nasty message on top of the dripping orange one she'd found on her dojo windows. Oh sure, Jim would be apologetic in the morning. That was the pattern. The unchanging, never-ending pattern.

She held her cup tighter. How had she ended up with him?

Her tea slid down her throat warming her with each inch traveled. She knew this mind path well. Every twist and every turn and yet, she'd never been able to find the answer. Jim had been different when she married him. Or maybe he'd just been able to hide it better. He'd chipped away at her—a hint here, a comment there—until she hadn't recognized herself or him for that matter. That's when she'd gotten out.

But had she? Jim turned up at the most inopportune moments, usually drunk and belligerent. Each time Casey poured him into a cab and sent him on his way. Maybe that was all the encouragement he needed. She twisted her mouth, took another sip of tea and watched the running lights of a small boat motor out west toward the Pacific. She sighed and set her cup down. Maybe Tory was right. It was time for Casey to take the final step—a legal one if necessary—to close the door on that part of her life.

Casey let her head droop against the wing of the upholstered chair. Lights reflected off the dark surface of the Fraser River below and tell-tale green and red markers plotted the progress of the lone vessel. She rubbed away the chill and sighed.

Flash. She froze.

Another. Down below.

She pulled forward, slipped her head out the window. Was someone down there? She swallowed her thundering heart and searched the darkness for an indication, some small hint of what was happening below.

Nothing.

She settled back in her chair. She was simply over-reacting. Who could blame her after all that had happened? Besides her own troubles, early reports called the latest fire down the street suspicious. And there'd been another building a couple of months ago.

She'd have to check on cause to be certain, but if she remembered correctly, each target had been on area heritage rolls. Alteration plans had been submitted and approved on at least the latest building. Neither of those buildings had upgraded fire systems. So why would the arsonist choose hers?

Maybe it was personal.

Fear inched its way up each vertebra. The man on the street made it sound personal. And the message tonight seemed to suggest something more than a random attack but—

Another flash lit the side of the building. She hadn't imagined that.

The cold window glass added to the chill and she rubbed her arms. Another flash emanated from somewhere near the ground but not directly below her. Bright light illuminated her neighbor's main floor window. Butterflies swirled in her stomach. She swallowed hard to keep them from escaping and dialed nine-one-one.

Something was happening next door.

"Now what?" Kieran cursed as the wail of sirens stopped outside his door.

His half-brother, Daniel, turned off his torch and stood beside the metal sculpture that lay across the floor. Like Kieran, the twenty-two-year-old had their mother's blond hair, but his male-model sleekness came from his father. He flipped up his welder's hood, his intense brown eyes turning toward the front of the building.

More sirens wound to a stop at the rear of Kieran's building and an insistent shake rattled the glass front doors. Red beacons drew patterns of light on the unfinished dining room ceiling as Kieran started toward the door.

"Huh? Did I set off some alarm or something?"

"I don't think so, but I better let them in before they break the door down."

Charlie Griffin's face stared at him through the glass. Damn.

"Got a call about a fire." Griffin took half a step forward as Kieran unlatched and opened the door.

"Everything is fine."

"You mind if we just come and check, do a quick run through?"

"Come on in." He let the group of firefighters pass and followed them back. "You said you got a call?"

"Yes, nine-one-one." Charlie's outfit looked cumbersome. "I guess with all of the activity of late, people are keeping a close eye on things."

What people? Few residential buildings overlooked his other than Casey's—

Casey.

She'd been angry when she'd left the pub. Her girlfriend had been amusing and when he'd noticed Casey's irritation, he'd played things up. He couldn't resist the tantalizing flashes of anger and icy-blue stares.

He rubbed at the bristles on his chin. Vengeance came in many forms, but he hadn't thought Casey the type. She certainly treated her ex-husband with more respect than he deserved. Kieran rubbed his knuckles.

Griffin cast a glance back over his shoulder before disappearing through the kitchen door. Kieran narrowed his eyes. What was that about? If he didn't know better he'd think that the fireman had turned up just to harass him. Maybe a call wouldn't be that hard to fake.

Okay, now he was being stupid. This wasn't some big conspiracy. False alarms happened all the time and with the recent fires, it was natural that everyone would be on edge. He supposed he should be grateful that someone was keeping an eye out for him, though it might take him a while to get there. Kieran yanked a couple of beers from the fridge as Griffin and his crew came back out of the stairwell.

"I'll be out in a minute." Once his crew was out of earshot, he turned to Kieran. "You've got some violations here."

Great. "What now?"

"Well, construction waste for starters. Looks like your contractor's depositing stuff on landings and in stairwells."

"Okay." Kieran had already spoken to the foreman about that. "And?"

"Flammable materials are being stored in your boiler room. Not a great idea."

Kieran narrowed his eyes. What materials?

"You need to make sure your stairwells are clear, make sure your fire doors are in good working order—and closed." He started toward the front. "And get those cans out of your boiler room."

Just what he needed. Another thing to add to his long list of to-dos. "All right. Anything else?"

"I'll be back to make sure everything is adjusted." He nodded toward the sculpture. "What are you doing there?"

"We need a couple more mounting brackets before we hang it on the wall."

"Why aren't you doing it outside?" Griffin pressed.

"It was too awkward to get through the doors in one piece," Kieran said.

"We've got this ready." Daniel held up the fire extinguisher. "And the tarp's fire resistant."

"Just be careful, all right. I don't want to come back here tonight."

Kieran let Griffin out and flipped the lock after him. He turned back to the room, leaned back against the cold glass. Bright light flashed from Daniel's acetylene torch as he adjusted the flame.

"What was that all about?"

"Someone called nine-one-one."

Kieran walked to the window and peered out toward Casey's.

"Your neighbor, the heritage woman?"

"He didn't say." The only lights illuminated in the building were those in her top floor condo.

"Women." Daniel smiled. "Always trying to slow guys down."

"You get that complaint a lot?" Kieran turned back to the room.

"Not me. I like to take things slow and easy."

"Yeah, that's not what Jen told me."

Daniel slapped the welding shield over his face at the mention of his girlfriend and connected the last few mounting brackets to the mixed metal sculpture laid out on the floor. The waves of hair would reach the length of the restored brick wall and Daniel's artistry intricately wove the goddess's features into the background.

Kieran handed a beer to his brother and twisted the cap off his own. Maybe the opening should be pushed back. He surveyed his surroundings. Stock would begin arriving in the morning and he'd begin training the kitchen staff, but the dining room was still incomplete and needed at least a month to build a rhythm. The opening was in two weeks.

He massaged his forehead and took a sip of beer. Now he had the list from Griffin and another fire inspection. He ran a hand through his hair; let it rest on the back of his neck.

"You don't like it?"

"Hmmm?" Kieran realized he'd been staring at the sculpture and shook his head. "No. It's amazing, Daniel."

"Great. Glad you like it." He took a swig off the long neck.

Kieran's relationship with his half-brother had been practically non-existent until five years ago when a seventeen-year-old Daniel turned up on his doorstep alone and in trouble. Kieran had taken him in, helped him get sorted and finish school. His brother's recent graduation from the Emily Carr Institute of Art and Design had been a source of great pride—for both of them.

Daniel picked at the label on his bottle.

"What's up?" Cool amber liquid bubbled down Kieran's throat.

"Mom's getting married again."

"How nice for her." Where did she find these guys? "And?"

Daniel shrugged, ripped half the shiny paper off the bottle.

"Let me guess, she wants me to cater."

Daniel nodded, drained his beer and set the empty of the stainless steel counter. He crumpled the label in his fist and fired it at a waste basket. "For free."

Casey peeped out her dojo window at the red beacons atop the hose truck. Firefighters traipsed around Kieran's building looking for signs of fire. She followed their progress around the side of the building, moved to another window for a better view.

No fire.

She chewed on a thumbnail. She'd seen something, she was sure of it. But—

Mumbled voices came through the window and she understood their meaning without hearing clearly. They'd been called out for nothing. There was no fire.

The firefighters moved back to the truck slowly, removed helmets and unbuckled jackets. The white hat spoke into his radio, got some reply and motioned his crew back onto the truck. Shaking his head, he climbed into the passenger seat and the fire engine pulled away from the curb.

A stray hair fell across her face and Casey tucked it back behind her ear. Through the darkened windows near the rear of the next building, she could just make out the shadows of fixtures in the industrial kitchen. She turned her attention further along the building where a figure crossed one of the illuminated windows. Kieran. He scanned her building and settled his gaze somewhere near the top floor. Another flash illuminated him from behind and he turned around.

Casey made her way through the dark dojo to the elevator at the back. She should have come down to check things out before she called the fire department, but if she had and there really were a fire, the time she'd wasted could have been costly. She sighed and glanced back toward the windows. Surely Kieran would understand that she had his best interests at heart.

Eventually.

A loud thump pulled her back out of her thoughts.

She hesitated at the control panel for the elevator. Listened. Something metal rattled across a sidewalk. Pop can? She stepped back into the dojo and held her breath. Waited. Listened. Nothing. She shook her head.

Imagination. That's all it was.

A dog barked in the distance as she stepped into the elevator. Traffic noise passed outside. Something thudded against the bottom corner of her building. She should go back upstairs, call—

Who?

Charlie? His wife would love that. Or maybe he was working

tonight and had already paid a visit to her neighbor for no reason.

Kieran? She laughed aloud.

She could go up and call Tory. Her friend would come in a heartbeat. Casey chewed on her nail some more. She'd be getting her friend out of bed—or the pub—for what? A bit of paranoia and runaway imagination?

No. Casey could handle it herself. She grabbed her flashlight and pushed the button for the basement. She'd simply pop downstairs, make sure that nothing was amiss and head up to bed.

The doors opened on a dark black hole that was once an antique shop. Hotspot Restorations had cleared the shop of burnt furniture and stripped the place nearly to bare bones, but the telltale odor of moisture and cleaning solutions constricted her lungs. The windows and doors had been boarded and the only light came from the small overhead in the elevator.

Casey clicked her flashlight on and started into the room. Something moved off to her left. She darted the flashlight that way. Nothing. Another step. Another movement. Her flashlight chased the sound. Still nothing. She edged a little further, leaned right and poked her light into a corner near the boarded windows.

Shadows played against the bare

plywood, the flashlight's beam partially obscured by one of the remaining support beams. Casey inched forward, leaning to catch a view of the hidden corner. Glowing orbs shone back at her and an angry growl rumbled behind it.

Casey jumped back as a raccoon scampered to the far corner. Her breath returned in the form of laughter. Just a raccoon. She adjusted her ponytail and turned back toward the elevator. This stuff was getting to her.

A truck rumbled by on the street, the road vibrations rattling plywood against the opening it protected. She crossed to what should have been the cargo door, circled her light around the doorjamb and stopped near the top. A jagged tear marred the right corner and splinters bent inward near the middle. Light pressure opened a space between board and jamb as the plywood moved easily away from the opening. She pulled her hand away as if she'd been burnt and the board sprang back with a thump.

It hadn't been imagination after all.

Chapter seven

Kieran admired the Victorian mansion from the sidewalk. The carefully-restored structure occupied a larger Queens Park lot and towered over the street. Planned chaos gnarled messy plants into beds resembling Monet's garden at Givenry minus the pond.

A wrought iron gate connected two sides of an old stone fence and Kieran pushed through, making his way along the sidewalk and up the old wooden stairs. Two wicker chairs flanked a small table on the porch to the left of the double front doors. He dug in his pocket for the paper to double check the address. Could this be the right place?

A twist of the ringer reminded him of an old bicycle bell and he stepped back from the door. Movement passed behind the wispy white window coverings and Cynthia Lenoch pulled the door open.

"Mr. Hennessy." She opened the door wider with her backward motion. Her smile revealed rows of straight white teeth. "Glad you could make it."

"I wasn't sure I had the right house." Surely Lenoch, with her damn-the-committee attitude couldn't be responsible for a home so meticulously restored.

She waved him through the door. If she noticed the hint of irony in his words, she kept it well hidden. "The others are in the great room."

Great room?

A stairwell rose upward from the far end of the foyer, its dark wood matching the panel wainscoting and ceiling. The room drew him in, enveloping him like a blanket despite the high ceilings and large square footage. Kieran ran a hand over the worn pineapple finial that capped the post at the bottom of the stairs and inspected the period inspired wall paper. Maybe if the Heritage Committee continued to block him—

He clamped his jaw against the thought. This wasn't the vision he had for Tethys. That top-floor view would best be seen without obstruction or distraction. It was imperative that he have that dining in the clouds atmosphere or he'd be just another restaurant.

"This way." She popped her head out of a room back to the right of the entry.

"Sorry." He took a last look

round. "Impressive. Surely you don't want to—"

Her eyes widened. "Oh no. My family has a place we'd like to offload down on Columbia, but with the limitations on its use, it's almost impossible to sell." She sighed and lowered her voice. "We'd have to find an idiot like my ex-husband. He went broke doing this place."

His journey into another time continued as he crossed the threshold into the great room. Warm morning sun filtered through gauzy curtains onto ancient hardwood. Two women occupied wingbacks near the fireplace and another sat on one end of a dainty couch that looked to Kieran as if it might collapse under her weight. The two men conversing in the corner turned as he entered and Kieran's body stiffened.

Jim Taylor.

"What is he doing here?" Jim snarled.

Kieran's question exactly.

"He's the man I was telling you about." Cynthia's brows narrowed.

"He's *her* friend." Jim took a step toward Kieran.

"Whose?" Cynthia's gaze ping-ponged between the men.

"Casey. They were out together the other night. He did this to me." Jim pointed to the scab on his nose and the yellowing bruises circling his eyes.

"You did that to yourself." Kieran spat.

"How? What?" Jim sputtered. "I punched myself in the nose?"

"You were drunk and obnoxious. You were manhandling—" Kieran's muscles tightened.

"I was with my wife," Jim snapped.

"*Ex*-wife," Kieran corrected.

"It was none of your business." Jim took another step forward.

"You made it my business when—" Kieran closed the remaining distance.

"Boys!" Cynthia pushed between them.

Kieran's balled fists shook. He itched to darken those circles with another blow, but turned on his heel instead and stormed from the house. The wrought iron gate rattled under his efforts to open it.

"Mr. Hennessy!" Lenoch called as she rushed out onto the porch after him. "Kieran."

He tried to blow his anger out on a breath and turned to her. She opened her mouth to say something, but seemed at a loss and closed it again, glanced down at her feet then back up at him.

So much for strength in

numbers.

Kieran was on his own.

Cool metal greeted the hand Kieran placed on the black rail cutting the middle of the stairs running up toward the Fifties deco building that served as the City hall. A gentle breeze swayed the flowers and hanging baskets flanking the recently widened cement and brick stairs. Halfway up the half-block climb from Royal Avenue wooden benches invited visitors to sit under Nineteenth Century gas lamps. He paused and gazed out over the lawns despite the raindrops dampening his hair. On another day he might be tempted to sit and ponder, but today he carried on to the top of the stairs.

Kieran hefted the heavy front door open and stepped inside, headed up the magnificent staircase off to the right. Any hopes of finding an alternate method of circumventing the Heritage guidelines had evaporated with the meeting at Lenoch's the night before. Since his application hadn't yet been outright rejected, he could add the few precedents he'd found for exceptions to heritage bylaws and resubmit. Who knew, if he made a good enough case he might have a chance.

He worked his jaw against his thoughts. He should have done this before he started. Permits for the interior alterations including the ground floor dining room and kitchen had been easy to get and he'd commenced the changes before obtaining permits for the rest.

Stupid.

If the building hadn't been designated heritage, life would be so much simpler. He had yet to figure out why his grandfather sought the heritage status in the first place. Or maybe he hadn't. Maybe the city thrust it upon him, Casey Michaelson leading the charge.

Whatever had happened, Kieran should have taken a closer look before he jumped in with both feet. But his dream had been to open his own restaurant and when his grandfather willed him the building, it seemed natural to make the move. His lack of experience had landed him in this mess. He'd have to find a way out of it, before it cost him everything.

"Kieran?"

Casey's smile broadened as he looked her way. Her golden blond hair hung down around her shoulders. The woman who stood beside her was at least five inches shorter and twenty years older.

"Jane." Casey smiled. "This is my neighbor, Kieran Hennessy." He nodded toward the woman in the cream skirt and matching jacket. "Kieran. Mayor Jane Brindle."

Kieran reluctantly shook the

offered hand and narrowed his eyes at Casey.

"I'll meet you downstairs." The older woman caught the attention of a passerby and carried on down the stairs with her.

"The mayor?"

"She's a friend." Casey nodded. "And she chaired the committee before I took over."

So much for his chances at changing the bylaw.

"Sorry about last night." She pinked and glanced at her feet. "I really thought...I saw the flashes and—"

He wanted to say it was all right, that he understood, that he appreciated her concern, but he couldn't. Her interference had set him back yet again.

"Your boyfriend has pulled my certification."

"Boyfriend?" Her forehead creased with thought. "Who, Charlie? He must have had a reason."

"Right."

"If you're implying I had anything to do with it—"

"*Your* phone call. *Your* boyfriend."

"He's not my boyfriend."

"Maybe you should tell *him*

that."

She shook her head. "Charlie wouldn't cite you because of me."

Kieran opened his mouth to say something else, closed it and opened it again. "Then why is he holding up my opening by another week?"

"Sorry?"

"He says it'll take him three weeks to get back."

"I'll talk to him."

"I thought he didn't do things for you."

She blew a heavy breath out. "I'm just trying to help."

"Help? Is that what you call it?"

Her eyes widened then narrowed and he thought she might shout at him, but she simply wheeled round him and pounded down the stairs.

"Kieran," Craig, his sous-chef called from the kitchen. "We need you back here."

What now? Nothing seemed to go his way over the week since Lenoch's meeting. Griffin's impromptu inspection had just been the icing on the cake. He steeled himself for the worst.

"What's up?" Kieran pushed through the door into the kitchen area.

"The produce that arrived this morning is horrible."

Produce. Kieran relaxed.

"Why didn't you just send it back?"

"I don't know," Craig snapped. "Maybe it was the inspectors and construction guys traipsing through the kitchen. Or perhaps it was the screwed up wine delivery."

Kieran raised a hand. "Sorry." He picked up a green pepper. "I'll go to the market *myself* in the morning. In the meantime, take my car and collect what you need. I'll salvage what I can of this." He tossed the pepper back into the box.

Craig pulled some message slips from his jacket pocket, traded them for Kieran's keys and threw his apron onto the counter. Kieran couldn't blame the young chef. He was experiencing some of the same frustrations. Craig had risked all to follow him on this adventure and if it didn't work out—

Kieran picked through the produce for the few decent specimens. He couldn't think about failure. Everything he had rode on this venture. Everyone who'd migrated with him from his old employer had taken a chance too. It wasn't just *his* future that hung in the balance.

He glanced around the kitchen. Stainless steel surfaces sparkled, new appliances waited and the funky geometric plates he'd found stood ready for plating. Tethys wasn't a mistake. Despite the setbacks, the kitchen crew was coming together. He and Craig worked well together. The staff they'd hired was green, but had potential—or so the culinary arts program had attested. Despite the shine on their kitchen whites and young faces, they were plating dishes—albeit slowly—he'd actually serve customers.

Kieran pushed through the kitchen door into the dining room. Daniel's sculpture reined over the large room where a lone table sat dressed in the construction zone. His maître d' Martin had taken everything in stride. He'd only need one table to instruct on set-up and service—though he'd need the rest soon.

"How long?" Kieran called to the painter working on the ceiling.

"Tomorrow." The man didn't look his direction.

"Better be." He pushed back through the doors into the kitchen.

He was going to have some of the best trained staff in the city by the time he opened. Three members of his kitchen staff pushed through into the kitchen, one young man wiping at something on his shoulder. Kieran narrowed his eyes. Paint.

Kieran pushed the kitchen door open.

"Sorry," the painter called before Kieran said anything.

He let the door close.

If he opened.

"What are you doing?"

Casey cringed. Jim.

Maybe if she ignored him—

He hopped out of his pickup and stepped up beside her. Had she walked under a ladder or something?

Jim closed in behind the contractor fitting Casey's Front Street Shop with roll-down security blinds. After a quick inspection, he stormed back across the sidewalk to her.

"I could have done this for you," he railed.

"I know."

"Well, why didn't you call me?"

"I don't want you here, Jim."

"I would have done it for free."

"Free?" She laughed. "Your *free* costs too much."

"What are you talking about?"

She could tell him, but she

wasn't going to. He'd never understand what continued contact with him cost her.

"We're not married Jim."

"I know that."

"Do you?"

"Don't be stupid."

"Don't call me stupid." Her jaw tightened around the words.

"You're being ridiculous."

"Ridiculous?" her voice pitched higher. "*I'm* ridiculous?"

His eyes widened as she turned on him.

"Ridiculous is being surprised that someone you've treated like crap doesn't want anything to do with you." She took a step toward him and he backed away. "Ridiculous is trying to build yourself up at the expense of someone else." Another step. "Ridiculous is trying to hold onto something you fought like hell to get out of." They'd reached the front fender of his truck. "Once and for all, leave me alone, Jim."

He ducked around the back to avoid squeezing between her and his truck at the front and yanked the driver's door open. "I was just trying to help you out, but I forgot, *you the man now*. You got everything."

Burnt rubber assailed her nostrils as he accelerated away from the curb. She followed his progress for half a block, covering her mouth in horror when he blew through a stop sign and barely missed a Smart Car with the right of way.

The silence behind her was deafening and she worked her jaw against the flush creeping up her face. First Kieran then Charlie and now Jim, it didn't seem to matter what she said, everything became a fight.

She sighed and glanced toward the river.

A saw kicked into action and the high-pitched whine sang against wood. Her glance at the storefront sent the gaping construction workers back to task and she picked up a long scrap of wood. She turned back toward the Fraser.

"Chase him away with that big stick?"

The deep voice pulled her back.

Kieran.

Hennessy's shoulder pushed against the corner of his doorframe. His relaxed body stretched into the small alcove and his arms rested across his chest, two cups fanning from fingers in his right hand and a carafe dangling from the other. His chef's whites were open at the collar and triangular flaps lay across his chest, the bright material a stark contrast to his tanned skin.

She spun the long thin scrap of wood. "Jealous?"

His mouth twitched into a smile, but he said nothing. He straightened and started toward her, hips swaying as long lean legs brought him forward in a few quick strides.

"Well you did have me flat on my back."

"You were easy."

"Bet you say that to all the boys."

An experienced flick brought the cups level and he filled both with liquid from the carafe before setting the stainless steel container on the sidewalk. The aroma of good medium roast coffee floated toward her and she accepted the cup he offered.

"What's this for?"

"Drinking." He took a sip from his cup and turned his attention to the construction zone in front of them. "I wanted to say thanks."

"For what?"

"Sending your boyfriend back." He glanced back at the building then settled his green eyes on hers. "He's in there now."

"Good." She blinked away the

connection. "And he's not my boyfriend."

He turned his attention back to the construction. His two-day beard was slightly darker than the blond hair that curled at his collar and added definition to his features. A hint of sideburn accentuated the high cheekbone and elongated his face to Hollywood perfection. The small scar that curved vertically through his jaw line near the chin added just a hint of mystery. His eyes trailed the workers' movements and she suddenly wished they'd follow her with as much interest.

"Coffee's best drunk hot." His cheek dimpled with the smile.

She flushed, took a sip too quickly, choked and got her wish as Kieran's eyes sparkled her way.

"You okay."

"Yes," she squeaked.

He turned back to the building. "What are you doing?"

"Choking."

He gave her a sideways glance, smacked her a few times on the back, the thuds reverberating through her rib cage and he stepped back to reassess. When her laughter brought renewed coughs, he lifted her empty left hand up over her head. Casey raised a brow his way and he let the limb drop.

"Better?"

"Much." She coughed a final frog from her throat. "Where'd you learn first aid?"

"Grandpa Fred."

Casey took a sip of coffee and savored the sapid liquid. She couldn't stop the pleasurable growl and Kieran's smile grew into a satisfied grin.

"A thoughtful man would have brought one of his cookies along."

His turn to growl.

He brought the mug to his lips again, nodded toward the construction workers. "Insurance pay out?"

The saw whined anew and she waited for the high-pitched after-ring to fade.

"I've all but given up on that." She shook her head. "Someone broke in."

His eyes widened. "When?"

She flashed him a sheepish grin. "The other night when I thought your place was on fire."

Kieran's jaw worked against some unspoken thought and ran a hand over his chin. The stubble grated like sandpaper until the buzz of a drill drowned it out.

"Any damage?" he asked finally.

"No. Thank goodness. I think the sirens scared him off."

"Same guy who tagged your windows?"

She hadn't realized he'd known about that. "Yeah, maybe."

A door banged shut and Charlie marched up from behind, clipboard in hand. He ripped off the top sheet and handed it to Kieran.

"You're good to go," Charlie said. "But keep an eye on those contractors."

Kieran scanned the paper in his hand and nodded. "I will." He lifted his gaze taking in both Charlie and Casey. "Thanks."

Charlie's nostrils flared and she edged away from his gaze. He hadn't wanted to recheck the building so soon and their argument had been a doozy. The firefighter wheeled round and started down the street, stopped and turned back.

His expression softened and he ran a hand through his short black hair. "The building down the street..." He glanced that direction as if he needed to show her where it happened. "It's a total right-off."

"And the cause?"

"Arson."

Chapter eight

"We need to talk," Charlie said and pushed through the door into her office.

"Okay." She stepped back to let him pass. "Stephen," she called to a blue belt nearing the entrance to the training floor. "Start the warm-up please." She closed the door behind her. "What's up, Charlie."

He opened his mouth, but hesitated. "This has to stay between us."

She nodded.

"You need to stay away from Hennessy."

"We've been through this before. I'm a big girl Charlie. I can take care of myself."

"It has nothing to do with that." He pulled an envelope from inside his gi and extracted some photos from inside. He flipped through a couple. "I found these sitting in a corner on the fifth floor of his building." He slid a picture of a box containing wind-up kitchen timers across her desk. "And empty plastic bottles at the rear exit from the kitchen."

"Okay." A question hung on the word.

"And he's got the burn."

"He's a chef. Chefs have timers and plastic bottles and burns."

"We found a jean jacket in the storefront downstairs. Trace found evidence of accelerant—the same accelerant used in the fire—on it."

"So why didn't it burn up?"

"Well, some of it did." He touched his right forearm. "It was found under an old mirror. We figure the mirror doused the flames and protected it. And the timer and bottles are similar to those used in the type of device the arsonist is using."

"So why hasn't he been arrested?"

He sighed. "The case is purely circumstantial right now."

"But why would he do this?"

"That's the question, isn't it?" Charlie rubbed his jaw. "There could be any number of reasons. Insurance for one."

"How so?" Casey shifted. "It's not like he can collect on my place."

"True, but if there is a precedent, some evidence of an arsonist at work already, then no one's the wiser if his place falls too."

"Come on. Whoever did this took a big risk with people's lives." She glanced toward the building across the way. Would Kieran really do that?

"Not really. He knows that the building is equipped with sprinklers. He's just been through all the inspections and upgrades himself. It's a requirement to retrofit these buildings during upgrade." Charlie followed her gaze then pierced her with a hard stare. "And he conveniently gets to your window in time. How does he know you're trapped?"

"Good question." She'd asked herself that question. "His window is across from mine. Maybe he saw me."

"Or maybe he slipped this into the sash." Charlie slid a picture of a small metallic object across the coffee table to her.

"You think he tried to kill me!"

"Why would he save me then?"

"Maybe he didn't realize that the electrical chase would act as a funnel for the smoke. Or maybe he thought playing the hero would get him in your good books. Does it really matter why?"

Did it? Casey lifted her fingers to her suddenly aching forehead and her mind travelled over her recent interactions with Kieran Hennessy. The cake. The visits to the dojo. The coffee on the sidewalk. His manner toward her had changed. Was that a function of guilt or was he simply trying to find a way around her? Or worse, through her?

She shook her head at that thought. He couldn't be that underhanded. He'd been above board every time she'd dealt with him as part of the committee. His drawings, plans and proposals, while unsuccessful had been earnest attempts at fitting within the guidelines. He'd even begun work on his restaurant.

"What about all the work he's putting into his place? If he was going to torch it, why bother?"

Charlie shrugged. "I don't have all the answers, but I have a lot of questions. Like how this," he tapped the picture on the table, "got wedged in your window frame."

The image showed a broken, brass number against a white background. Wear lines and scratches marred the broken end.

"Wedged?" She twisted the photo. A two.

He nodded.

Casey crossed her arms against the creeping chill. "Let me guess." Goose flesh bumped along her shoulders and she pulled the ice pack away from her face. "Hennessy is missing the number two from his address."

Casey's arms and legs pummeled the solid leather bag. Perspiration blurred her vision as physical exertion dulled, but didn't stop, her thoughts.

She clamped her jaw shut, slugged the bag again and caught it on the return swing. Why here? Why now? Her main floor dojo had been open for business for almost a year. Had she done something to cause this? She stopped. Maybe she was taking things too personally. Her building might simply have been convenient. Her fire protection systems should have made it less attractive, but maybe the arsonist hadn't known about them.

Then again the system hadn't been foolproof. She shuddered at the tightness in her chest. If it hadn't been for Hennessy—

Jab. Jab. Knee.

She grabbed the bag to stop the swing as the photographed half-number invaded her brain. Why leave evidence like that behind? Better yet. Why use it in the first place? Sure there were dumb criminals in the world, but in all her dealings with Hennessy, she'd not have chosen 'dumb' as an adjective to describe him.

A quick push sent the bag swinging and she peppered it with fists and feet. No. Charlie had to be wrong. Someone with an interest in derailing the committee could be responsible.

Or perhaps someone who simply wanted to get even. Bright orange letters flashed through her mind and she narrowed her eyes at the memory of the man with the cigarette. She hadn't recognized him, but that didn't necessarily mean anything. Applications regularly came through city hall and no requirements rested on applicants to present to the committee. The Heritage Committee passed its fair share of applications and frequently worked alongside owners and contractors to fund grants and find ways to meet the needs of both committee and community. Still there were many failed applications and inevitably lost revenue. Had there been someone particularly hard hit by one of the committee's decisions?

Hennessy.

She kept coming back to him. He and the committee had been back and forth over his plans more than any other proposal in her term as chair. The man had searched every loophole imaginable in a bid to get his way. And she'd effectively cut him off at every pass. A front kick rattled the chains and she sidestepped out of the way of the swinging bag. She'd have to keep him on the list.

Her gaze crossed the gap to his top floor windows.

Punch. Punch. Kick. Back-fist.

If this was about the committee, whoever was responsible would be sorely disappointed. While she'd been distracted since the fire, the committee had marched on without her. She was simply one vote of many.

Jab. Jab. Reverse.

Then again, revenge was said to be a great motivator in crime and as chair of the committee, she was most visible. They'd kept the Hennessy from completing his necessary renovations and forced him to make alternate arrangements for his dining room. The chill of anger froze those green eyes on more than one occasion. But arson?

Her eyes instinctively sought his window again.

A sliver of light grew to a slanted rectangle from a source to the right. His figure obscured a portion then stepped from the bathroom into the makeshift bedroom. A worn striped towel obscured his lower body and moisture glistened on his torso. He rubbed a smaller towel against his wet hair, ran it over his face and tossed it aside. He finger-combed his hair and grabbed at the towel knotted at his hips.

Casey forced her eyes away. Focus. Kick. Kick. Punch. Jab. Jab. She glanced sideways.

His bare bottom glowed white and round under his tanned back. Jab. Jab. Muscles flexed and smoothed as he readjusted the towel and rotated toward her. Kick. Reverse punch. Tingles vibrated her body as biceps flexed and his hands rested on the knot again.

Readying for another readjustment? Punch. Punch. Shove.

Her breathing quickened as she counted every six in his pack and she took half-a-step closer to the window. He bent, dropped the towel and lifted his head toward—

Air rushed from her lungs and she dropped to her knees as the bag struck her a second time, knocking her sideways onto the floor. Pain radiated outward from her cheekbone and rattling chains reminded her of children's laughter. She closed her eyes on the large bag swinging to and fro above her. She drew a few ragged breaths, rolled onto her hands and knees and started to stand.

Kieran leaned on the sill, head craning into the open space between their buildings in an effort to see what had happened. His concern turned to amusement quickly as Casey waved a hand his way and sunk back below his line of sight.

Smooth. Really smooth.

Her heart thundered with such vigor that she couldn't hear her breathing when it returned and her cheeks burned as if the arsonist had lit fire to each. Perhaps she should just crawl out of the room and find a rock somewhere.

"You okay over there?"

Crap. He was still there. She popped her head up.

"Just looking for something."

"What d'ya lose?"

Other than her pride? "An earring." She sat back on her heels, holding her earlobe as if putting an earring back in. "Yep. There it is."

He grinned and walked out of the room.

She gave herself a mental slap in and strode back to the heavy bag. Chains rattled as she threw combination after combination. Since the fire she'd slacked off on her training and she needed to get back into it. Her grading was just around the corner and her Japanese sensei would not be impressed with her lack of focus. If she failed her fourth degree black belt test—

She reached out a hand to steady the swinging bag and catch her breath. She grabbed a towel from the hook on the wall, rubbed the perspiration from her face and tossed the towel aside. She stepped up to the heavy bag.

Work. Don't think.

Casey switched stances and kicked. She counted off roundhouse kicks, backed off, went in again with the other leg. She practiced combinations of kicks and strikes until faded blue jeans carried Kieran's half-naked body back into the room.

He slid his belt through the loops on his jeans. Jab, reverse, elbow, roundhouse. He grabbed a t-shirt off the bed and tucked one arm, then the other, through the holes. Jab. Jab. Spinning back fist. He ran his hands the length of his torso, smoothing the shirt. Reverse, uppercut, step back, side kick. Casey moved around the bag, throwing blind combinations as his hands fiddled with his pants button and cinched his belt. He retrieved something else from the bed and grinned up at her.

She stepped behind the bag, arms pressed to her sides as if she were some cartoon character hiding behind a too-thin tree. Her face flushed and her breathing quickened.

What the hell was the matter with her?

It wasn't like she'd never seen a naked man before and yet here she was hiding like some...peeping Tina.

She ground her teeth and clenched her fists. How had she

gotten herself into this mess? A quick glance earned her another grin.

Better yet, how was she going to get out of it?

"Doing a little window shopping?" Hennessy called.

"Grandma always told me to make sure I was getting what I paid for."

"Like what you saw?"

She glanced around the bag, shrugged. "It's kind of hard to judge something so small from this distance."

His laugh echoed across the gap between the two buildings. He opened his mouth but closed it when a buzzer sounded further back in his apartment. He headed for the door, stopped and turned back.

"You better put some ice on that, before it swells any further."

Casey's hand shot to her right cheekbone, her fingertips gently exploring the puffy skin.

"Great." Bruised ego was one thing. How was she going to explain a black eye?

Three people stood in front of Casey in the line at the Planning Department and she yawned, checked her watch. Was it really almost lunch?

The young female counter clerk smiled at the man across from her. She flipped her hair back over her shoulder and giggled at something he said. They spoke in hushed tones and she slipped a piece of paper across the counter then watched him walk away.

"Why don't you just take a picture?" The other clerk snarled. Older. Heavier. Tired of picking up the slack.

Casey checked her watch again as the line inched forward. If Charlie was correct and the arsons were targeted, then it was just as likely to be anyone interested development of a property that fell under the committee's jurisdiction. All three buildings victimized by the arsonist—if the fires proved related—resided on the heritage rolls and those other than hers held failed renovation applications. Or at least they had until fire made them unsafe. After clearing the lots, owners could build to suit.

Convenient.

"Next." The older clerk still appeared impatient when Casey stepped up.

"I need to find out about planning applications that will affect these buildings." Casey slid the list across the counter.

She'd had difficulty sleeping after her discussion with Charlie and despite her vigorous heavy bag work this morning, thoughts of Kieran and arson running laps round her brain. She'd ordered title searches online. The rest—she stared at the pile of forms slapped on the counter in front of her—had to be done in person. So far it had taken most of her morning.

"Fill these out." The woman flashed a well-practiced smile.

"Thanks." Casey sighed, pulled the forms toward her and moved to the other side of the room.

In this day of technology, it seemed ridiculous that the stack of paperwork in front of her was necessary. The Permit Department clerk had handed her a similar stack. She pulled the chained-down pen from the holder and started filling in the blanks.

She paused and stretched, took a closer look at the aerial photos hanging on the wall above the counter. A quick run of her finger along the Fraser brought her to the rail bridge then beyond to the downtown area. Condos occupied the riverfront area now known as the Quay, though warehouses still flanked the neighborhood. She found her building further along, Kieran's right beside it.

Could he really be responsible?

A quick shake stopped her mind from the merry-go-round of possibilities from spinning her round again and she continued filling in the first two forms. Casey glanced toward the computer monitor sitting at each wicket, shook the pen in her hand and returned to her paperwork. The woman could probably push a couple of buttons on her keyboard and give Casey the answers she needed. But that's just not the way it was done.

Bureaucracies.

Casey scanned the bodies that queued around the canvas and chrome barrier keeping the line manageable. Near the front she followed a long pair of legs up over a curved bottom, past a narrow waist up to blond hair that curled at the collar. She snapped her head away and shot a hand up to her temple.

Had he seen her?

She glimpsed through her fingers as Kieran advanced another step toward the counter, his gentle nod an answer to her question.

Damn. She waggled her fingers in a half-wave, flashed an uneasy smile and turned back to the forms. What was he doing here?

Her heart sped up and she couldn't focus. Should she take her forms and leave? Should she look for him? Why wouldn't her hand stop shaking?

By the time she looked back at the line, he was gone. It was probably for the best. She sighed and turned back to her papers. Why did her man-sense have to be so bad? First Jim, the alcoholic. Now Kieran, the what? Arsonist?

"Lose another earring?"

Casey jumped at the voice in her ear and she snatched her papers up against her chest. He touched her slightly discolored cheekbone, brushed her hair back with his fingers and caressed the spot gently with his thumb. "That bag put up quite a fight."

Unable to put together a cohesive thought, she laughed.

He tugged at the corner of one of the forms, bent it back. "What are you up to?"

She pulled the forms tighter to her chest.

"Committee business."

Too quick. Too high.

She took a breath. "I was just checking on some bylaw applications."

"Dashing someone else's dreams, are we?" She opened her mouth, but his smile stopped the backlash. "Thinking about rezoning your building?"

"What are you talking about?"

"Well, the address on that application is yours."

She glanced down at the papers she held to her chest. "Well, not exactly."

"What then? You wanted to make sure you own it?"

"Yes. And apparently I do."

"Good to know." His eyes sparkled as he tilted his head and smiled. "So what are you really doing here?"

"I could ask you the same question."

"But you didn't."

"Okay, what are you doing here?"

"Talking to you."

"That's not what I meant."

"But it's what you asked. Your turn."

"Why are you checking into your own building?"

Now what? She could make something up, but she was a horrible liar. Lies, even the tiny white ones, hung on her face like portraits displayed for all the world to see.

Kieran raised his brows and pursed his lips.

Her shoulders drooped slightly. She was going to have to tell him the truth. As she opened her mouth to speak a cell phone rang and everyone checked their pockets.

Casey touched her pocket, signaled for him to wait a moment with her index finger and fumbled her phone to her ear.

"Hello?"

There was no call, but in this day of silent settings he didn't have to know that.

"Oh, hey Tory, how are ya?"

Wait. Roll the eyes. Blah, blah, blah.

"Tonight? Sure."

Another pause. Kieran's attention was beginning to wander. He was buying it.

"I'm just up at city hall. I could meet you out front in a couple—"

The classical music ring in her ear nearly deafened her and she pushed the send button to silence it.

"Hello?" She tugged at her blouse. When had it gotten so hot in here? "Uh, hi Tory. Can I call you back?"

She punched end and slipped it back into her pocket. Flashed a smile. Kieran's eyes widened and he raised a brow.

"All right. I was playing detective."

A quick laugh and both brows went up. "And you thought the

answers would just pop out at you?"

"Well, no. But I thought...well..." she let the comment trail off. "Wait a minute, what are you doing here?"

The corners of his mouth twitched with amusement, but he turned and threw a wave over his shoulder as he headed for the door. "Let me know how that goes."

Papers wagged out of his back pocket with each step and she snatched them.

"Hey."

She unfolded the papers and read the top.

He'd been one step ahead of her.

Chapter nine

Casey's gentian jacket made her pop like a color image against a black and white background as an impending storm turned the midday sky dark. Wind tugged at her hood, whipping her blond hair around the oversized material and she plopped one hand on her head.

Kieran tugged his own skimpy coat around him, cast a wary glance at the sky and jogged after her across the driveway to the park-like front lawn of City hall.

"What did you find?" she asked.

One blue eye peeked around the large hood at him and he resisted the urge to tug the bright blue fabric away to reveal the other.

Her. "Not much. Why don't we grab a coffee—"

The sudden downpour beat cold against his head and Casey screeched, stuffed her papers into her jacket. She hunched her shoulders and scurried down the rest of the stairs to the sidewalk. He hurried after, catching up with her as the traffic allowed them to cross against the lights.

She ran downhill, hooked a hand on a railing and swung under the awning that covered the tile entry to the businesses nestled on the side of the building. Casey flipped back her hood and peeked up at the angry sky. A flash of lightening sent her giggling backward into him and he wrapped his arms around her.

Casey clapped her hands together as if praying, pushed straight up through the circle of arms and broke his grasp. She spun, put a hand on his chest, hooked a foot behind his heel and pushed. His frame lurched backward and he scrambled to catch his balance, but his arms caught only air.

She grabbed his shirt front, tugged to change the direction of his fall and settled him on the ground, his weight pulling her down with him.

"Sorry." She grimaced. "Too many self-defense cla—"

Thunder drowned her words and they both turned toward the source. Another flash lit the sky and her lips moved as she counted three seconds. She jumped and squealed again, scurrying off him, extending a hand and helping him up. Her nearly purple eyes reflected the color of her jacket and sparkled with excitement.

He brushed a blossom from Casey's cheek, slid his fingers into her hair, cupping her cheek and caressing the soft skin just in front of her ear. The eyes that looked up at him were a deeper shade of blue than he thought possible and her breath warmed his wrist. He slid his hand round the back of her neck, brought the other hand up and cupped her chin.

Kieran lingered a moment, thumbs urging her face up toward his, knees bending to reduce the distance, lips touching, sampling, tasting. His tongue darted through slightly parted lips, tentative at first exploration and retreat, but growing in urgency with each foray. Her breathing quickened as her tongue jumped into the fray, battled his for position.

Her feathery touch tingled a trail around his waist and up his back to his neck where her fingers twirled and tugged at his hair. He slipped one hand around her waist and pulled her closer, carrying her toward the wall at the end of the narrow entryway cut into the side of the hill. A shiver rippled through her to him as her back touched the cement wall and someone groaned.

Was that him?

His nipples hardened under the thin fabric of his shirt as her hand brushed across his chest and settled in the middle. The pressure from her hand, soft at first became urgent and Kieran lifted his head. Casey's face flushed three shades to match the color of the soft, swollen lip she bit and she looked away.

The staccato of rain beating down on awning and cement invaded his hazed brain. Drops bounced off the sloping street beside them and ran in rivers along the sidewalk's edged toward the storm drain. Casey skirted him and adjusted her jacket before casting a hasty glance at the windows beside them.

Plate glass fronted offices where lights shone and open signs hung in the windows.

What the hell had he been thinking?

Raindrops fell cold against her cheeks and she turned her face up to the sky in an effort douse the flames that smoldered just under her surface. Better yet, maybe she'd drown.

What the hell had she been thinking?

She hadn't.

Those green eyes. Kryptonite to her senses.

It had been years since she'd kissed anyone in public and never had it been like that. A simple peck hello or goodbye. No. This 'hello' had been different. She'd buckled like some silly girl overcome by the weather—and those big green eyes.

She cast a glance over her shoulder. It was like a scene from one of those old fashioned movies where the couple takes refuge in some church or cave and fall into each other's arms and make love right there.

Her pulse quickened and she shook the thought away. If she could just get her knees to stop shaking and her lips to stop tingling...

Light shone through the window to her left. Two women worked quietly at their desks apparently oblivious to her incredible lapse of judgment. At least that was something.

Casey stepped back out of the rain and Kieran averted his gaze. He looked at his feet, the street, the building, the sky—anywhere but her. Was he trying to hide something or was he simply feeling as awkward as she?

"Sorry," he said finally.

Sorry? For what? For kissing her there? Or for kissing her at all?

What was she supposed to say to that?

She fumbled through her pockets for the scrap of paper with the address of Land Titles on it. Ninety-nine. She glanced at the doors and rolled her eyes heavenward. Figured. Not only had she lost herself in a kiss that obviously meant more to her than to him, she'd done it in front of the window of the office she had to go into. If she'd simply checked the delivery box on the title search order forms, she could have saved herself at least this little embarrassment.

Kieran reached for her but she ducked inside the office. The two women exchanged glances as she walked in and Casey's cheeks warmed. Had they seen?

An older redhead took her order numbers and searched under the counter for something. Casey cast a glance out toward the street. Kieran gazed back at her through the window, hands in his pockets, shuffling from foot to foot. At least he had the good sense to look uncomfortable.

She turned back toward the counter and touched her fingers to her lips. Warmth radiated outward despite the water that ran down her nose. She swiped at the drop before it could splat down onto the counter and glanced back at the window. Her breath caught in her throat. He'd gone.

"Here we are." The redhead slid an envelope across to Casey. "Funny weather we've been having."

A nod. "Yes."

"Cold and rainy one minute..."

The two women exchanged another glance. "Hot and bothered the next."

Casey's mouth slid into a wry grin. "Thanks." She waved the envelope at the women and pushed through the door, the women's laughter following her into the street.

The small round table in the corner of the coffee shop would barely hold the papers, but it was the only one available. Casey hung her jacket on the back of the chair and fished her wallet out of the pocket and turned toward the counter.

"Here you go." Kieran's deep voice startled her.

Her eyes traveled up the length of him, past the hand holding the coffee cup to his eyes. She contemplated a moment and took the cup. "Thanks."

"I wasn't sure you wanted me to wait."

"I wasn't sure I wanted you to either." She indicated the table she'd selected and settled herself in one of the chairs, dumped the contents of her envelope and the permit department documents on the table.

He took the seat and added the planning applications he'd gathered to the pile. Casey lined the papers up in by address then arranged the piles in order of fire dates. The firebug hit both ends of the downtown area as well as the middle.

"Anything?" Kieran asked.

"All of these places are on the heritage rolls."

"Would that be the connection?"

"Maybe." Casey shifted her chair and Kieran pulled his around beside her. "But given the area, almost all the buildings down here would fit into the heritage category."

"Then, there's got to be something else."

"There must be."

Kieran picked up the stack of forms and flipped through. Concentration pulled his features tight and brought out the angles in his face. He glanced in her direction and his eyes sparkled in the reflected light. Her heart quickened and she looked away.

Kryptonite.

"Ownership doesn't cross-over. The names of each property's owner is different."

Casey leaned in to see what he was talking about. The familiar aroma of spice and chocolate tickled her nose. Was that the beverage or him?

She gave herself a mental shake and turned back to the documents. Her eyes followed his finger down the page, but her fuddled mind wandered at the memory of his touch and she barely noticed what he was saying.

"Don't you think?"

"Sorry?" Damn. Focus.

"I can't see the connection." He pushed the papers away, leaned back in his chair and sipped at his cup.

"There's gotta be one. They're all happening here." She twisted the papers toward her, stacked them in order of fire date next to her pile. She perused the paperwork methodically. "There all owned by individuals except this one." She tapped the building that had housed the bookshop. "It's owned by some numbered company."

Kieran shifted his chair around the side of the table to get a better view. She reread the numbers. Something familiar there, but—

She chewed at her thumb and stared out the window.

"What?"

"I'm not sure."

He turned back to the paper read the numbers aloud. "You think it means something.

She shrugged and reached for

her coffee. She took a larger sip than intended and pain shot through her tongue. She drew a quick open-mouthed breath to cool the sting.

"Hot?" he said without looking her way.

Damn! He wasn't supposed to notice. "Yes, a little."

His smile brought crinkles to the corners of his eyes and he turned to her. "Want me to kiss it better?"

Her smile faded. "You did that up the hill, remember."

"Preventative medicine."

"Didn't seem to prevent much."

"Maybe we should try it again."

God. She was just as bad as he was. No wonder he'd ambushed her in the middle of the street. When had she become such a flirt?

His gaze remained fixed on hers for what seemed an eternity and she thought for a moment that he might actually kiss her right here. Worse. She might actually let him. She lifted her cup and busied herself with the papers on the table.

What would people say if they saw her kissing him? Talk about conflict of interest. She was the head of the Heritage Committee and he'd been attempting to get around the guidelines for months now.

Was that it?

Had all of this been some ploy to bring her round to his side, to give him an ally on the committee? Was his interest in her motivated solely by what it might get him?

Aside from her body, that was.

She flipped through the papers again. His application for bylaw variance was in the pile along with three or four others. Charlie's cautions played through her mind again.

Kieran's emerald eyes gazed at her over the top of his cup.

Definitely kryptonite.

She'd have to build a wall between them if she ever hoped to get through this.

"Could Charlie get you a copy of the arson reports?" Kieran asked as they walked across to the south side of Columbia Street. The heavy rain had tapered to a fitful drizzle.

"If he's got the reports, I doubt he'll give me a copy, why?"

"Well, I just wondered if we might find out something by looking at the materials used in the fires."

"Like some kind of forensic evidence?"

"Uh-huh," he mumbled and

nodded.

"CSI look out!" She smiled. "I can tell you they're all related."

"Charlie tell you that?"

"It was on the news."

They took a few steps in silence. Pedestrians moved along the pavement. Some hurried while others took their time, stopping at storefronts to survey the wares offered. Kieran followed Casey's gaze to the window of a bridal boutique and raised an eyebrow. What had she looked like in one of those gowns? Better yet, what had she looked like out of it?

Heat surged down low and he glanced away as he remembered the feel of her lips and body against his, the taste of her, the desire for more. He hadn't meant to kiss her like that. He'd been carried away by the moment, her giggles and the rain. And once sampled, her sweetness drew him in completely.

She'd been gracious about the ambush—if he didn't count the take down. Afterward, she'd been carried away, too. At some point though, her common sense had kicked in and she'd urged him to stop. How long had it taken for him to notice that hand on his chest?

And what was that in the coffee shop?

He would have locked onto her

right then and there if her quick coffee cup and flood of embarrassment hadn't brought him to his senses. It wasn't as if their relationship had been romantic. It hadn't even been personal. Until lately all their meetings bordered on antagonistic.

So, why had he kissed her?

Even though he knew he shouldn't have, he couldn't help himself. Her reaction to the storm had been delightful. The squeal. The laughter.

The smile.

He should have resisted. If he hoped for a future...

A future?

With Casey?

When had he started thinking along those lines?

The only future he ever thought of was business. Businesses didn't leave. They might fail. They might fly. But it was all numbers and money. Nothing personal.

No. Personally it had always been out with the old and in with the new, forming attachments that met the present needs and then moving on when the opportunity arose. It was better that way. Anything else always ended in disaster. His family was proof of that.

"What if we search financial records?"

Her voice brought him back as they stepped up onto the curb. Her blue eyes sparkled up at him. Her blond hair fluttered in the remnants of the wind. Those soft pink lips begged to be kissed. So why didn't he kiss her?

"If the fires aren't random, then there has to be a motive. Money is one heck of an incentive," she continued.

Focus. Forget the lips.

"True. But how would we find that out?"

She shrugged. "Know any hackers?"

"Only the kind that use a cleaver."

Casey smiled then frowned. Her features drew inward and he longed to caress the worry valleys out of her forehead. Stop. Focus. He forced his gaze up at the ornate corbels decorating his buildings front façade.

His building. His restaurant. *His future.*

God damn it.

He'd never been tied to anything, now—

They stopped in front of the door to Tethys.

"Do you want to come in for a minute?" Why had he asked that? "Sample some—"

"Cookies?" She smiled, glanced at her watch and shook her head.

"—Entrées. The kitchen staff is practicing service."

"Thanks," she said. "But I have a class to teach in about twenty minutes."

An odd rush flowed through Kieran. Disappointment?

Smile. Don't let her see it. He shoved his hands in his pockets and his gaze followed a pedestrian wearing a red ball cap down the sidewalk. What was it about this woman?

"Stop by later if you have time. There'll be lots of food." He walked with her a few steps toward her building, forced himself to stop.

What was his problem? He should just walk away. She'd made her preferences known. In the coffee shop. Just now. She wanted to keep her distance. "Some tasty desserts."

She turned back, craned her neck to look at him, the afternoon sun reflected in her eyes and on her moist lips. She took a step back and adjusted the angle of her neck.

"Okay, but my classes run until nine-thirty tonight."

Walk away. Give her the out.

"That's okay. It's not like I have anywhere else to be."

Why had he said that?

"Ten o'clock then?" And that?

She nodded. "Ten o'clock."

Kieran searched her eyes for hints at the thoughts behind, but the cool blueness revealed nothing. She glanced over her shoulder toward her door.

"I better go." She thumbed over her shoulder.

His eyes drifted to her mouth and when the moist lips parted he thought he might claim them once again. He forced his gaze up to her eyes. "Me, too. No telling what they've done to my kitchen."

Casey strode away, threw a wave over her shoulder and disappeared through her entry.

Kieran sighed.

Where had all this emotion come from? And why her?

He had to remember who Casey Michaelson was. They were opposites, adversaries in the fight for his building and business. They had different visions and desires.

Desire.

Infatuation more like. She was like a new dish, a wonderful

combination of ingredients. Spicy, rich and she smelled delightful. He should walk away, forget about her, but his taste early left him wanting more. He watched her into the building.

But would she give it to him?

Chapter ten

Casey sat across the stainless steel counter from Kieran while he prepared a light, late evening meal. The knife shone under the industrial kitchen's lights as he sliced vegetables. His movements were swift and his cuts precise. His abilities shouldn't have surprised her. He was a chef; he had studied in Europe. Still, he reminded her more of a construction worker. His muscular build, the deep timbre of his voice, the way he moved. He didn't fit the 'chef' mold.

She smiled.

She'd fought the 'mold' most of her life. She'd been one of only two females in her martial arts class when she started and the first female sensei in the organization.

"What made you buy a building down here?" Kieran's question brought her back to her stool.

"I grew up here and when this place came on the market, it looked like a great investment." She picked a carrot from the plate and took a bite. "Why'd you stay?"

He looked up from his work, but continued to cut, guiding the blade with the backs of his fingers. She cringed and he smiled. "Don't worry, this dish is purely vegetarian." He chuckled. "My grandmother would have a fit if she saw me handle a knife."

She raised her brow.

"You know, Fred's wife."

"Fred was married?" Stupid question. Change the subject. "Did she teach you how to cook?"

He nodded, but didn't say anything.

"Do you see your family a lot?"

"Not really."

"But you see your brother."

"Yeah, some."

"He's the one who made the sculpture. The one with—" she started.

"—the torch."

"Sorry." She wanted to hide. "How was I supposed to know?"

"Not a problem...now," he paused. "If I'd met up with you that night, the story might have been different."

"So...*why* was it you kept the building?"

"Changing the subject?" He grinned. "Smooth."

Casey's stomach fluttered. Had to be the peppers.

"Actually, I don't know. Fred loved it and left it to me."

"Nice grandfather."

He stopped his preparations and gazed over at her. "Yes." The vacant look in his eye suggested that Kieran took a quick trip to the past. "He had quite a sense of humor. I wonder if he thought it was some big joke." He returned his attention to food preparation.

"Joke?"

"Well, it hasn't exactly been easy around here. What with delays and disputes...I should have had the main floor open a month—" he stopped mid-sentence and looked across at her.

She worked her jaw. Where was he going with this?

"Wait." He held his hand up. "I didn't mean that the way it sounds. I might not agree with your position, but I understand."

Casey drew in a deep breath.

"I just meant ..." he stammered. "How about those Canucks?" He coughed out a laugh and forced a smile. "Think they've got a chance at the cup?"

"Changing the subject?"

"Worked for you."

"True."

The only sound was the knife as it sliced through equal parts peppers and tension. She hadn't come to discuss the Heritage Committee. Why couldn't he just leave it there?

Casey swiveled round on her stool.

A patch of unfinished greenboard above the sink awaited tiling. A box of junk left over from the kitchen construction sat in a corner. The far wall around the doors leading off the kitchen remained unpainted. She sighed. Kieran's renovations were still in progress, his business wasn't open as yet and her committee had had a part in all that. Why had she expected he'd avoid the subject?

"No chance."

"Huh?"

"The Canucks," she said. "No chance at all."

"Pessimist."

"Dreamer."

He raised a brow. "Optimist."

She laughed. A true Canucks fan.

Casey ambled over to the windows overlooking the waterfront. The view, though obstructed somewhat by the cement parking structure, offered a glimpse of the river and the lights on the opposite shore. Below, the sidewalk was hidden from clear view by awnings and shop signs. He was right about one thing. The view from the top would be a much better draw to the restaurant. The scent of warm olive oil drew her back toward the work table as vegetables sizzled in the hot pan.

"That smells great."

He smiled, shook and flipped the contents of the pan. "Wine?"

"That would be nice."

He nodded her toward him and she came round the counter. When he turned the pan handle toward her, she started back, shaking her head. Kieran's cheek dimpled under a mischievous smile and caught her wrist.

"Come on, you'll be fine."

"I don't know."

Her repertoire in the kitchen consisted of her mother's casserole, grilled cheese and anything that required the reheat setting on the microwave.

"I'm not—"

The warm arm that snaked around her middle chased the protest from her lips. He wrapped both his hand

and hers around the handle of the pan.

"Just shake..." Their bodies moved in time together, his hard body blanketing hers. "And...flick." His wrist action flipped the pan's contents over.

Her flustered giggle echoed through the expansive kitchen. If she could just move away a bit—

His free hand pulled her back into him.

"Whoa, watch out for the flame there."

Oh, God it was warm. Had she moved closer to the stove now?

Another laugh.

The heat radiating from the hand on her abdomen competed with that from the stove and perspiration kissed her brow. After repeating shake-flick with the pan a few more times, Kieran removed his hand from the handle, but kept her secured with the other.

Shake. Flick.

His body hunched over hers. His strong chest wrapped round her shoulders like a shawl, his hand inches from hers, ready to repeat the instruction if need be.

Shake. Flick.

The hand on her abdomen retreated to her hip; a trail of

gooseflesh followed the movement. She drew a quick breath and the pan hand stilled. He pulled back tight to her, wrapping her body like a glove—a warm, masculine glove.

"You have to keep it moving."

His breath was hot on her ear. Her body tingled. God, but he felt good. She tried to force her attention back to the cooking vegetables, but failed miserably. How could she think of anything else when he was touching her like that?

Peppers.

His body swayed. She went with it. Shake.

Garlic.

His hips moved, took hers with them. Flick.

Carrots. Peas. She searched for something else to focus on, but found only his warm body, the hand that still directed hers, the smell of spice and chocolate.

No. That must be imagination.

He tucked his chin down over her shoulder and released her hand. "That's it," he encouraged.

Kieran's cheek brushed against hers as she glanced his way and she sought contact despite the roughness of the burgeoning beard. She inhaled his scent again.

Definitely chocolate.

She followed the scent a moment, leaning back into him, enjoying the contrast of strong muscles and soft touch. Though it seemed impossible, he moved closer to her, enveloping her body with his. She shifted her weight, pushed back into him, seeking even more. God but he was—

Kieran straightened and stepped back.

Heat crept up Casey's face in contrast to the cool emptiness left by Kieran's quick retreat and her heart thundered. His brows knit deep furrows into his forehead and he thumbed awkwardly over his shoulder.

"I'll go get the wine."

What had she been doing? Everything had been going so well until she'd taken a cooking lesson and turned it into some strange one-sided mating ritual. She'd practically thrown herself at him.

And he'd walked away.

"Shake. Flick," he called from across the room and waved a relaxed arm.

She sighed turned back and snatched a carrot from the pan. A piece snapped off behind her teeth and she crunched it as he disappeared through the door.

Maybe she should have just stayed home.

Cool air helped little with Kieran's fight to maintain self-control and he vowed to stay in the wine cooler for as long as it took. Had she done that on purpose or did she really have no clue what she did to him?

And why had he walked away?

Her widening blue eyes trailed him when he'd abruptly moved back. She'd turned, but not before he noticed the deep crimson coloring flooding her face. She'd wanted him.

Any other woman would have elicited a totally different response had she brushed up against him that way. Yet here he was hiding in the wine cellar like a teenager camping for the first time, uncertain whether to crawl in; afraid that one false move would bring the tent down. He extracted a bottle of Italian Pinot Grigio, touched the cool bottle to his forehead. Something was seriously wrong with him.

Casey waited just outside the door. Ready. Willing. *Wanting*. All he had to do was walk out and pick up where he—or rather she—left off. So why didn't he?

Because she'd regret it in the morning.

And then so would he.

He blew a mocking laugh out his nose and continued down the racks in search of an appropriate wine.

Since when had regrets mattered? She was a grown woman. Hell, she'd even been married before. It wasn't like she didn't know the consequences of her actions. So what if she'd regret it in the morning. It wasn't like they had a future.

Men and women were not designed to stay together long-term. With life-expectancies lengthening, people were bound to get sick of each other. Just look at his parents. His mother—queen of the brides—embarking on marriage number four. Or was it five? She'd left a trail of disappointed grooms—his father the king of them all. Kieran played witness to a feast of jealousy and self-loathing that only ended with his father's death.

Kieran would not follow in those footsteps.

He selected a bottle of chardonnay from the rack and took it with the pinot toward the door. Each was different, one light and crisp, the other full and bold. Both reminded him of Casey.

Damn it.

She'd invaded his mind. His heart quivered with the memory of widening blue eyes as he'd pulled away from her. Warmth travelled the length of his body to his groin.

Maybe regrets did matter.

"Dinner was wonderful." Casey lifted her glass. "Here's to the chef."

Kieran nodded. "Glad you liked it." He leaned an elbow on the stainless steel counter they were using as a breakfast bar.

"Sorry about the vegetables." The soft glow of the candle enhanced her grimace.

"What? You don't like blackened peas?"

"Black-eyed peas maybe." She laughed and sipped at her wine.

"Maybe you should stick to breaking boards," Kieran teased.

"Eating that," she poked at the plate, "would be very similar."

He laughed aloud. His trip to the wine cellar had taken him longer than expected and Casey's shake and flick had degenerated into a shimmy and nudge. He'd tried to salvage something, in an effort to save her feelings, but the questionable mess lay untouched on the serving dish.

Silence fell over the room as he leaned against the stool back and enjoyed his wine. None of the earlier tension remained between them and the warmth of alcohol brought comfort to his body. He filled his lungs and released a long, slow breath. He could stay here all night.

Casey leaned forward on her

elbows and held her glass between her hands. She took a lazy sip and turned to look at him. Her eyes sparkled under relaxed lids. His hand twitched under the impulse to brush the stray strand of golden hair from her forehead. When she smiled the desire to taste the wine on her glistening lips swelled up inside him.

He stood and walked over to the window.

"I wonder what they have in common," she said.

What? Her lips? "Sorry?"

"The buildings."

In the dim candle light Kieran could make out the tongue that slid along her lips and he followed its progress. He caught a shift in her expression and realized she'd said something more. He nodded, not quite certain what he was agreeing to, but unwilling to break the moment.

"I was hoping the common factor would jump up and bite us. Maybe a lien, or a common owner—something."

Focus. "That would've been too easy."

He cast his gaze back out into the night. Reflected light from across the river lay in long lines across the water's surface and the ding of a lowering train barrier sounded off to his right.

Slits of light danced through

the spaces between the freight-cars and he tried to let the strobe-like sensation lull his mind, but each new strobe was like a petal on a child's flower. I want her. I want her not. Round and round. Over and over. He should just walk on over there, wrap his arms around her and kiss the wine off her lips. After that—

"Got any ideas?"

Definitely. He shook his head.

Kieran peered into his empty wine glass and rubbed his face. He couldn't remember the last time alcohol had such an effect on him.

"Are you okay?" Casey asked.

A nod.

Why wasn't his mouth working?

He crossed to the table, held the bottle up to offer her more wine and dumped the remnants of the bottle into his glass when she declined. Sobriety would have been the more sensible option, but sensibility had never been his middle name. The hunger to touch her, to wipe the concern from her brow overwhelmed him and he gripped the neck of the wine bottle tightly.

"I'm fine." He forced a smile. "Just a bit tired."

Tired. That was a new word for it. He set the bottle down on the table and downed the last half glass of pinot. He shifted his weight as his loins stirred and sparked. He stared into his empty glass. The wine. That had to be it.

He set the glass down.

"What were you saying?" Focus on the conversation.

She hesitated, stared at him through squinted eyes. "Have you got any ideas what to do next?"

He could think of a few things, but none of them had anything to do with finding the arsonist.

"I thought your idea about finances was good." He crossed to the sink, filled a glass with water and downed half of it. "Water?"

Casey shook her head. Lips pursed in thought called to him from across the kitchen. He drank a few more gulps.

What was the matter with him?

"Yes, money is as good a motive as any," she said and stared as he drained the glass of water in one long swig. "Are you sure you're okay?"

Another nod.

Another lie.

She glanced at her watch and stood. "Oh my God. Look at the time. I should let you get to bed."

Bed?

She swallowed her last sip of

wine and extended the glass toward him. His hand wrapped round hers on the stem as he closed the distance between them. Her gaze dropped to the glass and climbed slowly back up his chest to his eyes. His free hand brushed that lock of hair back from her face and his breathing slowed then quickened with contact.

Emotion swirled behind eyes that had deepened to almost indigo in the candlelit kitchen and despite the open industrial nature of the room; the walls seemed to close round them. Her mouth opened slightly and her hot breath sweet with wine caressed his face. Was she inviting him?

Did he care?

He inched forward, tentative, cautious. Not at all like the urgency of the afternoon. He set the wine glass aside and cupped her face in his hands. He moved closer still praying she wouldn't resist.

By God, he did care.

Another inch closer and her mouth came up to meet his. Heat flashed through his body as their lips met in a kiss, at the same time tender and urgent. He followed the edge of her mouth, tasted her sweetness and the remnants of wine. She mirrored his movements, trailed her tongue after his. When their tongues touched, the kindling burning in the pit of his desire burst into flame and he groaned.

He ran his hand down the curve of her body to her hip, then followed the line to her bottom and pulled her into him. His excitement grew with the contact and his breathing quickened. Her heartbeat thundered under the caress of his hand.

Pull away.

Stop.

He wasn't going to do this.

The fingers that up over his shoulder, along his neck and found the curls at the nape of his neck chased all thoughts of stopping from his mind. She tugged, twirled and tugged again. He pushed harder against her and the two danced across the kitchen to the counter behind them.

God, she felt good.

A brilliant flash brightened the room beyond the glow from the candlelight. Two seconds later a thunderous crash rattled the windows. The trance broken, Casey's body tensed under his touch. She pulled away and headed to the window. He fought to regain control and followed her, stepping up behind her to gaze out over her head. An old wooden warehouse down by the river's edge was consumed by flame.

What had happened?

It was as much a question about the activity inside his building as outside it.

Chapter eleven

Embers from the fire floated past Casey where she stood on the sidewalk beside Kieran. While the spring night chill ran up her spine, the heat from the fire warmed her face in an odd sensation that reminded her of camping on a damp summer night. But she wouldn't be roasting marshmallows tonight.

She shivered.

Kieran reached his arm around to give her shoulder a gentle squeeze. Warmth filled her and she let herself lean into him. She touched her lips with her finger tips. The cooking lesson had been a nice touch and she wondered how many other women had succumbed to his frying pan. She twisted her mouth.

Had he planned it?

Had she?

It wasn't like she hadn't thought about the possibilities. After this afternoon, she'd done nothing but think about them. She shook her head. What the hell was matter with her? Since when was she such easy prey for a pair of green eyes and Teflon?

A loud crack brought her attention back to the burning warehouse. Steam rose from the back of a firefighter whose protective jacket lay on the blacktop beside him. His grimy face showed signs of exhaustion and he took a long swig from a bottle of water. The arsonist should be proud, fire demolished the structure. He should have stayed to watch.

Had he?

Unfamiliar faces abounded around her. Two women engaged in animated conversation a few feet down the sidewalk. A man leaned against a parking lot support pillar. A small group lingered on the other side of the road. Casey glanced around and up at Kieran. She didn't even know him that well.

She wrapped her arms around herself and took a step away. Charlie's warnings rang through her head until she shook them away. Kieran had been with her. He couldn't have had anything to do with the fire—

"You okay?" The whoosh of fire hoses nearly drowned his voice.

A line cut through the middle of his forehead where concern pushed his eyebrows together. She bit her lip against the compulsion to reach across and smooth it away. Reflected flames danced in his eyes and her stomach swirled like water down a drain and she longed for his steadying touch.

Why had she stepped away?

She gave herself a mental shake.

Her marriage to Jim had taught her two things. She didn't need a man and she didn't *need* a man.

So what was it about this one?

She blinked away from his probing eyes and her gaze settled on her basement storefront. Plywood still covered the entrance and repairs had given the place a patchwork appearance, new and fresh against the old and damaged.

Was that what Kieran was? Repairs?

She hadn't thought she needed any.

"Casey?"

"I'm fine." His eyes widened at her harsh tone and she took a breath. "I think I just need some time to myself." She started toward home, then spun around. "Thanks for dinner and..." She let the thought trail off. "I'll talk to you tomorrow."

Casey waited for a truck to pass, then cut across the street and disappeared into her building. Kieran pulled his collar up to shield his neck from the sudden chill as the door closed behind her. He shoved his hands into his jacket pockets and kicked a stone across the pavement at the railway tracks.

Damn! That hadn't gone right; nowhere near according to plan. But then, he hadn't had a plan. Maybe that was the problem. He'd set out to seduce every other woman he'd taken an interest in. His method had been perfected over the years. Attraction. Plan. Seduce. Split.

He couldn't do that with her. He wasn't even sure why. Still, he couldn't seem to keep his hands off her either. He shook his head. His self-control had gone up in smoke along with her basement.

Damp from the over-spray of fire hoses his hair flattened when he ran his fingers through it. He drew in a deep breath and let out a low frustrated growl. She confused him so intensely that from one moment to the next he didn't know which way to turn. He kicked another rock, sent it careening close to a parked car and headed for his place.

"It must have been the wine."

He punctuated the statement with a hard shove at his service entrance door. It opened with a bang. The alcohol had depleted his defenses and he'd been drawn in by those wine-soaked lips. "Right."

The latch on the door clicked into place and Kieran reset the alarm. When he pushed the button for the elevator, the motor clanked and grunted as the old gears limped into action. How long would it take to get down to him? A new elevator was bound to cost a mint and changing it would probably be against some Heritage Association rule. The wry laugh that followed echoed off the lobby walls.

Days of late nights and stress took their toll, made him bone weary. He leaned against the metal handrail affixed to the elevator wall for support. His eyelids were heavy and he let them close. Things would get better after Tethys opened. He lifted one lid and stumbled out when the elevator ding indicated his arrival at his destination.

His cot beckoned from the back room and he heeded the call. A deep yawn caught him as he pulled his shirt over his head and kicked his shoes and socks off. He leaned on the thin mattress. Right now, nothing mattered but sleep. The arsonist and the fires. Casey. The elevator. All of it would wait until the morning. He closed his eyes and inhaled deeply. Sleep, when it came, would be welcome. He yawned again.

Kieran opened his eyes and sat up. The elevator. Why had he had to wait for it? When he and Casey left, the lift sat at the loading dock entrance. In newer computerized models, the cars would head to a preprogrammed floor to cut wait-time. His model predated computers and required a call to move. No one else was in the building. Shouldn't the elevator have waited?

He ran his hand down his face and rubbed his chin. Common sense told him to call the police, but what if it was a false alarm? The last time the fire department arrived on a similar fool's errand, they'd yanked his permits.

He'd be damned if he'd let it happen again.

The voice mail signaled a message. "Ms. Michaelson? Jason Newfeld from Newfeld Insurance. The underwriter won't process your claim right now. It seems there is some discrepancy with the paperwork. And, since it's a suspicious fire...Well, you can call me, or I'll just get back to you when we get it sorted. Thanks."

Casey sat on the barstool at the window. Orangy-red embers were periodically visible when the wind cleared the steam or the firefighters stirred the rubble. She shook her head. Her energy dwindled. If it was earlier in the day, she might wrap her hands and beat her heavy bag senseless. She drew in lungful of air and let it out.

Then again, maybe not.

Up until a few weeks ago, the control of her life rested, without question, with her. Since the fire, an eddy of circumstances had spiraled her in new directions. She couldn't remember the last time she'd felt this out of control.

Why had all of this happened now, when things seemed to be coming together for her? The dojo. The lofts. Her life. Her grandmother once told her the challenges in life kept it interesting. Casey had to agree, but she could do with a little boredom right now.

Her loud sigh broke the silence as she hopped off the stool.

Kieran's window was dark, but it held her attention anyway. Where did he fit in all of this? And what *had* he done to his arm? Maybe if she'd asked him tonight, he would have told her.

The echo of tingles brought by his kiss still resonated on her lips. She flopped across the arms of her favorite reading chair—a cushy monstrosity she hid in a corner by the window—closed her eyes and inhaled. His scent still lingered in her nostrils and she breathed deeper trying to draw the memory in. Drew in something else.

Alcohol.

She opened her eyes and twirled around. The shadows loomed large in front of her and hind-sight slapped her for not switching more lights on when she arrived home.

Don't panic. Be aware.

All the things she told her students flashed through her brain, but fear still crept up her spine and settled at the base of her skull.

Who was here with her?

Light from the street below peeked through the fifth floor windows to throw long thin shadows across the hardwood. Kieran flipped the switch by the door. An annoying buzz followed, but no light came on. He'd have to thank his grandfather, when he saw him, for his bequeath of a structure in such terrific shape.

He inched toward a door and stopped. What was he supposed to do if he found someone? Maybe his reunion with his grandfather would happen sooner than planned.

A two-by-two he found propped against the wall near the door to the stairwell would be a decent equalizer and he thanked God for untidy contractors. Kieran picked it up and headed down the hall. A squeal announced the swing of the door and he cringed.

So much for surprise.

He crept across the room. Step. Wait. Listen. He heard nothing. Another step and another. Pause. Still nothing. He continued across the floor until he reached the stack of plywood leaning against the wall. Kieran lifted the board above his head in preparation, leapt into the open, arms swinging down, but the blow met only subfloor. He steadied himself and turned to a door leading out from the back wall.

He moved within inches of the slightly ajar barrier and reached for the knob. A noise, a crinkle of cellophane or plastic, emanated from the room. He froze mid-motion. Listen. Nothing. He reached again, stopped with the renewed rustle.

Kieran's heart thudded against his ribs and he strained to hear the movement in the other room. Nothing.

Had they heard him?

Was there another door through which the intruder could sneak around and get the drop on him?

His hands shook slightly as he moved closer. The breath he drew was noisier than intended and he held it while he listened for a response from within. He exhaled in a long, slow gust and pushed the door hard with his foot. A flurry of movement followed the door's crash and Kieran readied the two-by-two for a downward strike. No one came out.

Damn! He jumped to the other side of the door jamb to get a better view. Darkness and shadow obscured much of the room, but no projectiles flew his way. Was that a good thing?

Kieran angled through the doorway, careful to keep a wall behind him for protection. A high hiss bounced around the near-empty room as a beat-up tabby swatted a paw his way. Kieran let the breath he hadn't realized he held out and leaned against the wall.

"Caroline," he said to the cat. "I thought you were dead." His grandfather had found her on the train tracks one day and brought her back to the antique shop. "Time hasn't tamed you any." The cat growled. Kieran laughed.

Relief coursed through his veins and the tension eased from his body when he checked the other rooms and found them empty. Maybe his imagination had worked overtime. It wouldn't be a surprise. Still, he doubted he'd sleep until he knew for certain his place had not been breached.

The cluttered, dark stairwell at the end of hall beckoned and he heeded the call with dread. While it was better than before, Kieran was going to have to talk with the contractor again before Charlie Griffin decided to pay another visit. Building materials and other miscellaneous bits cluttered the way down the stairs. Dim emergency lights illuminated the way and he thanked his grandfather for that little upgrade as he picked his way around the junk. He traveled the stairs to the fourth floor by twos stopping to listen occasionally, but hearing nothing out of the ordinary. The door broke open after a few hard yanks and he fell back with the movement.

"Damn!" he cursed, his voice echoed down the stairwell.

He clamped his mouth shut and grabbed his foot. Why hadn't he put his shoes on? Careful not to put pressure on the ball of his foot, he hobbled onto the fourth floor, leaned against the wall for support and checked for blood. A trickle of dark liquid ran across the skin and dripped onto the floor.

He ran a thumb over his foot to assess the damage and continued his search. He still had three floors to check, four if he counted the restaurant and store though motion detectors would alert him if anyone was about down there. His foot throbbed and he contemplated hobbling down to the first floor kitchen to access the first aid kit, but opted instead for his makeshift apartment.

Using the heel of one foot and the ball of the other, he managed to climb the stairs. He found some cologne, packing tape and a take-out serviette. His wound stung when he doused it with cologne and he quickly applied the impromptu bandage.

He glanced toward Casey's window. She'd be asleep by now and he could almost picture her golden blond hair splayed across the pillow, breasts moving slightly with each relaxed breath. She'd be warm and—

Something moved in the condo across the way.

What was that?

He leaned forward into the glass pane in an effort to see. There it was again. A shadow? No. A person. Casey?

He squinted toward the dimly lit room, straining to make out the images. When the figure passed in front of the faint light from somewhere deeper in the condo Kieran froze.

"Oh, God," he screamed at the closed window then sprinted for the exit.

Kieran took the stairs three at a time, swung around railings and smacked into the walls along the way. He paid no heed to the pain when his bare feet struck ragged edge strips on the old stairs. He pushed past it, ran through it. Over and over, his mind replayed the shadowy image of a body, limp and perhaps lifeless as it was dragged across the floor.

Was she hurt? Was she dead?

No! He couldn't let himself think of that.

A high pitched wail greeted him when he pulled the door to his service entrance open. He punched the code to silence the alarm and flew through the door. If he went in through the boarded area at the bottom of Casey's place, he could gain access to the elevator lobby. Once he got into the elevator it would be a few short seconds to the top and her side.

The board covering the burned-out loading dock slid to the side with an ease that surprised him. The intruder must have entered this way. He hopped from space to space across the blackened floor in an attempt to avoid the materials most hazardous to his bare feet. He kicked himself for not taking the time to pick up his shoes before racing over here. It saved him thirty seconds at the outset, but cost him now.

His bare feet shot sideways on the smooth concrete in the elevator lobby and the air rushed from his body when he slammed into the hard brick wall. He fell to his knees and coughed as he forced air back into his lungs. Pain enveloped him, but he pushed up onto his feet toward the elevator. Nothing could—no, nothing would—stop him.

Except the lock on the elevator pad.

Damn!

How could he forget that? Anger pumped blood through his body and converged at his temples. He massaged the pulsing veins with his fingers. Panic threatened to rob him of reason and he struggled to control his mind.

"Think!" he said aloud as he tried to break through the emotional cloud in his brain. "Come on! She could be dying up there!" His voice echoed off the walls, then fell flat on the floor.

He spun in circles a few times before he moved toward the stairwell. Why hadn't he thought of it before? The intruder had to get up to Casey's loft somehow. Maybe the assailant left a trail of open entries that Kieran could follow to the penthouse.

Although he reached the stairwell door in a few long strides, his approach seemed to take forever. What if the door wasn't open? What would he do then?

Don't think. Just do. He shouldered the door out of the way and stumbled through the opening.

He gave silent thanks as he took the stairs by twos. How much time had passed since he viewed the scene from his window? Was there any point to his efforts? He shook his head. He had to stay focused; to get to the top. There'd be time to think about things later.

From the fourth floor landing where he paused to catch his breath, the railings seemed to go up forever. His lungs hurt. A trail of bloody footprints followed behind him. The pain in his feet pounded under his weight. He pushed off the wall, forced his aching thighs into action. Casey needed him.

By the time he reached the door at the top, his breathing was so ragged he feared the noise would give away his position. He stepped back from the door and struggled to draw long, slow inhalations to decrease his heart-rate. Blood covered his feet like a pair of socks and the warm liquid made him slide on the polished cement landing as he moved toward the door.

Relief coursed through Kieran's body at the silence with which the handle turned. If he'd been at his place, the screech of rust would reveal his presence to the whole building. He allowed himself a fleeting smile and pulled on the door.

When he stepped back to allow for the swing of the door, his foot slipped off the toe of what could be a boot and a hard object pressed into the back of his skull. It couldn't be. It wasn't possible. In his panic, he'd missed the approaching footsteps. But where had they come from?

All adrenaline faded from his body.

How would he help Casey now?

Chapter twelve

"Kieran?"

He raised his head and met Casey's eyes. Confusion and fear rested behind them. His emotions mirrored hers. If she stood in front of him, whose body had been dragged across the room? His mind flipped back to the scene he'd viewed. Had he seen her face or had assumption led him to think it was her?

"I heard a ruckus in the stairwell and waited. Look who fell into my grasp," the deep voice behind him chuckled.

Ruckus?

Kieran turned his head. A hard object pressed into his cheek pushing his face toward the front.

"You just stay where you are. Hands where I can see them and don't move." The stern words were artificial, 1950's cop-show deep.

Kieran raised a brow at Casey. Her expression remained hard and she bit her lip. Was she going to tell the guy he was her neighbor or what?

"Casey?" he said, his voice a little higher, more pleading, than he'd intended.

"Uh? Oh, yes. He's my neighbor." She broke eye contact to look at the person behind him.

"Your neighbor?"

She nodded, but the man didn't move. He pushed the object into Kieran's back.

"You sure?"

"Yes."

"Huh."

"Can I put my hands down now?" Kieran asked.

"I guess." The guy sounded disappointed.

"Thanks." Kieran twisted around as the man clipped his flashlight back onto his belt.

Behind Casey no evidence of anything amiss existed. Her demeanor showed no signs of agitation except what he seemed to have caused. He took a step forward and his foot slipped toward the door jam. Casey reached out to grab him.

Her eyes opened wide and she placed her hand under Kieran's arm to usher him across the marble foyer. He shook his head. Blood smears covered the space below his feet. Staining the foyer floor would be one thing if he'd had to rescue her, but she was in no immediate danger. He stepped back and sat on a stairs to the roof.

"Do you have a towel or something?" he asked.

The man in the black and white security uniform eyed Kieran's feet with amusement. A slight smile played on the guard's lips and his eyes sparkled.

"Glad you're enjoying this," Kieran clamped his jaw. "Don't you have somewhere to be?"

"Oh. Yeah." He coughed, dropped his voice again. "I'll just wait over there with my partner." He took a step. "For our brothers in blue."

Despite the pain in his feet, Kieran nearly laughed aloud. Where did they get this guy?

The rent-a-cop took up his post a few feet to the left of a partner whose eye roll was visible from across the room. Casey's ex-husband sat head lolling against the wall.

After security had hauled her ex out the door, Casey poured bottled-water over Kieran's feet to wash away the blood and debris. He drew in a sharp gasp over gritted teeth. She winced with empathy, but continued to bathe the wounds. What had he been thinking traipsing through the night without shoes?

He made no sound as his bare chest heaved under deep inhalations. Bits of debris protruded from the gashes in the soles of his feet. None required stitches, but some extensive cleaning and disinfecting was in order.

She pulled a ripped piece of packing tape from the top of his foot and he sat up. Her nose wriggled at an unexpected aroma. Sweet. Masculine. Chemical. She hesitated. Tried to place it then continued with her machinations. His expression shifted from pain, to amusement, to pain again and he laughed.

"What?" How could he find this funny?

He opened his mouth to speak, but closed it again. He leaned his head against the metal rail and closed his eyes. Exhaustion made the circles under his eyes deeper. She reached out to caress the dark spot under his eye with her thumb, but pulled back.

Why had she done that?

She ducked her head back down at her work hoping he hadn't noticed.

"Inside joke," he whispered. "I'll share it with you sometime."

"You better." She longed to kiss his forehead, to ease the

creases forming there. She shifted her gaze back to his feet. Keep it to business. "Uh...you have a lot of junk in your feet. There's not enough light here."

He looked across the landing toward the door planted a sly smile on his face. "Are you inviting me in?"

She sighed in response. Smart ass.

He pulled himself up to lean on the rail and she reached around to help him up. The contact with his bare skin sent shocks through her body, igniting the smoldering desire burning deep within her. Her cheek brushed his muscular chest as he leaned into her and she wrapped her fingers around the area just above his waistband.

"Who samples your cookies?" Because it certainly wasn't him.

"I don't bake cookies," he growled, but he was smiling.

Keep the conversation neutral.

"What are you doing here anyway?"

His face relaxed as he sat on the bench in the foyer and took the weight off his feet. He looked off down the hall and then back at her. Was he having trouble bringing himself to tell her what happened or simply concocting a new version of events?

"I thought . . . I came . . ." He dropped his head into his hands. "I thought you were hurt." Emotion tightened his voice. His green eyes, icy with fear, pierced her with their intensity.

"And you came to help me?"

He nodded and broke eye contact. She put her hand over her mouth to hide the smile she couldn't help. Half-naked and barefoot, he'd risked life and limb to rescue her. She pulled a bit of wood from his foot and dabbed the area with a cloth. He winced.

"A heck of a rescue," she said with a hint of sarcasm.

"No problem." His tone was grumpy, but he let a quick laugh cross his lips. "Anytime." He frowned.

"Don't complain to me. Next time put shoes on before dashing into the fray."

Idiot. Who did he think he was; some comic book hero?

Casey smiled and coated the bottom of his foot with antiseptic cream then folded gauze into small pads for the more damaged bits. A couple of quick turns of the gauze roll secured everything and she clipped the bandage from the role. She wadded an extra thick pad for his heel and secured it with tape. Not pretty, but it would do.

"What made you think I needed rescuing anyway?"

"I saw—" He shrugged. "I thought you were in trouble."

He'd been looking through the window.

"Why Mr. Hennessy. Perhaps we should change your name to Tom."

Casey had never seen a man blush before.

"I...just...glanced over." His eyes narrowed and sparkled. "I seem to recall a recent training accident—"

Casey coughed loudly.

The gentle pull of his hand under her chin drew her up on her knees between his legs. Heat sizzled through his eyes to hers and the warmth spread throughout her body. Her mind flashed back to the street, to the kitchen.

Why start something neither of them could finish?

In a split second that seemed to last an eternity, he closed the distance between them and his mouth claimed hers. The carnal battle of tongues sent shock waves rippling up from her depths. Her hands splayed on his chest for support and heat flamed through her.

That was why.

Shivers pulsated in time with

the rapid pounding of her heart and his hand followed the line of her arm, over her shoulder and down her back to the bare skin where her shirt had pulled up. A groan.

Was that him—or her?

He pulled his head back toward the wall, his hands gently restraining her. A fire of a new sort rushed her senses. Was this some sort of game? Was he intentionally playing with her? She started to push away. He grabbed her wrist.

"Look Mr. Hennessy." She found it difficult to breathe. How could he suck her in so easily? "I don't have time—"

His features contorted and he used her biceps to shift her to the left slightly then let out an audible sigh. Oh, God. His feet. How could she have forgotten?

"Are you okay?" She drew a breath through her teeth. "I'm sorry about your foot."

"What foot?"

He wrapped his arms around her and pulled her tight against him. She drew a sharp breath at the urgency of the contact, tensed. He wanted her, but what waited around the curve? She'd travelled this road before, driven happily off the cliff into an abyss of heartache. Was the ride worth the risk?

His mouth claimed hers again and any idea of pulling away vanished. His taut, warm flesh flamed against her, igniting her passions like dry grass in a field. With a practiced shift, he hooked his fingers around the hem of her camisole and tugged it up over her head, breaking contact with her lips for barely a second before shirking her of the garment. He ran a hand down her bare back, pulling her tight to him, breasts pressed against his abdomen. He cupped his hands around her buttocks and pulled her upward, nudging her legs open with his and settling her across his hips.

Kieran groaned when she settled against him and he deftly opened the front of his jeans to release his tension before finding the nook between her legs. His green eyes smoldered as he cupped her breasts in his hands. She inhaled deeply as he took each nipple into his mouth.

She should ask him to st—

All coherent thought left her when he reached down the back of her loose cotton sleeping pants, slid around her hips to the nub that ached for him and gently massaged it with his thumb. She dug her fingers into his shoulders and lifted her face upward as a wave of pleasure washed over her. He moved round her hips and pulled hers tight to his. He leaned forward and she wrapped her arms and legs around him and lowered her to the floor.

Heated travertine was smooth against her back and buttocks as he pulled her bottoms off and settled her on the floor. Her stomach twittered as he shed his jeans and boxers, readying himself to slide up between her legs. Her hand ran down through his hair along his shoulder and back. He used a knee to part her legs then settled his erection against her.

She drew a sharp breath, might have whispered something—or not.

Kieran smiled and covered her mouth with his. He thrust his tongue into her mouth sweeping, curling, exploring. He withdrew and thrust again. She shifted her hips and opened her legs wider as desire demanded satiation, but he simply meandered up her garden path, inch by inch.

He ran a palm roughly over her nipple then cupped her breast in his hand and she drew in another deep breath, pressed forward into him. His eyes widened and he breached her borders with one hard push. Her breath caught as he withdrew and plunged again. His eyes sparkled like gemstones and his mouth slanted over hers, drinking quickly and running kisses over her chin, neck, shoulders and breasts.

Her fingers tangled in his hair as she pressed his face into her and she lifted her hips to meet his. He seemed to hesitate, but she wrapped her legs around him and pulled him deeper, again and again until he arched upward, finding release and pulsing in time with her.

"Oh my God," was all she could manage.

Kieran rolled sideways off her and pulled her up tightly against him in one fluid motion. God, but she was amazing. Soft and silky, yet hard and strong. How could both things fit so wonderfully in one package? A trick of nature.

And what a trick she was.

A smile played on the lips he brushed over the top of her head. When had things changed between them? They'd started out on opposite sides of the fence, but somehow the fence had gotten shorter, easier to hop over. He twisted his mouth.

Was he doing the hopping or was she?

Did it matter?

Casey shivered and he drew her closer into him. She snuggled further down into his shoulder, tangling one leg with his. He grabbed a throw from the back of an overstuffed chair nearby and settled it over her. She fisted the material and sighed.

He ducked his head down, caught a glance at her expression. A relaxed smile played on her lips.

Would she be as content in the morning?

Would he?

He should have planned this better.

Scratch that. He should have planned period.

If he had, they'd be on a bed not a tile floor and he'd have taken his time with her, played, teased, enjoyed. Next time, he'd make it up to her.

Next time.

When had he started thinking about next times?

He'd made an art out of finding women who, like him, simply enjoyed the moment and moved on. Casey had blind-sided him. Somehow he'd found this woman whose emotions stretched beyond the now and her immediate needs. If things didn't work out for them where would she be? Where would he be?

He shook the thought away. None of that mattered now.

Casey snuggled closer at his movement and her warmth radiated through his body. He ran his hand over her hair and along her back to her bottom. Round and soft, he loved its shape. He brought his hand to her face, hooked a few blond strands behind her ear and caressed the soft skin in front it. She lifted her nose into his neck, mumbling something in her sleep.

Kieran closed his eyes and rested his chin against the top of Casey's head. He'd never been one for futures and yet, something told him his was about to change.

Casey drew in a deep breath and exhaled slowly. Kieran's scent brought a smile with it and she shifted closer. His warmth spread across her thicker than the blanket he'd pulled down over them and amplified the heat radiating from the floor. She smiled. Not exactly what she'd had in mind when she ordered the radiant heating.

Her fingers trailed his midline to his nipple, rounded it and moved across his chest. He brushed his hand upward, grasped hers and flattened it against his body. He grumbled something low in his throat, shifted slightly and drifted back down into sleep. His chest moved up and down in a relaxed rhythm and she rested her cheek against it.

How exactly had it happened? One minute she'd been tending wounds and the next—

She sighed. She wasn't going to think about the how or even the what. She was just going to go with the feeling. And what a feeling it was.

She smiled into his chest. It

had been a long time since she'd woken up beside a man and even longer since she'd woken up so relaxed. She shifted and propped her chin on her hand. Stubble covered his chin and she ran a finger along it. The rough fibers rasped with her touch and Kieran's shoulders moved in a wave. Relaxation made his features boy-like, but below them he was all man.

Casey tingled down low and shifted against him. Would he wake if she—

A sound outside pricked her ear and she froze. Her eyes narrowed as she strained to hear anything unusual, but heard nothing. As she started to relax back into Kieran's warm chest, she heard it again.

What was it?

She sat up, tugged her camisole over her head, slipped into her sleeping pants and moved toward the window. She flattened herself against the pane, but could see nothing below. Cool air bit at her bare legs when she tugged the sash up and she shivered instinctively. A bang of something being blown in the wind pulled her attention downward as she popped her head and shoulders out the window.

The plywood covering her entrance swung open and clattered against something unseen on the ground. Something moved toward the building, the makeshift door swinging with it.

"Hey!" she yelled into the darkness.

The figure took a step back, looked upward and turned away. She caught a quick glimpse when the streetlight illuminated the figure, but a hoodie and ball cap effectively obscured the facial features. He fled across the train tracks toward the river and the dilapidated warehouses.

Casey sighed and cast a glance back at Kieran. His chest moved up and down rhythmically and she longed to climb back under the thin blanket beside him but that would mean leaving his place and hers vulnerable. She finished dressing, grabbed her cell phone and flashlight. She hefted the small tool kit that had become a permanent fixture in her back foyer and stepped into the elevator.

Whatever happened to sleeping the night through?

Chapter thirteen

The bell chimed into the darkened space as the elevator opened on the ground floor. Casey flicked on the flashlight and scanned the area before taking the first tentative steps out into what remained of her basement.

Empty.

She let out a breath she hadn't realized she'd held and walked across to the doorway. It sat half-open, a sliver of light from the streetlamp slicing the darkness. She exited quickly, set her tool box down and assessed the damage. Splinters jutted from a broken corner and she flashed the light around the opening looking for a solid piece through which to sink yet another screw. If the new security door didn't arrive tomorrow she'd have to go after another piece of plywood.

The screwdriver twirled the wrong direction and she flicked the switch before picking up the screw that fell to the floor and bounced under the plank. She growled. By now she should be a pro at this. How many times was it she'd had to repair it now?

She pulled the plywood sheet back open and bent for the screw. Casey fixed the screw to the end of the power screwdriver and glanced across the darkened space to Kieran's building. Was the door open? She shifted sideways to double check.

Damned idiot. He must have left it open in his haste to get to her. She set her tool aside, grabbed the flashlight and crossed the short distance to the open doorway. A light glowed from inside and she pushed slightly against the door. An enticing aroma emerged from within and suddenly famished, she contemplated a trip up the stairs to the kitchen.

Kieran and his staff had been working madly practicing dishes for the restaurant. Maybe he'd even prepared another one of those fabulous—what had he called it—tortes. She smiled and headed up the stairs picturing his face when she woke him up to share some 'cookies' with her. Maybe she'd even let him eat them in bed.

Her giggle echoed up the stairwell as she detoured into the kitchen. She crossed quickly to a large stainless steel door, yanked the handle. Goosebumps sprouted instantly at the icy air kissing her bare arms and she stepped inside. She stole what looked like a creampuff off a wheeled dessert rack and popped it into her mouth.

A grumble of appreciation rolled down her throat with the second treat she stole. She resisted the third treat that called to her wondering suddenly if she were stealing something more than test-runs and found the elusive torte halfway down a second cart. She tested it with a swipe of her finger and hummed in appreciation. A quick tug pulled it and the waxed doily under it onto her left palm.

Now if she could just find a—

She caught a quick movement from the corner of her eye, grabbed her flashlight and rotated. Shining orbs glowed at her from the shelf in front of her and an angry growl turned quickly to a near hiss. She struggled to keep her chocolate, caramel, pecan booty from tumbling to its demise while backing away from the angry raccoon on the counter.

"Shoo."

The animal appeared possessed with the glowing eyes and Casey shifted the flashlight.

"Go on, get."

Or was that *git*?

It didn't really matter either way. The animal simply stared at her.

Now what? She scanned the room for signs of a mop, broom or any other means of encouragement, but found nothing. She glanced down at the torte and contemplated a moment before reaching for the handle to the walk-in. She, tucked her flashlight under her arm, grabbed a bowl of sliced fruit from the shelf and inched toward the stairwell.

"Come on. Hmmmm. Smells good." She set the bowl down on the landing.

After what seemed like forever, the raccoon inched toward the bowl. Casey's grip on the doorknob tightened. If she could startle it downward, it would have nowhere to go but out. As she straightened in preparation, something soft began circling her ankles and froze as the raccoon started toward the bowl.

A cat. What was this place, a zoo?

The cat's back arched. Pffffft. The raccoon growled. And the two animals hightailed it up the stairs. Casey whirled back out of the way and the torte headed for the floor.

"Stop," she yelled more at the torte than the animals, but neither listened.

Damned animals. She should let them kill each other, but she took off up the stairs after them. She paused at the top of the first flight, listened, heard something topple on the next floor up. She scrabbled upward and into the main hallway of the third floor.

Period ceiling paneling had been split symmetrically by new walls that cordoned off future lofts from the central corridor. The original hardwood of the hallway floors carried on through the doors that led off to the left and right. She nodded in appreciation. The place had good bones and Kieran was taking advantage.

Renewed conflict drew her further down the hall and she turned into a room off to the left. The cat chased through her legs and the raccoon scampered past right on its heels. Who knew such a fat creature could move so quickly. She chased down the hall after them, caught a toe on a mismatched board and skidded along the floor.

She winced and grabbed her knee. Damned cat. If the stupid thing had just stayed away for another five minutes she'd be up in her condo sharing cookies with Kieran, but no. Something clattered overhead and renewed thuds echoed across the floor above.

Casey shook her head and started to stand. A faint rhythmic sound came from her left and she turned her head toward it. She stepped into the room.

Tick. Tick. Tick...

A clock? She took another step closer, ducked her head around a pile of wood and the ticking got louder. Her heart thudded harder, nearly drowning the sound in the room. She took a steadying breath and shone her flashlight farther along the pile until she saw the kitchen timer and the plastic jug.

"Charlie!" Casey jumped at him as he pulled up against the curb moments after her call. "There's at least one device on the third floor the last room on the left."

"What did it look like?"

Casey did her best to describe what she'd seen as he rummaged through his trunk for some equipment.

"Wait here for the others and tell them I'm inside."

Charlie rushed in before she could stop him and he was already through the door by the time she thought to tell him about the stack of lumber. She bit at her thumb a moment before following him in.

She took the stairs at full speed and burst into the hallway behind Charlie. He spun round toward her.

"I told you to wait outside."

"I forgot..." she struggled to catch her breath, "to tell...you about the lumber."

"Of all the stupid bloody things to do." His voice shook with fury as he pointed her back to the stairs. "Get outta here."

She moved out onto the landing, caught sight of the cat a few stairs up. She inched toward it, but it retreated drawing her up onto the next flight. She grabbed the feline at the top of the flight and hesitated at the familiar ticking she heard from deeper in.

A few steps into the hallway pinpointed the source to the first room on the right and she retreated quickly into the stairwell.

"We got another one Charlie," she yelled when she stepped into the third floor hallway.

He popped his head back out into the hallway. "I thought I told you—where?"

"Fourth floor, first room to the right. Let me—"

"Out! Now!"

She turned to follow his orders as the distinctive sound of a flare igniting invaded the stairwell and milliseconds later, the smell of melting plastic and raw fuel assailed her nostrils. She leapt down the stairwell as flames whooshed behind her. She cast a glance back over her shoulder. Only the amber glow of reflected flame greeted her.

Where the hell was Charlie?

Sirens stirred Kieran out of sleep. He wrapped his arm around air and sat up.

"Casey?"

No answer. She'd probably gotten sensible and moved down the hall into her bedroom—without him. He ran a hand over his face to rub the sleep away as another siren whirred to a stop right outside the window. Red light swirled around the ceiling and he jerked up.

He tugged on his pants, hobbled over to the window despite the drying wounds tugging at the bottoms of his feet. He blew a heavy breath at a particularly painful step, but continued unabated until he perched on the windowsill.

"What the—"

A hose truck blocked the street below and a crew of firefighters dragged a long hose in through the back of his building. Smoke curled out a few of the upper floor windows and flames shot out some of the lower ones. He limped down the hall into the training room, shoved the heavy bag roughly aside and tugged at the window sash.

He fumbled with the latch and cursed.

Damned windows.

By the time Kieran freed the sash and popped his head out, two lower floors of his building seemed fully involved in the fire. He tried to push himself back from the window, to cover his eyes, to imagine that it wasn't happening, but he couldn't. His dream was literally going up in smoke before his eyes.

He set his jaw and shook his head. Why here? Why *now*? If he'd been an early target, it could have saved him all the time and energy he'd spent getting the place ready. They'd begun dry runs. Tomorrow night would have been their first test service. Kieran closed his eyes on the carnage and shook his head again.

He'd known something was up earlier. If he hadn't come screaming after Casey, he would have finished his search, found the devices. Instead of saving her, he should have been saving his building. She didn't need his help, hadn't wanted it. She'd made that clear every time he'd gotten involved.

What the hell was the matter with him?

Love 'em and leave 'em had been his mantra since he was old enough to know what a mantra was.

And he'd lived by it—until now.

Casey. This was her fault. She and that silly-ass husband of hers couldn't manage their divorce like normal people; like his parents. Leave and be done with it. Cut all contact. That's the way people did it when they were finished with someone. Just walk away and forget about them. He'd done it a million times. It wasn't so hard.

So why hadn't he walked away from Casey?

He instinctively glanced toward her bedroom window and was surprised to find the window tightly shut. His stomach jerked in response. He dodged the heads popping out of windows to get a better view of the action to search the ground, but he found no sign of her.

She couldn't possibly have slept through the commotion, could she?

Ignoring the bite in his feet he hurried down the hall and pushed open her bedroom door. Empty. He carried on down the hallway, searching every inch of the place.

He stuck his head back out the window. "Casey?" he yelled. Heads turned, but none of them hers. At ground level, he spied what looked like the plywood that had covered her entrance angled away from the building. Had she gone down to fix it?

"Casey?" he called again, trying to keep the panic from his voice. He crossed the living room and called again, "Casey?"

Nothing.

He pushed the button for the back elevator, but gave up when no motor rumbled in response. Had she locked it off meaning to come straight back up? He spun quickly round. Smoke billowed out the windows of his top floor and the amber glow was visible even from this angle.

She wouldn't have—couldn't have...

He let the thought trail unable to allow its completion.

Glass shattered into the space between the buildings and Casey's fire alarm sounded as he stepped into the hallway. He cupped a hand over his ear and pounded the elevator button before realizing that they'd already been locked off.

Damn. He was going to have to hoof it.

His barely crusted wounds cracked in protest as he started down the stairwell. He growled as he landed at the bottom of the first flight and he grabbed the railings with both hands opting to swing down the whole flight. It couldn't be worse than—

But it was and he clamped his jaw against the hot pain. Still he swung again and again until a mother carrying one child and towing two others blocked the way. Panic sent the children's eyes darting despite the mother's encouragement and Kieran scooped the older two into his arms, speeding their decent to street level.

He set the children down beside their mother and limped along the sidewalk toward the crowd being held back by police. A quick search revealed nothing and he turned his eyes to the flames licking the fourth floor of his building. His heart jack hammered against his ribs.

Where the hell was she?

Casey spun frantically on the sidewalk. Had the firefighter heard her when she'd said that Charlie Griffin was in the building? She hurried up the hill toward Columbia and the other fire crews. Maybe one of them would listen.

"Charlie Griffin is in there," she called as she rounded the corner.

"We're taking care of it."

What did that mean? Did they know where he was? Had they gotten him out? What?

The firefighter's sooty expression offered no answers. "You need to speak to the chief, the guy in the white helmet over there."

She nodded and started to thank him, but the firefighter was already engrossed in his job. Broken glass showered the sidewalk behind her as the firefighter broke the etched doors to Tethys. Her heart sunk, but she continued along the sidewalk and waited for the firefighter in the white hat to look her way.

"Have you found Charlie?" Casey preempted his question with her own.

"What were you doing in the building?"

Casey flushed. "My friend Kieran Hennessy owns it." She couldn't bring herself to tell him the whole truth. "What about Charlie?"

"And do you know where Mr. Hennessy is now."

"Upstairs in my condo. Charlie?"

"And you live?"

If he didn't answer her question about Charlie soon, she was going to explode. "Next door. Now what about Charlie?"

"I can't release any information at this time."

"But I was just in there—"

He held up a finger to stop her, listened to something that resembled static to her untrained ear and spoke quietly into the microphone. "Now. Explain to me exactly what happened."

Casey launched into a play by play that started with her entering the building, left out the part about the stolen desserts and wound up at being chased down the stairs by flames.

"And Griffin was right behind you."

Casey shrugged. "One minute he was and the next, he wasn't."

"Thanks." He started to walk away then turned back. "Wait over there and I'll let you know the minute we have news."

A hand on her shoulder startled her and she was ushered under the tape away from the building. A tall man in a dark blue suit stepped up beside her.

"Detective Orin Mitchell."

She inspected the badge he extended. "Casey Michaelson."

"I need some details from you."

Casey gave him her personal information and recapped the story she'd told the firefighter.

The detective nodded. "And why had you gone down there at this time of night?"

"Well, I heard a noise—" The image of the man in the hoodie flashed through her brain. Had she seen the arsonist?

"Yes?" he prodded at her change

in expression.

"I think I saw him."

Mitchell's eyebrows shot up.

"I was in my place when I saw him, he was wearing a hoodie and ball cap, but—" She spoke so quickly her words were tumbling over one another.

"Hold on, hold on. Slow down. Tell me from the beginning."

"Okay." A breath. "I heard a noise and popped my head out the window. I yelled at him to get him away from my entrance."

"And where was this?"

"My condo's on the top floor of that building."

"Okay, but where'd you see the guy?"

"Oh, round the back. At the freight entrance."

"Do you think the guy was trying to break in?"

"That's what I thought originally. When I yelled, he ran off."

"And where was Mr. Hennessy during this?"

Her cheeks warmed slightly. "Sleeping at my place."

"And where is he now?"

Good question. Probably worried sick about her. She looked over her shoulder toward the crowd. "I'm not sure."

"But he was in your apartment the whole evening?"

"From about midnight."

"And why didn't he come down with you?"

"He was sleeping and he hurt his feet earlier when he came rushing up to my place."

"He came...*rushing*?"

"I had a problem with my ex earlier and Kieran, Mr. Hennessy came to help me sort it out."

"And how exactly did he do that?"

"Well, he didn't really." This was sounding more ridiculous by the minute. "Security was already there."

"Could it have been your ex you saw?"

"I don't think so." Could it have been?

"What's his name?"

"Jim Taylor. He's a contractor here in town."

"And do you have his address?"

She opened her mouth then closed it. Where was Jim staying

these days? She shook her head.

"Any reason why he might wish to do you or Mr. Hennessy harm?"

Casey shrugged. "You'd have to ask him."

The detective made notes on his pad. She glanced up at the burning building. Jim. Would he do something like this? Oh he'd break into her place all right, had proven that again tonight, but torch Kieran's?

She shook the thought away. He was sleeping it off in the cop shop at the moment. Security had taken him down to hand him over. Or had they?

"Anything else you want to add?"

Casey started to shake her head, but stopped. "Any chance you could find out if my friend Charlie's safe?"

"I'll see what I can do." He ducked under the tape.

Glass rained down on the detective and he hooked an arm over his head, but continued on. Smoke billowed from a third story window. Flames shot from the building.

Oh, God. Where was Charlie.

Chapter fourteen

God she was an idiot.

Casey covered her face with her hands. No respirator. No protective gear. If something happened to Charlie...

Grime and sweat obscured the features of the young firefighter who slipped off his protective jacket and sat on a polished metal edge of a fire truck. He grabbed a bottle of water from inside, drank half and poured some over his head. Casey wove her way through the crowd of onlookers until she stood across from him.

"Is Charlie Griffin okay? Did he get out?"

"Can't say."

What the heck did that mean? He wasn't allowed or he didn't know? Frustration pushed at her temples.

"Who *can* say?"

He ran a hand through his blond hair and motioned toward the chief. She'd already been down that route.

"Any news, Chief?" She moved back through the crowd again. "Any news on Charlie?"

He held up a finger for her to wait a moment and listened to some chatter over his radio. He turned away and spoke into his mike then looked back at her. "Sorry?"

"Charlie Griffin!"

"Yes," the firefighter started, then glanced around. "He singed a few hairs, but he's fine. He was here a minute ago."

Relief swept through her veins. Even if she couldn't find him, he'd survived. She was going to kill him for not showing himself to her, but he was okay.

Casey glanced up toward her windows. Now for Kieran. He wasn't going to be a happy man, but there was no sense making him unhappier, adding her to his worries about building and business. She fought her way back through onlookers. Where had all these people come from? It was the middle of the night for crumb's sake.

"Casey! Over here!"

Kieran sat on the edge of a cement planter near the sidewalk edge. His wave drew her attention through the sea of bodies and he dove in to meet her in the middle. He pulled her to him and wrapped his arms around her. Heat from his embrace contrasted the chill in the air and she shivered. He stepped back, looked into her eyes and pulled her close again.

"I guess we won't be opening next week." He laughed, but his body tensed.

Flickers of light reflected in his eyes as his attention flitted between her and the burning structure. She turned in his arms and leaned into his chest.

"I'm sorry, I tried to stop it."

He spun her back to him. "What do you mean, you tried to stop it?"

"I went down to fix the plank over the entrance and..." she dropped her gaze to her toes. "Well, your door was open." She wrapped her bottom lip under her teeth.

"So you went in?" Kieran's eyes clouded and his expression hardened.

"I shouldn't have, but...Anyway, this raccoon—"

"Raccoon?"

"Yes. And then I couldn't very well let it get the cat."

"Cat?"

"Yes, a cat." Why was he having so much trouble following this? "But when I went after them, I found this bomb thingy."

His eyebrows shot up. God, she was making a mess of the

explanation. "You found a bomb?"

"Okay, well, not really a bomb, but it looked like one, sort of." She waited for more questions, but when confusion contorted his face again, she sped on. "Anyway, Charlie got there right away and he told me to get out, but I had to grab the cat, don't you see."

He shook his head. He clearly didn't see.

"But then I found the second device and then it exploded, but Charlie wasn't behind me."

"You were in the building with Charlie?"

"Yes, that's what I've been telling you."

"And there was an explosion?"

"Well, explosion might be a little exaggerated, but the device caught fire."

His scowl deepened. "What were you doing in the building in the first place? Why didn't you just shut the door?"

Heat rushed her face.

"I was looking for cookies."

"Cookies?" he growled. "I don't make cookies."

Casey set the coffee on the table in front of Kieran. He

attempted to stifle a yawn, but didn't succeed.

"Don't do that," she said, yawning herself. "It's contagious."

"Sorry." He laughed. "It's been a while since I stayed up all night with a woman."

"I seem to remember a snore or two," she quipped then seemed to regret it.

"You wore me out."

She smiled and her blue eyes sparkled with mischief. "It wasn't my idea to...uh, sleep on the floor."

"Was that what we were doing?" He grinned and took a gulp of coffee. The hot liquid burned his tongue and he drew in an open-mouthed breath to relieve the pain.

"Hot?" She smirked. "You should be more careful."

He raised his eyebrows her way and she giggled.

Sunrise lightened the sky and Kieran leaned back as Casey sat in the chair alongside his. He sighed. It was hard to believe the beauty of the morning given the disaster of the night before. A good portion of his second, third and fourth floors no longer existed. The etched glass doors were spread in pieces across the dining room floor—if there was a dining room floor. He took another sip of coffee.

An orange hue colored the sky over the hills across the river and the darkness provided an interesting, albeit momentary, contrast as it retreated against the rising sun. Streaks of light shot from behind the hills and blue replaced the gray haze of the early morning sky.

Casey's eyes reflected the colors as she gazed out the window. Fatigue kissed her face and her blinks stretched into longer moments of closed lids. He smiled and touched her cheek. She turned to him, lips parted, full and inviting. He leaned over and covered her mouth with his in a quick, intense kiss then pulled away.

"I should go," he said and shifted back toward the river that now danced in the sunlight. "You need some sleep."

"Yeah, right. Where?" she asked.

She grabbed his collar and pulled him into another kiss. She was brazen, probing, becoming more familiar with every thrust of her tongue. He groaned and shifted in his seat at the underlying promise. When she pulled away a mix of disappointment and hunger rushed through his veins.

"You want another coffee?" she asked.

How could she sound so calm? Didn't she know what she did to him?

She threw a glance over her shoulder and started toward the kitchen. The glint in her eyes answered his question; she knew exactly what she did.

"Hell no." He grabbed her arm and pulled her back to him.

"Something else, then?"

He covered the innocent smile on her lips with his and did his best to show her exactly what he wanted.

The phone rang and she pulled away after the third ring. "I better get that, it could be important."

"Not as important as this."

"Get over yourself." She laughed and tugged free.

He watched her scurry across the room before he glanced back out the window. The sun was full up in the sky. A tug motored down the river. Rush hour had just begun on the Patullo Bridge. Nothing had changed from the night before, but the dawn of a new day gave him hope.

Things were looking up.

The door rattled under a heavy fist. The pounding echoed through the condo as less than a minute passed before the noise repeated. Casey stirred in Kieran's arms. She pushed up off his chest, moved her head from side to side in rapid motion, eyes wild, searching. Kieran's muscles screamed when he moved. This wasn't exactly how he'd envisioned waking up with Casey.

"Casey!" A male voice yelled between thumps. "Open the door!"

Jim.

Kieran shook his head. When would the man get the idea she'd moved on? Casey buried her head in his chest, the tension in her body revealed the emotion that coursed through her. He ran his hand over the back of her head and down her hair. He massaged her neck. She deserved better than this.

"I can't believe it," she mumbled then rested her chin on Kieran's chest.

"I thought he was in jail."

Her eyes narrowed. "Me too."

Jim hammered on the door again.

"I better go shut him up before he wakes the whole building." She sighed heavily as she pushed herself off the couch and him.

His rapid upright movement left him dizzy. He steadied himself a moment before he attempted to stand. His feet protested, but seemed to ease some with the movement. If Casey needed him, he'd be close by.

"What's he doing here?" Jim moved past her toward Kieran.

Kieran braced for the contact, but the man stopped a short distance away.

"This is my house Jim, I'll have whoever I want over."

Casey stood with her hand on the doorknob, the door open to elevator lobby. Anger drew her eyebrows together and her eyes shot daggers at Jim.

"Get out. Or I'll call the police." She gnawed at her bottom lip, as if she bit off the desire to say more and she lifted the phone she held in her free hand.

Fury in his eyes, Jim wheeled around to her, his hands drawn into fists and his body rigid. Kieran took a step closer, ready to pounce if need arose.

"You'd like that, wouldn't you? Have me carted away for nothing."

"For nothing?" She fought to keep her voice even. "You broke into my home last night and you're back again this morning."

"I had a key. I didn't break into anything."

"A key you had made without my permission."

"I'm your husband."

"*Ex*-husband."

Kieran stepped a little closer. Adrenaline pumped his heart with alarming speed and the discomfort in his feet faded to nothing. If Jim made any threatening movements, he'd have to go through Kieran to get to Casey.

"I mean it, Jim. Get out." She opened the door wider.

"Why? So you can play house with your neighbor?" He sneered. "The man without a house."

Anger surged from the depths of Kieran's body. He balled his hands into fists and tightened his jaw. He was being baited, knew it, but didn't care.

"I think you should leave now," Kieran said through clenched teeth. "Or-"

"Or what?" Jim sneered. "You'll beat me with your wooden spoon?"

Kieran lurched forward.

"Knock it off." Casey's daggers shot Kieran's direction now too. "Get out, Jim. You are not welcome here." She placed the hand with the phone on her hip. "Can I make it any clearer for you? We're not married. There is no chance we will get back together. Leave or I'll have you arrested."

Jim's mouth opened and closed as he seemed to struggle to find an appropriate comeback. "I made the biggest mistake of my life the day I married you, why would I want you back?"

"Well, then. I guess you won't need to show up here again, will you?" Her expression matched her words. Both were hard, biting. "Now, get out."

Jim looked from Casey to the door to Kieran as though the words he heard surprised him. His eyes narrowed, he set his jaw and took a step back. He turned and pulled the heavy metal and wood weapons from their place on the wall in Casey's foyer and crashed them into the glass shelf beneath, shattering it. The whole lot clattered onto the marble foyer floor. He grunted and headed toward the door.

Kieran shot forward, but Casey's raised hand stopped him in his tracks.

"Don't."

Jim turned and asked, "Does he fetch too?"

Casey slammed the door in her ex-husband's face. She made her way across the entrance, knelt and started picking at the broken bits on the floor. Her breathing sounded artificially rhythmic as she struggled to maintain control. Kieran went in search of a container for the shattered glass and porcelain to give her time to regain her composure.

He leaned on the counter in the kitchen. Why had he let Jim get under his skin? Just what Casey needed—another hothead to worry about. She'd made it clear enough she could handle Jim without his help. But then, how many women thought the same thing about their ex-husbands and ended up dead? He shuddered at the thought.

His tangled hair pulled as he ran his fingers through it. He should have hung back, just out of sight where he could step in if necessary, but wouldn't become extra fodder for Jim's verbal attack. He'd hoped to calm the situation, but in the end, he'd only intensified it.

Disappointment coursed through him. He'd just demonstrated his lack of self-control to a woman whose ex-husband was the king of bad behavior. He'd be lucky if she didn't kick him out on his ass.

"Bright, buddy," he said aloud. "Really, brilliant."

Chapter fifteen

Tears fell onto the debris covered foyer floor despite Casey's best efforts. She reached up and massaged her brow before she wiped the moisture from her cheeks.

What was going on?

Her stomach swirled into a knotted mass and she thought she might vomit. Her ex had turned into a raving lunatic and she'd become—

What? A one night stand?

She hadn't expected things to get so...intense, hadn't been prepared.

Her memory carried her back under the awning where her heart had beaten in time with the rain drumming the canvas. And the cooking lesson. They'd been cooking more than vegetables. She'd felt the shift, noticed the change and let things happen. She'd encouraged it.

Why had she done that?

Glass tinkled into the container she dragged over and she

turned to retrieve more. She stacked some broken porcelain inside a large piece of urn, caught a sharp edge and slammed her finger into her mouth. She dragged her other hand across her damp cheeks and tried to dam brimming tears with the palm of her hand.

Stupid. Stupid. Stupid.

She should have kept her distance, sorted things out with Jim and the committee before letting anything happen with Kieran. She sniffed and rubbed her nose with the back of her hand, drew in a ragged breath. This morning, he'd simply been trying to protect her. Who could blame him? He thought her weak. Impulsive.

What the hell did he know?

She tossed more pieces into the canister. She could take care of herself, had been taking care of herself for ages before he came along. He turned her into someone different, someone she wasn't, someone who needed—him.

"Here," Kieran knelt across from her and held out a white trash bag. "It's all I could find."

Casey snatched the bag, dumped the shattered pieces from the canister into it and set the bag inside. She slipped in the bigger pieces and narrowed her eyes his direction. He picked tentatively at some of the larger bits scattered further across the floor, reached across her to drop them in the can.

She backed up to avoid his stretching arm, gathered a few more pieces and ducked out of the way of his next pass. She clamped her jaw and slid the canister toward him. Her collected fragments slammed against the others and she hesitated.

Kieran's eyes widened and cocked his head.

Why was she so angry?

He shifted onto his feet and retreated back into her living space. She dug her fingers into her forehead, just above her left eye.

And who was she angry at?

Kieran reappeared with a broom and dragged it across the tile floor. His eyes spoke volumes when they locked with hers, it wasn't his fault that she wasn't sure what they said.

Why was it things went wrong every time he was around?

She grabbed the dustpan and readied it for loading. "Thanks," she managed.

He looked at the broom and let out a self-conscious laugh. "No problem."

"Not for that," she said. "I meant about Jim—" She hesitated.

An uneasy smile flitted across

his face. He took another turn with the broom. She tucked her head down over her task and gathered a few more big pieces and a few steadying breaths. Her cheeks blazed.

"I know you were just trying to protect me. But I—"

"—don't need my help." His words were rapid, defensive. He waved a dismissive hand. "I know. I know."

"What do you know?" Her knuckles whitened around the dustpan handle.

Did he know how embarrassing it was to have her ex-husband show up all the time and have people wonder how she could have been so stupid as to marry him in the first place? Or having someone feel the need to defend or rescue her all the time? She was a black belt. A sensei. If there was any defending to be done, she should be the one doing it.

She sighed and wrapped her fingers around the sheath of the ceremonial sword he'd retrieved from the pile and shifted nervously from hand to hand. She set it against the wall.

Did he know how grateful she was that _he_ had come to her rescue? Or how much she liked having him around?

How about how much that scared her?

He stared at her for a moment, blinked and looked away. "Time to go," he said.

He handed her the broom and walked away. She wanted to follow him; to put a hand on his arm, to apologize, but her feet remained rooted to the floor. She'd chased after Jim too many times during their marriage; apologized for things that were not her fault. She wouldn't start that with Kieran. She couldn't.

But was he asking her to?

She threw a glance over her shoulder in the direction of his building. It lay in ruins. His business, at least two floors and who knew what else damaged possibly beyond repair because he'd come to her rescue.

She tossed the broom aside and hurried toward the elevator.

"I was just trying to say thanks," she called at the closing doors.

Casey pressed the elevator button. If she'd been two seconds earlier, she'd have caught the doors before they closed, but it had been too late. The elevator descended without her. She turned toward the stairs, stopped. She'd have to find her keys to get through the locked lobby doors.

She pushed the button again, as if the action would hasten the elevator's return. She blew a breath out over her lips.

"Where is the stupid thing?" She pounded on the button then held it in. "Come on. Come on!"

Kieran would be long gone before she even got on the contraption. His damaged feet might buy her some time, but not much—adrenaline and emotion did funny things.

Inner doors to the elevator rattled as it stopped at her floor. She bit her lip and slapped the metal frame impatiently. As soon as room to slip between the doors developed she jumped into the lift—straight into waiting arms.

"We have to stop meeting this way."

The low voice. The familiar scent.

Kieran.

She steadied herself against him, shifted her head upward. Why—

"You're welcome." He pulled her even closer though she wasn't sure how.

"I'm sor—"

He put his finger to her lips to stop the words she spoke and shook his head.

"You have nothing to be sorry for."

He held her close while he ran a hand down the side of her face, hooked her hair behind her ear. His eyes sparkled and roved between her eyes and mouth until he brushed her lips with his. Their bodies swayed as the lift sprang into motion.

He raised his brows.

"We could push stop."

A floor indicator dinged and the doors opened. Casey spun around to put her back to Kieran. Kate West hesitated before she stepped in. She flashed a confused smirk and pushed the button for the lobby.

"Morning, Casey."

"Morning." She struggled to control the grin. "You know Kieran Hennessy?"

Kate nodded at him and gave a quick wave. When the doors opened she shifted her purse under her arm.

"Sorry about your restaurant, Mr. Hennessy." Kate walked out the front door without another glance back.

Casey depressed the sixth floor button. "Think she was uncomfortable?"

"Nah." Kieran pulled her to him and stared down into her eyes. "Let's see if we can make your other neighbors think about taking the stairs."

The warmth of Casey's body against his drove Kieran mad on the ascent to the sixth floor. She giggled at his proposal, but maintained her position. She fit nicely into the space under his chin—as if she were made for it. He draped his arms over her shoulders, interlacing his fingers with hers and brought their hands to meet in front of her.

As the doors opened on her floor, he let go with one hand and used her forward momentum to spin her round to face him. He closed the gap between them; her fiery body fueling his flame as he pressed her up against the door jamb and took possession of her mouth.

She gave over to the contact, parting her lips and allowing his tongue to sample her sweetness. Her hand burned a trail across Kieran's chest and down his ribs to his waistband and his heart pounded. A low growl rolled in his throat and he pushed harder against her.

Casey pulled away at the loud buzz that emanated from the elevator control panel and glanced inside. Kieran put his arm around her waist, pulled her tight against him and shifted into the lobby away from the door.

"Saved by the bell."

"Saved is it?" That would be a matter of opinion.

He started toward her, but she

ducked away and into her condo, retreating down the hall toward her bedroom.

He twisted his mouth.

Damn. Apparently it was hers.

Why had she run away?

The man was going to think her a lunatic and she completely understood. Only an insane woman could walk away from those brilliant eyes and talented lips.

When *had* she lost her mind?

Casey shook her head and filled the sink with cold water, but splashing her face did little to cool the heat still burning within her. She reached for the shower knobs. She needed the big guns.

A shudder rippled through her body as the cold water stung her skin. Her knees still wobbled as if they were jelly-filled and the tingling of his touch reverberated through her body. Heated with remembered kisses, she contemplated adding more cold, but twisted the hot instead to stop her teeth from chattering.

Her shivers abated and she crossed her arms over her chest trying to stop the stream of memories. Kieran's touch, so warm, so gentle, so comforting. The urgency in his movements. In hers. The need for more. She slowed the hot water a little more and shivered under another shock of cold.

She'd been right to walk away.

Definitely.

She closed her eyes and pushed her face up into the icy jets. She'd been out of her marriage more than two years. Certainly the time for rebounds was over. But she hadn't wanted to date, hadn't had a rebound. If she dated Kieran now, would he be her rebound?

She twisted her mouth. Did it matter?

Whatever he was, it couldn't be good. Arsonist's flames had pushed them together, but what would happen once outside fires were doused?

Sounds from the foyer caught her attention as she rubbed the chill from her body and wrapped herself up in her soft terry robe. She grabbed an extra T-shirt from her drawer and headed back toward the clatter.

"Feel better?" Kieran asked as he dumped the contents of a dustpan into the garbage.

"Um-hum." She leaned against the arched doorway. "You didn't have to do that, but thank you."

"You're welcome." He checked for bits of remaining debris before turning back to her.

"All right if I use your

phone?"

"Sure."

"I've gotta get a hold of the staff and let them know not to bother coming in." He cast a wistful glance at a window facing his building.

Tethys. "I'm sorry."

He shrugged.

"Maybe we should phone Charlie to see if they've got anything yet."

"It would be good if I could at least get in and get some stuff."

She picked up the phone and dialed as he tugged the shirt over his head. The shirt, large on her, covered his chest without disguising the definition of his muscles. She hung up when the machine clicked in. She pulled her hair into a ponytail and fastened it as she walked back into the main living area.

"No answer." She chewed on a thumbnail. "We'll try him again later."

Kieran slipped up onto a stool at the breakfast bar and glanced down at the shirt. "Your dojo?"

"Yes." Their eyes locked for a moment and electricity zinged through her bringing with it a kaleidoscope of remembered touches and images from the night before.

Stop. Focus. Think of

something—anything—else.

Breathe.

She turned to the coffee pot, filled the carafe with water.

"Better let me get that." His eyes sparkled as he flipped open the well of the coffee maker and relieved her of the carafe.

"Fine." Her voice was high and sharp. She extracted a couple of yogurt pots and some fruit from the fridge and slapped spoons beside them. "I have to get ready for class anyway."

He picked up the no fat yogurt and twisted it in his hands. "What's this?"

"Today's special. Bachelor breakfast."

He grumbled something that sounded like "not this bachelor" and she laughed. Had he already forgotten 'veggies a la Casey'?

Back in her bedroom, she shed her robe in favor of a tank top and slid her bright white gi pants up over her hips. She yarded on the heavy fabric drawstrings and tied a neat bow at the front. As she freed, dried and brushed her hair a wonderful smell invaded the still moist bathroom air. She stuck her head out the door and inhaled.

Was that aroma coming from her kitchen?

She grabbed her gi top off the back of the door and headed back down the hall. Where had he found the ingredients?

Two plates waited on the island across from the stool where Casey settled herself. Kieran turned, used the flipper to slice through what he'd concocted, slid half onto each plate and set the pan aside.

"Hope you don't mind."

"Mind?" She laughed. "You must be joking." She picked up her fork in anticipation as he slid the plate across to her. "I don't think my kitchen has ever smelled so wonderful."

Casey waited for him to sit beside her, but he simply picked up his fork, leaned a forearm on the counter and sliced a bit of omelet off. The shine of the moment dimmed a little, but returned with the first bite of omelet. It all but melted in her mouth and she groaned. He smiled, slipped a forkful into his own mouth and glanced up at the India ink drawings decorating the small patch of hallway wall that bordered the kitchen.

"Nice." Another smile. "You?"

She shook her head. "Grandmother."

Bittersweet sorrow rushed over her.

"Gorgeous." He slid down the

counter to get a closer look. "Does she still draw?" He touched the signature in the corner where her grandmother's artistic hand had drawn numbers in the curl beneath her name.

Month. Day. Year. Casey's birthday the year she and Jim had purchased this building.

"No. She passed away about six months after she drew that."

"I'm sorry." He paused.

She forced a smile. "Thank you."

Kieran inspected the drawing of her building closely, giving her a moment.

"What are these numbers above the door? Not your address."

Casey sighed. "My grandmother thought it would be nice to commemorate my marriage in some way so she added the date to the brickwork."

Kieran made a scraping motion. "What's this?"

Casey's eyes widened. She hopped off the stool and scooted over to him. She drew up close to the picture.

"Oh, just a bit of white out." He grinned.

"Funny." She shouldered him out of the way and headed back to the stool. She probably would have obliterated the evidence if it wouldn't have ruined the drawing.

"Mind if I hop in your shower before I head off?" he asked.

"Not at all." Her gaze dropped to her omelet. One quick flick into her lap and she could join him.

His eyes narrowed as if he could read her thoughts.

"Extra towels are in the cupboard," she added.

What a sight he'd make wrapped in one of her bath towels. She swallowed a bit of omelet to fight the thoughts, but the food just couldn't compete. Her gaze roved his torso, climbed the mountain of light stubble on his chin. He shifted again, enticing her probe downward. When he shifted a third time, her gaze shot back up to his face.

He smiled arrogantly back at her and she nearly choked on her egg.

"There are flip flops by the door." She managed finally and set her dishes in the sink. "Stay as long as you like, use the phone, watch TV." She pulled a set of keys out of a kitchen drawer and set them on the marble counter beside him. "Lock up before you go."

Her heart beat in time with the waggling eyebrow.

She slipped her bag over her

shoulder and started toward the rear elevator. "I'm having the place rekeyed today," she threw back at him.

His laugh followed her to the elevator and he joined it a second later. Gooseflesh radiated from the place where his hand snaked round and pulled her back to him.

"Go kick some butt."

He covered her mouth with his, pressing hard and opening again and again. His tongue swept over hers, exploring with carnal urgency. What resistance she'd mustered faltered and the sparks of her desire flamed. When he pulled back, she stared blankly up at him.

What was she supposed to be doing?

He pushed the button for the elevator and left her there waiting for it. Kicking butt would be difficult with knees that wobbled like gelatin.

Casey turned away, bit her lip and staggered into the elevator. She lifted her gaze, locked onto his sparkling gems and nearly hopped back out. She pressed the floor selector and waited for the door to close then ran her fingers over the place where Kieran's whiskers touched her cheek.

Would he be there when she finished class?

Did she want him to be?

She hooked a thumbnail on an eye tooth, glanced upward and smiled.

God help her, she did.

Chapter sixteen

It had to be a false alarm.

A fire bell competed with the shrill siren of a smoke detector and the offices of the local paper erupted into chaos around Kieran. Two fires in two days? It couldn't happen.

Could it?

Gerald Belkin, the squat reporter who'd been interviewing him, shot out of the windowless office with unexpected speed as the distinct aroma of burning plastic curled around Kieran's nose. He moved toward the door, collided with Belkin who headed into the room to grab a file folder and camera off his desk then push back by him.

Kieran hurried after the reporter through the maze of partitions that divided the paper's offices. He coughed against the thickening smoke, tugged his T-shirt up over his mouth. Shouldn't the smoke be getting thinner?

The air closed in around him.

Tight.

Smoky.

Hot.

A low rumble of hungry flame grew into a roar as smoke reached like tentacles past him. He wiped the perspiration off his brow and glanced back over his shoulder. They were headed the wrong—

The reporter stumbled forward, righted himself and lifted his camera. Kieran clamped his jaw.

Idiot.

He pulled at Belkin's shoulder. The man tugged free. Kieran grabbed a fist of material, whirled the man around and yanked the camera out of the man's hands. The file folder tucked up under the reporter's arm fell to the floor, photos and documents scattered in every direction. The man dropped to retrieve them

"We have to..." Kieran's raw throat and lungs protested, "...get out."

As Kieran tugged a sudden whoosh of flame pushed the reporter forward didn't wait for Belkin's agreement. He yanked the folder from the reporter's hands and locked onto his arm, pulling him back the way they'd come. Kieran's eyes stung with salty perspiration and smoke as he searched for the appropriate pathway. He resisted the urge to run and crouched a little lower.

Where the hell was the exit sign?

Hot smoke scorched his lungs and he covered his mouth and nostrils with his T-shirt and palm. He coughed, checked a door off to the left and continued down the hall. Weren't there supposed to be exit signs at the end of each corridor? Damned fire inspectors had been hell on him and yet, this maze of walls and blocked pathways passed inspection.

"How the hell do we get out of here?" The yell ripped his throat raw, but emerged a scratchy whisper.

The reporter merely waved him on.

Kieran turned right at a T intersection of corridor, travelled twenty feet and came to a dead end.

Now what?

He turned back to the reporter who shrugged and spun in panic.

Idiot. How the hell did a person work in a place and not know it—

Dizziness robbed him of the rest of the thought and Kieran pushed past in the other direction. Smoke poured into the corridor and followed the T outward.

Which way—

Now what—

He had to get—

He inhaled a lungful of the acrid air, sputtered and landed on all fours. A stronger wave of dizziness overtook him and wracking coughs shook his body. Belkin flopped onto the floor in front of him.

Heat wrapped Kieran like tangled blankets and the room began to narrow.

Damn.

He closed his eyes, tried to force his lungs to draw on the little oxygen left. The exit couldn't be far.

If he could only—

Young heads turned upward toward the lone balloon caught in the limbs of a nearby tree. The light breeze blew the white balloon to and fro a moment, before the thin ribbon slid through and the orb floated skyward after the rest.

Celebration of life. Casey smiled at the photograph of Al Weiss. It had definitely been that.

"Look," one mother said to her youngster. "Grandpa stayed to say goodbye."

The little girl squealed in delight and waved a hand at the

straggling balloon. "Bye Grandpa!"

Casey smiled and dabbed at the tears that brimmed the corners of her eyes. It had been a wonderful afternoon at the park, family, friends and fond memories. Al would have liked it—well everything except the fond memories. He'd never really been one to dwell in the past as far as Casey knew. He'd have waved off the praise and suggested another round of bocce.

A small white Cavalier pulled into a parking spot across from the picnic area and Tory waited behind the open driver's door as Casey said a few quick goodbyes.

"Nice service?"

Casey's glance instinctively sought the balloon in the tree only to find it had freed itself and now soared upward after the others. She tugged open the car door.

"Lovely."

"Sixty-three?" a disembodied voice spoke from the black box mounted on the Cavalier's console.

Tory held up a finger and keyed the mike. "Six-three."

Casey's gaze drifted back to the mingling crowd, a mix of friends and family. The little girl ran a few yards and jumped, eyes still following the last balloon.

"I have a couple of drops to make down at the Quay."

"Sure sounds good." They had an hour and a half to kill before their self-defence workshop at a local senior's center was due to start.

Tory wheeled through the park and out onto a street lined with some of the oldest houses in the city. Casey liked to imagine the city back in the days of horses and carts, milk delivery and—

"So...?"

Tory yanked her back to the present.

"So...what?"

"Where is he?"

"Who?"

"Your *butler*."

"My *what*?"

"Your houseboy, you know, the guy who answered your phone."

"Oh."

Kieran.

Why had he answered her phone?

"A guy answers your phone in the wee hours and all you can say is 'Oh'?"

She could add a few choice things right now.

Tory turned a corner and zipped along a side street to bypass a line of traffic. "Your chef, right?"

"He's not *my* chef, but yes, it was Kieran."

"Did you sample his cookies?"

"Tory!" But she laughed.

"Ah. You did." Tory's whoop echoed around the car. "Tell me you did."

Casey shook her head. She was never going to live this down.

"Deets girl!"

"Not much to tell really."

"What, he doesn't know what to do with his spoon?"

Casey's eyes widened and she smiled, but she didn't reply.

"Oh come on. Mr. Plaid Boxers in your condo all night..." Tory shifted gears and sped around another corner. "...and there's not much to tell. You must be doing something wrong girl."

"You didn't hear?"

"Hear what?"

"The arsonist struck again."

"Kieran's?"

"Yeah."

"Much damage?"

"At least the bottom three floors."

"His restaurant?"

"Totalled."

"Ah, that's not good." She shook her head. "What's he going to do?"

Casey shrugged. "I don't know."

Tory pulled into a loading zone, shifted her car into park and leaned over her seat into the back. She brought an envelope forward, double checked the packing slip and stepped out of the car. "Be back in a sec."

What *was* Kieran going to do?

If they condemned his building he'd be free to build what he wanted, providing it met the height restrictions. If they didn't, he'd have to rebuild to old specifications. Could he survive that long without having the restaurant up and running?

Casey chewed at her thumb. She hadn't really thought of that. She'd blocked him at every turn, thinking only of the preserving the neighborhood. If she hadn't, he might have had restaurant up and running already. She chewed on her thumb. She hadn't set the guidelines, but she'd worked them to the letter. Had she cost him his dream?

What had he found out today? Was the place salvageable? Did he have enough insurance? Would he stay with her—

Where had that thought come from?

Did she really want that?

She twisted her mouth and checked out the window for Tory. Two weeks ago such stupid thoughts would not have entered her mind. Sharing her place with somebody? Unlikely. With Kieran Hennessy? Unthinkable.

She did what she pleased, when she pleased and treasured her freedom. There was no one to consult or answer to on any decision. No ramifications. No 'I told you so's. That's the part she liked the best. Home was a safe place—her safe place.

She enjoyed her independence.

A sigh escaped into the car as her mind flitted back to breakfast.

She'd enjoyed that too.

A lot.

And waking up in Kieran's arms—if she skipped the ex-husband screaming in the hallway part—had been warm and comforting.

But she was getting ahead of herself.

Last night didn't mean anything. It had simply been a reaction to all the things happening lately. The two of them had been together for one raw moment of passion and wonderful as it was, it was just that—a moment. Nothing more. Nothing less. It didn't mean anything.

But he'd kissed her goodbye.

Casey shook her head against that thought.

Stop.

It had simply been a kiss, a brush of their lips. So why had her legs trembled? And why had her heart threatened to jump out of her chest? Better yet, why was it speeding up now just thinking about him?

Maybe she should phone to see how he was doing. She tugged her cell phone out of her pocket and noticed the text icon. Two texts from Tory explaining that she'd been delayed by extra deliveries. One from Charlie. 9-1-1. Call him.

She hit the call icon. He picked up on the second ring.

"Charlie? It's Casey. What's up?"

"We're just finishing up at the News."

"At the news?"

"The News offices burned this afternoon. We found two people inside. Thought you ought to know."

Her heart skipped. Why would she need to know this? "Are they all right?" Was all she could think to ask.

"One's alive. The other's not

so lucky."

Oh, God. Still what did it have to do with her?

"What? Who—"

"A reporter named Gerald Belkin and...Kieran Hennessy."

The emergency room was teeming with activity as Casey flew through the doors and up to the information counter.

"Kieran Hennessy?"

The nurse glanced at the queue that waited behind the line-starts-here sign, but said nothing. Casey shoulders slumped and she walked to the back of the line. Had everyone and their cousins been injured today?

She'd been so relieved at the news that Kieran was alive that she'd hung up on Charlie without waiting for explanation. Now, standing in this line, she longed for more information. A tidbit to let her know what had happened.

What had Kieran been doing at the paper? He hadn't mentioned going there at breakfast. Maybe he'd gone to place and ad about the postponement of his opening. Or maybe he needed to cancel one.

She gave herself a mental slap.

It didn't matter what he'd been

doing there. All that mattered was that he was here now, in the hospital, in God-knew what shape.

The line surged forward as five people moved into a tiny cubicle in front an admitting nurse. Casey bounced uneasily on the balls of her feet, leaned back and tried to get a peek through the square glass windows that resided in the tops of the doors barring entrance into the triage area.

"Any news?" Tory's voice startled her.

"I haven't got to talk to anyone yet."

"He'll be fine. It'll be all right."

Her friend's words did little to calm the fear waves crashing around Casey's mind. Why did Kieran always have to be the hero? She clamped her jaw against the question.

He'd saved her from certain death in her own fire. And he'd come to her rescue—unnecessary as it might have been—last night. Would she want him any other way?

A space opened in front of the first nurse she spoke to and Casey leaned forward on the counter.

"Kieran Hennessy? He should have arrived here a short time ago. Fire victim." Her heart sunk at her last words.

"Hmmm."

Hmmm, what? *Hmmm*. He's dead. *Hmmm*. She couldn't find his name. *Hmmm*. He's just about to be released. What the hell did *hmmm* mean?

Tory's hand in hers stopped the panic rising with each second.

"Are you a family member?"

Casey's heart thundered again.

"His fiancé," Tory supplied.

The woman glanced down her nose—though that seemed an impossibility given the woman's perch on her chair. If she didn't give them some sort of answer soon, Casey was going to scream.

"Mr. Hennessy is in ICU at this moment."

"ICU." Casey repeated. Did they usually move emergency patients through so quickly? "Is that a good thing?"

An IV hung from a hook above Kieran's bed and liquid dripped through a tube down to his left hand. Bandages covered his right forearm and hand while an oxygen mask obscured his pale face. His chest moved up and down slowly under the speckled fabric of the hospital gown, but Casey found little reassurance in this.

The lack of response when she touched his arm worried her and she slipped her hand under his, lacing her fingers through his. "I'm here." She whispered.

Tears pricked at the edges of her eyes, but she chased them away with the back of her hand. He was here. He'd be fine.

He had to be.

Tory set her hand on Casey's shoulder. "Charlie says he needs to speak with you outside."

Charlie stood on the far side of the glass looking in; face still grimy from fighting the fire, eyes tired from too many similar fights. She waved him in, but he shook his head in denial. Casey sighed and looked back at Kieran. She didn't want to leave him. Why couldn't Charlie just come in here?

"I'll be right back." She brushed the hair back and touched her lips against his forehead before walking out into the main ICU area. "What is it Charlie?"

A uniformed police officer took up post at Kieran's door and the strawberry-blond detective · she'd spoken to the night before moved to the far side of the bed. He said something that Casey couldn't make out. She turned from the cops to Charlie.

"What's happening? Why are they here?"

"For Kieran."

Casey opened her mouth, but no words came out. What the hell was going on?

"Where do they think he's going to go?" She gestured at the guard on the door. "The nurse said he'd be sedated at least until they can assess the swelling in his airways." She tore her eyes back to Charlie. "What's going on?"

"The fire at the News is suspicious and he was found in possession of the dead reporter's camera and a file folder."

"So..." She felt a little like a fish out of water, her mouth opening and closing at her inability to form a coherent statement.

"Belkin was the reporter that covered the fire at Hennessy's too. And the one down the road."

"Okay, but what does this have to do with Kieran?"

"The reporter..." Charlie cast a glance at the floor, at Tory and then settled back on Casey. "He called this morning. He said he had information on the fires."

"And you think Kieran broke in there to get the evidence and set the place on fire?" Casey's raised voice drew an angry stare from the duty nurse and she lowered it. "Come on."

"Come on nothing." He drew his

features tight. "We have reason to believe Kieran Hennessy is the arsonist."

Chapter seventeen

"Maybe he has an explanation." Casey took a turn around the small waiting room.

Charlie shrugged. "This wasn't my decision, but it doesn't look good, Casey."

"Still, innocent until proven guilty, right?"

"In a perfect world."

"Don't give me that perfect world crap." Casey worked her jaw against the anger. "What have you got? A burn and a stolen camera? A few missing pictures?" She shook her head. "And you don't know if he even had anything to do with it."

"It's more than that. All of this started after his first meeting with the Heritage committee—after your first denial of his plans."

Tory flashed a sympathetic look. Had Casey done something to start all of this?

No.

"Now you're blaming me?" She glared at Charlie.

"I didn't mean it that way, but the first fire happened the day after the committee's first denial of Hennessy's proposal."

"Okay, but he kept reapplying with new plans. He wouldn't have done that..."

But he might have. Casey plunked down on one of the vinyl covered couches that lined the wall. It could still be coincidence.

"While doing an inspection, I found timers and accelerants."

Tory sat down beside her, placed a hand on her shoulder.

"But you said those weren't the same."

"No, I said those were similar. And—" He held up a hand to stop her next argument. "They were exactly the same as the ones used in his fire and at the News."

"Did you find his fingerprints? Maybe—" She was going to suggest that the arsonist took advantage of what was on hand, but even she didn't believe that.

Pent up energy forced her off the couch and she crossed to the vending machine. The memory of Kieran's touch, the warmth of his naked torso against her chilled body played through her. She felt safe in those muscular arms, certain that he wouldn't let anything happen to her.

She'd liked the feeling.

"Why would he save me and not Al?"

Charlie shrugged. "Maybe he didn't know Al was in the building."

Fair enough. "What about the guy I saw last night?"

"Probably a vagrant, just taking advantage of the loose plywood." He ran a hand through his hair. "How long was Hennessy at your place before the first delay device went off?"

"I'm not sure." How long had he been there? "Maybe the arsonist set stuff up after..."

Even she knew she was grasping at straws. Charlie had an answer for everything and his answers fit. The timing, the access, the materials. The sick feeling in the pit of Casey's stomach swirled up her throat. Tears pricked the back of her eyes and she shook her head, her gaze moving from Charlie to Tory and back again.

"And why would the arsonist try to sneak into your building after setting up next door?"

Good point.

"He couldn't have done this," desperation made her voice weak.

"Why couldn't he?"

Because she loved him.

She loved him.

When the hell had that happened?

Casey leaned back against the passenger seat of Tory's car and tried to stop her head from spinning. And how—if he was the arsonist—had she been so completely fooled?

Charlie had to be wrong. That was all there was to it. Investigators had been wrong before. The news was rife with stories of wrongly convicted individuals. Okay, rife might be a little overboard, but it *did* happen.

"Casey." Charlie put a hand on the empty passenger door's window frame.

She shook her head and turned away. She didn't want to hear anymore. She didn't want to talk. Her body and mind tingled against a numbness that radiated outward. This couldn't be happening. It wasn't possible.

Tory slid in behind the wheel and turned toward her.

"Can you just drop me home?" Casey preempted Tory's comment.

"Sure."

They drove the short distance

to Casey's in silence. Her hasty exit was delayed when the auto-lock wouldn't disengage and she slammed her shoulder into the door repeatedly before Tory laid a calming hand on her forearm. Casey looked up into her friend's eyes and the little composure she maintained fell away in a monsoon of tears. Tory pulled Casey to her.

Damn it. She trusted him.

The flood tapered to a hiccup sometime later. Tory hooked Casey's hair back behind her ear and peered up at her.

"Better?"

A sniff. "Yeah." She took a swipe at her damp cheeks then rubbed her friend's shoulder. "Sorry."

"S'alright." She gazed down at the damp darkened fabric of her uniform shirt. "Gives it some character."

Casey gave a short laugh and sighed. "I really know how to pick 'em, don't I?" She gazed at the coffee shop across the way. "I think I'll become a vegetarian."

"Huh?"

"Men are pigs."

Tory laughed. "Not all of them."

"No," Casey agreed. "Just the ones I'm interested in."

She drew a ragged breath and pushed the button to unlock the door.

"I'll grab a couple of coffees and meet you upstairs." Tory pulled the keys from her ignition.

"Nah, thanks. I think I just need some time to myself."

"You sure?"

"I'm fine."

"Call me later?"

Casey nodded and stepped out of the car. The light evening breeze carried the stench of burnt wood across the street from Kieran's building. She glanced further down the street to a thin strip of yellow police caution tape that flapped in the wind. She closed her eyes.

Why?

Kieran's head pounded out a heavy beat and he lifted his hand toward it, stopped at the pain that shot up his arm and looked down. White bandages encased his right forearm. He narrowed his eyes against bright light and blinked to clear the haze.

Where was he?

"Mr. Hennessy." Harsh. Male.

Kieran cringed against the words echoing in his head and closed his eyes again. Dizziness spun him.

He grabbed at the blankets. Something covered his mouth and nose and he sounded a little like Darth Vader when he breathed. Tubes trailed his left hand as he brought it to his face to pull the mask away.

"Leave it." Another voice. Gentler. Female.

Casey? He opened his eyes.

The woman who leaned over him smiled gently as she pulled his hand back. "Oxygen. You inhaled a lot of smoke."

He tried to say something, but was unable to form sounds.

"You've been intubated. Your airways were slightly swollen." She smiled reassuringly. "I'll get your doctor."

He must be in the hospital. What had happened? He searched the room for Casey, but the only other occupant of the room was a tall man with strawberry blond hair and freckles across his nose. His grim expression contrasted the kind face and he straightened his blue suit jacket as he stepped up beside the bed.

"I'm Detective Orin Mitchell," he started. "I'm investigating a string of arsons including yours and this latest one at the News."

Right. The News.

Had the reporter made it out?

"Are you up for a few questions?" Mitchell asked.

Kieran nodded.

The detective pulled a camcorder out of his pocket and set it on the rolling table that sat off to the side of his bed. He took out a pen, unscrewed the cap and made a notation at the top of the page. He stepped toward the door and Kieran spied a uniformed officer through the window.

Kieran would have laughed if he could. What was the guard for? Had they thought he'd run? Where was he going to go connected to these contraptions?

The cop picked up the camcorder, checked that it was working and pointed it toward the bed. The detective stepped into frame and stated the particulars of place and date for the record then turned to Kieran.

"You are being interviewed in connection with the series of arsons..." The rest of Mitchell's statement filtered slowly into Kieran's brain.

They thought he was involved.

He closed his eyes against the thunder that pounded with renewed vigor at his temples. He tried to swallow, but couldn't and the dull ache in his chest intensified.

Did Casey know?

Did she believe it?

He closed his eyes and pushed back against the pillow.

Was that why she wasn't here?

The buzz of power tools wafted through her bedroom window. Repairs on the antique store would take months, but at least the security gate for the loading bay had arrived. Maybe she'd finally get a decent night's sleep.

Then again, maybe not.

She glanced over toward the window that opened onto Kieran's temporary sleeping quarters. How could she have been so stupid? She should have noticed...something. The shift in his demeanor had occurred after her fire when he'd rescued her from the flames. Had he wedged the piece of metal in her window? Is that how he'd known she was trapped up there?

A shudder rippled through her and she rolled over in her bed. Maybe she could just wrap up in her down duvet and hide for the rest of the day. One of her black belt students would surely pick up the slack for her and teach this afternoon's classes just as they had for the last few days.

Her phone blasted the two quick rings of the intercom and Casey pulled her pillow over her head.

Maybe if she ignored it whoever it was would go away.

The ringing stopped and Casey stared at the silent phone.

Good. She plopped her pillow under her head. At least something could go her—

The renewed ring nearly sent her off the bed.

"Hello," she snapped.

"Can I come up?"

Jim. What did he want?

"It's about the crew."

She hadn't seen much of Jim since he broke into her condo, but he'd sent a crew over that morning to start work on the store front. His form of apology. She sent them packing. Damned if she'd accept anything from him.

"I've made my own arrangements." Or she would as soon as the insurance paid out.

"Casey, please."

"Go away Jim."

Casey clicked off the receiver, tossed it down on the bed and sunk back against her pillows. The last thing she needed was her ex-husband—

The double-ring stabbed at her brain. She snatched the phone up and stabbed at the receiver. "I said get lost."

"Casey?"

A woman's voice. Kate. "I haven't got my new door key yet."

"Sure, sorry. Come on up. I have it here."

Casey buzzed the door and headed down the hall into the kitchen to retrieve Kate's key. She was going to get herself together. This was ridiculous. Lying in bed for days. Snapping at unseen intruders on the phone. Granted she'd thought it was Jim, but...

"Sorry Kate." Casey stepped back and let the woman into her foyer. "I thought you were someone else."

"You okay?" she asked as she'd signed for her new key.

"Yeah. Just a touch of something." The other woman looked as if she was going to add something, but Casey cut her off. "I'm fine. Really."

Kate hesitated before smiling. "Call if you need anything?"

"You bet."

Casey flipped the lock and walked back toward the kitchen. She pulled the carafe from the coffee maker, moved to the sink and froze.

"Why wouldn't you let me in?" The stench of hangover told her more than the voice. Jim.

"What are you doing here?"

His features tightened at the sharpness of her tone.

"You don't have to be so bitchy," he whined.

"How did you get in?"

"Your security conscious crew let me pass and I came up the back."

"Give me the key."

How could she have been so stupid? She should have had the rear elevator redone when the guy came to rekey her suite and the common doors. She kicked herself for not having the building's security entirely reassessed.

She held out a hand. "The elevator access key, Jim."

"Fine." He snaked his hand into his pocket and handed it over. "Why won't you let my guys help out?"

"When are you going to get this through your thick skull? I don't want anything from you."

"I just wanted to say I was sorry for the other night."

"And you just thought you'd break in again? You've got a funny way of showing how sorry you are."

He balled his hands into fists. "I'm just trying to apologize."

"Fine. You've apologized. Now get out."

She followed him to the front door careful to keep him in full view. He yanked it open and headed through, but turned back before she could shut it behind him.

"Where's *Lover boy*?"

Good God, that's all she needed. She shoved the door closed, but Jim jammed his foot in the opening.

"Get out of the way Jim." Her heart threatened to pound out of her chest and her stomach sent bile up her throat. Why couldn't he just move on?

He shouldered his way back into the condo, sent the door into Casey's forehead and carried her backward onto the floor. Streaks of light competed with threatening darkness and she tried to focus, to think. Something damp and sticky moistened the fingers she put to her forehead and she pulled her hand back.

Blood.

"Is he here?" Jim stormed past her and into her place. "Is that why you wouldn't let me in?"

After what seemed like an eternity, Casey managed to push herself upright against the wall. She had to get into a more advantageous position before Jim returned. Jim caught her off-guard. She wouldn't give him the chance to get the upper hand again.

With one palm pressed against her forehead and the other against the wall, she stood. A quick exit might be prudent if she could reach a lower floor, but when she pushed off the wall a wave of dizziness threatened to topple her.

Using the wall and furniture for support, she inched down the hall toward the rear where a second phone sat on a table. If nothing else, she could get a call out to emergency services. The throb in her head kept time with the beat of her heart and a wave of nausea engulfed her.

Concussion?

She squinted against the pain and reached for the phone. Instead she collided with Jim's shoulder as he stepped in front of her.

"Are you nursing him back to health?" His eyes flitted from one area to another before coming to rest on hers. "Where are you hiding him?"

"What are you talking about?" She tried to shake the cobwebs from her brain, but the movement only increased the vertigo. "Who?"

He grabbed her shoulders, pushed her back against the wall. "Hennessy."

Explosions of stars accompanied the agony gripping her and she fought to focus. Why wouldn't he just go away? He had his life, he'd told her so on numerous occasions. When would he go and live it?

"Kieran isn't here. And even if he were, it's none of your business." The pain eased slightly and she exhaled heavily. "Is this...really...why you're here?"

Jim seemed to take her in for the first time since he barged through her door. His eyes widened and he extended his arm toward her. Reflex caused Casey to pull away. Jim let his arm fall to his side. He dropped his gaze to the floor then took in the room. His hands found his pockets and his features reddened.

"Ah, Casey, I didn't . . ." He looked away again. "You should have just let me in." He scowled.

"I'm not to blame for this." She pulled her hand down to examine the blood on her palm. He opened his mouth, but she cut him off. "Just go."

Halfway down the hall he stopped and glanced over his shoulder. He ran a hand through his hair as if contemplating a return to her side. She shook her head and pointed toward the door. Relief passed through her when, obedient for once, Jim moved down the hall and out the front.

She inched after him, clicked the lock and moved toward the bathroom. Her hand trembled when she pulled it away from her forehead to glimpse the damage in the mirror. A small stream of blood trickled from her hairline and she leaned in to get a closer look. An inch long slit snaked up into her hair. Casey sat on the edge of the tub, pressed a wet towel against the wound and let the cloth cool the area.

Nausea hit her anew as she pushed upward. She grabbed a towel hanging off the rack to steady herself. Rhythmic breathing calmed her and she shifted her back to the wall. The door hadn't hit her that hard, had it? She winced against unexpected pain when she leaned back to let her head rest against the cool tiles. Instinctively she reached to the back of her skull and tested the area.

"Damn!"

She should have been better prepared. Why had she let her guard down? Jim had shown again and again that he couldn't be trusted. Maybe that was her gift...caring for men who couldn't be trusted.

Angry tears spilled from her eyes.

What was the matter with her? She could counsel women to keep their wits about them, to be aware of their surroundings, to use their heads, but when it came to her, all common sense seemed to vanish.

"Stupid! Stupid! Stupid!" She headed to the kitchen for an ice pack.

The double phone ring of the enter-phone sounded as Casey stepped close to the handset and the bell reverberated through her head. "Hello?"

"Casey?"

Kieran.

Her heart did a little flip and she clamped her jaw against the feeling. "I thought you were in jail."

Stupid statement.

"Obviously not," he growled.

Relief started through her, but she chased it with measured anger. This man had tried to burn her out of her home and when that failed, he lit a fire that took someone else's life. She shouldn't—wouldn't care for him.

"Leave me alone."

"I have your keys."

"Leave them at the dojo."

"There's no one there."

She drew a breath and blew it out. She didn't want to invite him up, was afraid her resolve would crumble if she did. She shook her head in disappointment and immediately regretted the movement.

Al. All she needed to do was think of Al.

"I'll just drop them outside

your door. You don't even have to open it."

A hesitation and the phone disconnected. She pushed the door release, listened to the shrill signal on the phone and hung up. Casey leaned against the door, until the elevator arrived and watched through the peep hole as Kieran stepped up to the door. She inhaled deeply at the sight of him despite the distortions of her viewer. He raised his hand to knock, but dropped it back out of sight. A second later she heard her keys clatter to the floor.

Casey inhaled deeply as he turned away from her. She couldn't let him go. She had to see him one more time. Just a quick peek. Something to last her until everything was sorted—forever if it had to.

She shook her head. That bump must have really done something to make her so dramatic, but she unlatched the door anyway. The door seemed heavier than usual and she tugged hard, staggered back when it moved. Kieran turned, his frown deepened.

"What happened?"

"Nothing," her voice was a whisper.

Vertigo spun like an eddy when she tried to pick up the keys and she gripped the door handle tighter. She gulped air to combat the bile that invaded her throat and fought to regain control. Kieran retrieved the key ring from the floor.

Fingers touched her chin, drew her face toward him. Caring warmed his emerald green eyes while his thumb drew circles just in front of her ear. The tenderness in the gesture surprised her and confusion swirled inside to further heat her cheeks.

She shook away from his touch. "Keys?"

He set the keys in her hand, grabbed her wrist. Her heart thundered. What was he doing?

"How many fingers?"

"What?"

"Fingers? How many?"

She gazed toward the hand that faded in and out of focus. "Three?"

"What day is it?"

She opened her mouth to answer, but hesitated. It was Tuesday, wasn't it?

"We're going to the hospital," he said and scooped her up into his arms before she could protest.

Not that she could have anyway. She closed her eyes on thumping head and the world swirled. Kieran's scent comforted her and despite her earlier admonitions, she leaned her head into his shoulder.

"Open your eyes!" The voice came through as a distant echo, despite the familiar timbre and tone. Her jumbled memory led off in criss-cross paths, Jim, Al's funeral, the shadowy figure outside her shop. Kieran. He was with his brother...the thought floated away.

"Casey! Open your eyes! Wake up!"

She forced her eyelids open to find herself inside a car. How had she arrived there? She had no recollection of leaving her condo.

"That's it. Keep 'em open." Why was he yelling? She squinted against the pain and allowed her eyes to droop again. "No, come on. Stay..."

A peaceful blackness enveloped her and she drifted away from the voice.

Chapter eighteen

Tires squealed when Kieran applied extra pressure on his breaks to avoid slamming into the car in front of him.

"Not good. Not good."

His heart thundered and he fought to control his still-aching lungs. An accident would only complicate matters.

Casey's head lolled and bobbed before it found support against the passenger window. He ran his fingers through the blond hair touching her shoulders, clamped his jaw and focused on the road. His palms sweat under his tight grip on the steering wheel.

Green. Kieran transferred his foot to the gas. "Come on. Come on." He pulled out around a sluggish vehicle and sped down the left lane toward the hospital.

"Kieran?" Her voice was weak.

"Yes?" Hope rose then fell. No response. "I'm right beside you."

She mumbled something incomprehensible, shifted. Was movement good? Was she coming round?

He came back to the road. Slammed on his brakes.

"Every red light."

He inched forward. He could see the hospital. It was right there. His car shook as a tractor-trailer narrowly missed the front end. He jammed on his brakes again.

Come on. Come on. Come on.

His tires squealed off the stop line and round the corner into the lot. He flew out of the driver's seat and yarded Casey's door open.

"You can't—" The nurse's eyes widened and he threw his smoldering cigarette butt aside. "I'll get a gurney!"

Kieran met the nurse half-way into the ward and placed Casey down.

"What's her name?" the nurse demanded. "What is her name?" Louder more forceful.

"Casey," Kieran muttered. "Casey Michaelson."

"What happened?" Another man.

"I'm not sure...she hit her head." Kieran's stomach clenched.

A hand restrained him as they shoved her through the swinging doors into emergency. He blocked the door's swing with his arm then let the limb drop to his side.

"Sir?"

Kieran glanced to his right. A young woman sat in a chair at a wicket style desk. She motioned for him to take the seat across from her and his legs moved almost automatically, carrying him to the chair. His gaze stayed with the doors.

"Just a few questions," she said, her voice light but matter-of-fact.

He answered her questions mechanically only periodically shifting his gaze to the nurse. Casey's name, address, phone number. Those were easy. Carecard number. He didn't know. Next of kin? Unless her useless ex-husband counted, he didn't think she had a next of kin. Kieran fought to maintain control.

"Nature of the accident?"

The question brought him out of his reverie. "She hit her head."

"Yes, but how did it happen?"

How *had* she hit her head? Was it a fall, or had someone helped her fall?

Did Jim have a hand in it?

"Sir?"

He shook his head and shrugged. "I don't know. It happened before I got there."

The nurse nodded and fired a few more questions his way.

"When will you know how she is?" he interrupted.

"The doctor will come out and speak to you," she answered and continued her cross-examination. "Do you and Ms. Michaelson live together?"

What did that matter?

He shook his head.

"How long ago did the injury occur?"

"I told you. I don't know."

Why did she keep asking him questions? Didn't she know that he wanted answers too? What the hell had happened? Had she slipped? Or had someone hurt her?

Jim.

"If you'll just have a seat, the doctor should be out shortly."

There was nothing more he could do, except wait. Hard chairs lined walls in the room where he settled. He grabbed a magazine, thumbed it half-heartedly before throwing it back onto the corner table. He leaned forward, twisted the heel of his hand against his closed eyes to relieve the growing fatigue. People didn't die from concussions, did they?

Kieran leaned back in the

chair. He used the wall as a head rest and closed his eyes. Damn he was tired. He took out his puffer and drew some medication into his aching lungs and held it.

Had it only been a few days since he was here himself? So much had happened since then. And he still didn't understand.

How could anyone think he'd done these things?

They must see some connection between him and the fires, but they hadn't arrested him. Still, they must have something in if they convinced Casey. He clenched his jaw. And someone <u>had</u> convinced her. If they hadn't, he would have been there to help her, to prevent this from happening.

Not that she would have wanted his help.

He took a couple of turns around the waiting room until a woman holding a sleeping baby stared him into a chair. He forced himself back into the contoured back, but couldn't control his agitation and leaned forward again. He gazed toward the swinging doors that divided the waiting from triage areas.

What the hell was taking so long?

Was she okay back there?

Kieran pushed up off the seat

and walked toward the reception desk. A woman nearing six feet stepped through the swinging doors. She wore a white coat over green scrubs and a stethoscope hung over her neck. The receptionist pointed his way and the doctor veered his direction.

"Are you Ms. Michaelson's fiancé?"

He didn't correct her. "How is she?"

"We're sending her for some further testing, but she is awake and responsive—"

"Can I see her?"

She glanced down at her watch. "Only for a moment. Bed six."

He winced at the purplish bruise that peeked from under the bandage covering Casey's forehead. He longed to touch her, to caress her injuries away, but he hesitated.

How would she receive him?

Casey's eyes fluttered open and she blinked against the light. After a few moments her eyes seemed to focus on him and she smiled. He closed the distance between them, clasped her hand in his.

"How are you feeling?"

"If you could get the buzz saw out of my skull, I'd be great."

Kieran brushed her hair aside

before bending down to give her forehead a gentle kiss. She seemed so small there in the middle of the bed, so defenseless.

"What happened?"

Her eyes clouded with emotion and she shifted her glance to the curtain beside her bed. Didn't she trust him? He'd understand. He'd do what needed to be done to help her out; to make things right. She looked back at him and his heart ached. Why wouldn't she let him in?

"It doesn't matter."

"It damned-well does matter!"

Her hand came up at the angry tone and she slid her tongue over parched lips. She inhaled deeply and her brow creased. Pain or worry? Maybe he should leave it. He rubbed his face with his free hand as he shifted his weight on the bed, but couldn't shake free of the anger. Something or someone had caused her injury. He blew a calming breath over his lips.

"Tell me it wasn't Jim."

The slightest change in her body told him he'd struck a chord.

Jim.

Stupid bastard.

His body tensed and she drew her thumb over his hand. "Let it go." Her voice was barely a whisper.

A nurse tugged the curtain back. "We have to take her up," she said.

Kieran nodded.

Casey's brow furrowed and she tightened her grip.

"I'm here," he whispered and drew his thumb across her forehead to ease the lines.

He touched his lips to her forehead and she stirred, shifted and nestled herself down into the pillow. Her features relaxed as if his touch sent her worries packing. He walked alongside her bed as far as the nurse would allow and watched her into the elevator.

Kieran turned on his heel and headed back through the emergency room. She'd asked him to leave it alone, but he couldn't. Someone had to do something to stop Jim from hurting her again.

Locked.

Kieran hammered at the door again.

No answer.

Jim's pickup truck sat next to the construction trailer, but the man was nowhere to be seen. Kieran hammered the door a final time then stepped down from the platform.

He leaned against his car's

front fender mulling things over before pocketing the keys. Kieran knew of at least six watering holes—and they were holes—within a short walk from the construction trailer and one of them was sure to yield Casey's ex-husband. Logic told him to skip the search and head back to the hospital, but he wasn't feeling particularly logical at the moment. He tugged his jeans jacket collar up and headed off down the sidewalk.

Thunder crashed in the distance and the wind picked up a notch. Rain soaked through to his shirt before he reached the first pub entrance and he shook great drops off his hair. Smoke-filled air stung his eyes. Hadn't these guys heard about the anti-smoking by-law? A few heads shifted his direction, but returned in fluid motion to their previous position. No one cared about the newcomer. Kieran, happy with his anonymity wandered toward some tables at the back, searched faces along the way.

"What are you staring at?" a gruff male voice barked.

Kieran brought his gaze around to the source of the voice. A heavy-set man pushed up from the table to send his chair to the floor with a crash. Kieran tensed.

He'd come looking for a fight.

Just not this one.

He spread his hands out in a conciliatory gesture and shook his head. He opened his mouth to speak as he was roughly shoved aside.

"You!" A spindly twenty-something with a two day beard and dirty jeans rushed past him. "Gonna do something about it?"

"Yeah!" The first man wobbled a few steps forward before he gained his balance.

Feet flew over the bar as the bartender cleared it and headed toward the sparring match. Another man—a bouncer Kieran thought—emerged from a back door to join the melee. Kieran ducked out of the way and skirted the tables scattered around the middle of the room. He gave the room a last survey and headed for the door.

No Jim.

Outside the bar, the storm had tapered to a light drizzle. The wind carried the spray into Kieran's face and tempered his mood during the walk to the next bar. Despite the calming effect of the weather, his desire to find Jim still burned inside him. The bastard hurt Casey. She'd avoided his questions, but her body language and quiet plea to leave it be had told him everything.

The thought of Casey in her hospital bed furrowed his brow. Hurt. Embarrassed. She deserved better. He balled his hands into fists and pushed into another bar.

"Hey!" Kieran turned toward the

voice from his left. An olive-skinned man who resembled a linebacker held a hand out toward him. "Five dollars."

Kieran fished in his pocket for the bill and slid it across the counter. "You know a guy named Jim?"

The man laughed before sliding the five dollars into his own pant pocket. "Yeah, sure. There's a Jim at the bar, two in the back and probably one in the can."

Funny.

Kieran wiped the rain off his brow then moved inside.

The dim room provided the perfect atmosphere for a person to drown their sorrows, perhaps even promoted it. Patrons—bobbing and weaving with intoxication—filled much of the available space and Kieran picked his way past the booths and tables to the bar.

"What can I get ya, sweetie?" Female bartender. Not what he'd expected in a dive like this.

"D'you have something red on tap?"

She nodded, stuck a glass under the spigot and pulled. Another patron staggered up to the bar. He grabbed a stool, leaned on it for support then moved his body around to climb on top. After depositing Kieran's beer, the bartender slipped down the bar to a far corner, crossed her arms and waited.

The drunk raised his head after a long period of struggle. He cast his gaze around haphazardly as if looking for something in to settle on and slapped his hand on the bar. Kieran turned at the loud crack, but the bartender remained relaxed, arms crossed over her small frame.

"G-g-gimme a b-beer will ya, Trudy?"

"Sorry, Stan," she smiled. "You're cut off..."

Kieran rotated away from the exchange and a room full of drunks stared back at him. Carbonation and hops bit as he swallowed the amber liquid. Kieran scanned the crowd, but couldn't see Jim.

Maybe it was better that way.

"Hi."

Kieran shifted his gaze toward the woman who'd come up beside him. Her smile was tentative, but she gave the impression she'd done this before.

She winked. "Buy me a drink and I'll help you find what you're looking for."

"Who says I'm looking for anything?"

"Everyone's looking for something." She seated herself on the stool next to his.

Did this line usually work? Kieran spun back to the bar. He took another gulp of beer before he placed the glass on the counter. "I'll buy you the drink, but I'm not interested."

A noisy breath whistled through her nose and she hopped off the stool. "Don't flatter yourself. I was just being friendly." The woman stormed off across the room to an empty table.

Kieran shook his head. Had he looked lonely? The mirror behind the bar would give him the answer, but he avoided a glance. He already knew the answer.

He pushed the half-drained drink across the counter and rubbed his eyes. Why was he chasing through bar after bar instead of waiting for news about Casey? What would he do when he found Jim? Beat him up? She'd be so disappointed in him if he did.

Kieran fished in his pocket for some money. He should head back to the hospital and be there when her tests were finished. He could keep her company or bring her home, if the doctor's said it was all right.

But would she let him?

He turned back to the bar, hooked a hand around his glass. What if she thought he'd done all these things? Would she want anything to do with him? His whiskers scratched against his hand as he rubbed his jaw. He'd just have to convince her of the truth.

But how?

He spun away from the remainder of his beer and headed for the door. He'd have to figure out a way, find something to convince her.

"What're you doin' here?" The familiar voice originated from the right. "Who do you think you are? Comin' here, messin' things up?"

Jim sat at a booth, empty glass on the table in front of him, flame from a lighter illuminating his face. His eyes closed for a long moment. He flicked them open wider than usual and let the flame die. He pushed himself up off the beat up bench seat, balled one hand into a fist and shook it at Kieran.

"You know what he did?" Jim's balance wavered slightly. "He stole my wife."

A chorus of supportive name-calling rang out from the nearby tables. Kieran's worked his jaw against words he longed to speak.

"I oughta . . . I oughta—" Jim staggered forward to wave his unsteady finger in Kieran's face. "Why don't you..."

The last line trailed off into an incoherent drunken mumble when Jim's head bobbed to one side. Kieran drew a breath and turned to exit. No matter how attractive the thought of slapping Jim silly appeared at the moment, hitting this pathetic drunk would serve no useful purpose.

A fist grazed his cheekbone as Jim traveled past him with the force of the movement. Kieran extended a hand, which Jim swatted away in favor of a fall to the floor. He hooked his foot behind Kieran's knee, toppling him and threw himself on top pounding away with his fists. Kieran deflected a number of blows before he gained the upper position and pinned Jim to the floor with one hand. He'd landed three hard blows on the man's face before a set of strong hands pulled him off.

"Break it up," a stern voice yelled in Kieran's ear. "Knock it off!" A hand held his collar and another twisted his arm up behind his back and shoved him toward the door.

The cold wet metal of a car hood brought him back to the reality of his actions. How would he explain this to Casey?

Chapter nineteen

"What the hell do you think you're doing?"

For the first time, Kieran took the time to focus on the person who'd hauled him out of the bar. His brother Daniel stood a few feet away, hair askew, eyes wild with anger.

"You're lucky it was me and not a cop." Daniel crossed his arms, shifted his weight, then jammed his hands in his pockets. He shook his head. "Tell me you're not like *him*."

Him, meaning Daniel's father.

Kieran shook his head. "He hurt someone I care about, but I was wrong to go there, was going to leave..."

He let the excuses trail off. No matter what he said now, he'd proven he'd resort to violence if he thought it necessary.

"Casey?"

"Yeah." Kieran walked down the road toward an all night diner that served mediocre coffee and stale donuts. "Come on, you can buy me a coffee and I'll tell you what happened."

"Who was that guy?"

"Casey's ex-husband. She's in the hospital tonight because of him."

"I should have let you keep going."

Kieran shook his head. What was happening to his plans? He was going to come here, build the restaurant of his dreams and live happily ever after. Instead, the restaurant of his dreams lay in charred ruins and the woman he loved lay in a hospital bed.

The woman he loved?

He cast a gaze out the window. He cared for her, enjoyed being around her, but did he love her?

No. He didn't love anyone—wouldn't allow it. Love just got people hurt. That's what it had done for his father. Love made him weak and vulnerable. He trusted and in the end, it killed him.

The waitress set a couple of cups on the table in front of them and Daniel smiled up at her. His brother watched her walk away and grinned back at him.

"Nice."

"Hmmm? Right. Yeah."

"What's the matter with you?"

He shrugged.

"Come on, what's up?"

"I think I'm their prime suspect."

"For what?"

"Arson."

"They think you're responsible for these fires?"

"Looks like."

"That's crazy."

"Tell them that." His brother looked as if he might get up and do just that, but Kieran slid his coffee cup in front of him. "Sit."

The brothers drank in silence a moment.

"So how'd it feel?" Daniel asked finally.

"What?"

"Bashing that guy in the nose like that?"

"It was immature."

"Yeah, but I bet it felt great."

"Yeah, it felt good all right." Kieran took a sip of his coffee and smiled at his brother. "I just wish you'd turned up about two minutes later."

Pain pounded at Casey's temples. She kept her eyes closed in an attempt to avoid the light from the overheads as they wheeled her down the hall. In and out of consciousness her entire time in the hospital, she had no clear recollection of events. How had she managed to get herself here? Or had she?

Something pinched at the back of her hand when she tried to touch her forehead. She opened her eyes and blinked against the light. Tubes ran up from an intravenous needle to a bottle hanging above her. A nurse pushing at the side of the cart, placed a hand on Casey's shoulder and smiled.

"It's all right, you'll be fine. We're just headed to your room."

Her room?

Casey dropped her hand on top of her stomach and closed her eyes again. Kieran. His concerned features flashed before her eyes. When had she seen him look like that?

"Here we are," the nurse interrupted. "We just need to slide you over." Was she talking to Casey? "Careful, on three." No, to someone else. No need to answer.

Casey could barely hear the words over the thumps in her head, let alone form a coherent sentence. Focus. She had to get her thoughts straight, clear. Too many things were at stake. At the moment, she couldn't even remember what those things were.

Kieran.

He'd been so upset the last time she saw him. About what? He'd yelled at her. What was it now? Oh, yes, he'd brought her to the hospital. Maybe he was here waiting for her to look at him. She forced her eyes open. The IV. A control panel above the bed. Pale green walls. A chair.

Empty.

A single tear rolled down her cheek. Why wasn't he here?

Kieran stepped up to his driver's door and twisted the lock open.

"I'm heading back to the hospital." Kieran pulled his driver's door open. "Can I drop you somewhere?"

"Nah, I'm meeting some friends at the pub." Daniel pointed toward the water front. "I have a couch if you need it."

"Thanks, I'll call if I do."

His brother slapped him on the shoulder and took a step toward the corner. Stopped. "What's that guy doing?"

Kieran followed his brother's line of sight. Charlie Griffin tripped over a stair that jutted out into the sidewalk and tumbled forward, landing on all fours. The firefighter struggled upright, weaved and headed for the street. A car narrowly missed him as Kieran sprinted across the road.

"Whoa, Whoa." Kieran took hold of one arm while Daniel caught the other and they steered him back onto the stairs. "Where you headed there?"

"Hennessy," Griffin spat.

Kieran pulled away from his breath. "What did you do, drink the brewery?"

"What are you doing here?" Griffin closed one eye in an attempt to focus.

"Keeping you from getting killed." Why exactly, he wasn't sure. "What are *you* doing?"

"Bastards." Griffin waved toward some invisible source of anger. "Wouldn't let me in!" He shoved upward, but alcohol-rubbered legs dropped him back to the stair. "I'll show them. I'll..." What he was going to do was lost in his shirt as his chin dipped.

"We better get him out of here." Kieran slid his hand back under the firefighters arm.

"Isn't this the guy that had you arrested?" Daniel asked.

Kieran nodded.

"I say leave him." Daniel pulled his hands away. "He deserves whatever he gets."

Kieran couldn't help but laugh. "We can't leave the guy to wander into the street."

"Why the hell not?" Daniel asked, but he'd already hooked a hand under the firefighter's arm and was helping him to his feet.

"Whe' you takin' me?" Griffin mumbled.

"Home." Kieran settled the firefighter on the back seat and left Daniel to belt him in. He yanked open his driver's door and slid behind the wheel.

"What's this?" Dan handed an old butane lighter over the seat back.

Kieran twirled the silver object in his hand. Flicked it open. Clink-click. It sparked on the first try and the blue and yellow flame flickered in the car. He closed it and slipped it into his jeans pocket.

"Where's home, Mr. Griffin?" Kieran asked.

Griffin screwed his face up and said, "Got no home."

Daniel fished the man's wallet out of his pocket, tossed it to Kieran. He checked the seatbelt securing Griffin and the firefighter slumped sideways. His snores rumbled as Dan closed the passenger door on him.

"At least order pizza on the guy's visa."

"Sometimes I worry about you, Dan."

"Have fun."

Fun. Right.

What could be more fun than playing chauffeur for the guy who thought you'd burned down half the city and killed two people?

Kieran pulled into the driveway beside Griffin's truck. The Victorian house at the lot's front dwarfed the garage, a near miniature of the larger structure. He shivered against the chill air as he stepped out of his warm car.

A violent shake brought Griffin around enough to get him out of the car and halfway up the walk between the fence and garage where a gate partitioned off the backyard. The six foot fence opened into a small but well-stocked play area. A jungle gym complete with swings and a rope bridge took up most visible space. In the dim illumination from the porch light, the structure inspired awe.

Griffin shook off Kieran's help and crossed the distance to the wooden support beam. He ran a hand over the weather worn wood and leaned against it a moment.

"I built it for my son," Griffin said, his voice cracked. He coughed and stumbled toward the garage.

Fluorescent lights flickered a moment before casting bright light over the cement area. Workbenches lined two walls, tools hung on pegs, ready for the next project. Kieran tripped over a plastic bottle and kicked a few others as he tried to keep from falling. "Sorry. I bin meanin' ta ge' rid o' those." Griffin motioned to the containers that lined the wall. He fumbled and flicked another light switch. Light blazed at the top of the steep stairs.

Griffin started up the stairs, slid back down into a heap at the bottom. Kieran contemplated leaving him there. He'd be safe, but he'd probably die of hypothermia on the cold cement floor. He hooked a hand into the firefighter's belt and hauled the man upward. He made slow progress up the stairs, making it up two and resting momentarily between each pair.

They fell through the opening at the top, sweat pouring off Kieran, while the fire fighter rolled away and curled into a ball on the wooden floor. Dormers on three sides provided light from streetlamps and space to move without the need to crouch. An old chest of drawers sat beside a queen-sized brass bed, the footboard marking the pathway into the room beside a couch that ran under one window. A set of sheets, along with pillow and blanket sat on top the unmade bed. He knelt in front of a baseboard heater, tested its temperature and fiddled with the knob.

In the opposite corner a fridge, hotplate and sink suggested a kitchen, though Kieran would be hard-pressed to agree. A bag of groceries sat on the counter next to a coffee maker and he glanced over at the sleeping man.

Trouble in paradise?

Kieran settled himself on the couch. He yawned and let his head fall against the soft cushions. He should phone the hospital again. Casey should be back in her room by now. Was she all right? Had she wondered about him? Asked?

He pulled his cell out of his pocket and dialed the number. Same song, different singer. She was stable and in ICU. No visitors. No information.

He should be there. He could help her, comfort her.

She'd probably tell him to go bake cookies or something. He

smiled. She was all bluster. When it came down to it, she melted into his arms. Warm. Soft. Beautiful. He loved the contradictions. The other night had been unplanned and—carnal. The next time they'd take it slow.

Would there be a next time?

He massaged his temples. Did she really think he'd done all the things he was accused of? Could she think him capable of it? His body tensed and he raised one brow toward the firefighter. Maybe he *should* have left the man to fend for himself.

Kieran shifted positions and relaxed. He laid his head against the arm of the couch and stared through the window at the sky. A peephole had opened in the clouds and a few stars twinkled down at him. He stretched his legs across the other armrest, crossed his ankles and linked his hands behind his head. Was Casey looking at the same sky? Was she feeling better?

God, he was tired. It had been one helluva week. His building was toast. His restaurant—his dream—was gone. None of it mattered. His thoughts kept coming back to Casey, so small and frail against her pillow.

What would he do if she didn't believe him?

Hard rain drumming on the roof

and the gurgle of a drip coffee maker brought Kieran out of his slumber. He enjoyed the aroma of the freshly brewed java a moment before he sat up.

Damn. He'd fallen asleep.

He yawned and ran both hands through the hair at the sides of his head, tugging gently when he neared the ends. He cast a quick searching glance for the firefighter. Gone.

How could he have fallen asleep here?

Laughter drew his attention outside and he shifted to get a better view out the window. The large jungle-gym sat empty, while two children dressed in rain coats and hats chased around the neighbor's yard. Oblivious to the downpour, Griffin stood beside the large wooden structure in his yard watching the children play. After more than a minute, he walked back toward the garage.

Kieran pulled back from the window and stretched out on the couch as before. The firefighter ducked in through a door to the right of the stairs and emerged with a towel draped around his neck. Griffin poured himself a cup of coffee and stood at the counter, droplets falling from his hair into his mug. His shoulders slumped and his body shook as he stared down at the counter. Kieran tensed.

Griffin glanced his way, set

his coffee cup down and rubbed his face with the towel. The sip of coffee he took seemed to straighten his shoulders.

"Morning." Dampness sparkled just under his eyes and he lifted a cup toward Kieran then filled it.

"Yeah, thanks."

Kieran swung his feet round, accepted the cup and leaned back. He sipped the dark liquid while Griffin emptied the grocery bag, avoiding eye contact. He arranged items around the makeshift kitchen. He turned back suddenly.

"Why didn't you just leave me there?"

A shrug. "You nearly got yourself run over." Griffin narrowed his gaze and Kieran thought he knew what was going through his mind. "Contrary to popular belief, I'm not that callous."

Kieran set his coffee cup down roughly, sloshing the contents onto his hand. He shook the hot liquid off, stood and started toward the door, remembered the lighter and turned back.

"Here," He tossed the lighter at the firefighter.

"What's this?" Griffin twirled it in his fingers.

"You dropped it outside my car last night by the construction trailer."

"No, I didn't."

Kieran shrugged. "Keep it."

He half-climbed, half-slid down the stairs into the garage. Stupid SOB. He should have left him to get run over and killed. At the very least, the idiot might have had some sense knocked into him.

Kieran kicked at a plastic bottle that blocked his path and the unmistakable aroma of gasoline invaded the space.

"Crap!"

He shook the dampness from his shoe, pushed out the door and got into his car. He slammed the gears into reverse and glanced up at the garage loft window. Stopped.

Griffin stood in the window, lighter in hand. The flame flickered on and off again twice before the firefighter backed away.

What was that about?

Chapter twenty

By the time Kieran reached the corner store to pick up some flowers all he could think about was Casey. A call to the hospital admissions desk had informed him that she'd been moved to a regular ward and that had to be good news. He smiled into the review, adjusted his hair and hopped out of the car.

The fragrance from the bouquet filled the elevator as it groaned into action on its ascent to the general ward and Kieran jumped with nervous energy. He'd given up worrying about how she would receive him, resigning himself to letting events play out as they did. She was getting better and right now, that was all that mattered.

Kieran just about leapt through the elevator when the doors opened on her floor and a man flashed an annoyed glare as he pulled a small child out of the way.

"Sorry, Sunshine."

Sunshine? Where had that come from?

Kieran shrugged and continued on down the hall.

A couple of women stood behind the counter at the nurses' station engaged in a hushed-tone discussion. Another two stood in front of a rack on the wall, one rested a hand on a closed metal chart and appeared to be giving instructions. Kieran stopped at the counter and waited. A fifth nurse came around the corner into the station area and flashed a smile his way.

"Can I help you?"

"I'm looking for a friend, Casey Michaelson. Can you tell me which room she's in?"

He followed the nurse's directions down the hall to the end and started in.

"Get out." Casey's voice was shrill with tension. "You're not supposed to come near me."

"But—" Jim stood beside the bed arms flailing.

"Just leave." Her fists bunched, body tight, blue eyes shooting angry daggers.

Flowers and good humor forgotten, Kieran crossed the room to yank Jim away from the bedside. He placed himself between Jim and Casey.

"Back off," Kieran commanded.

"What are you going to do?" He

sneered at Kieran, flashed an innocent smile toward his ex-wife. "Hit me again?"

Kieran opened his mouth to speak, hesitated and closed it again.

"See, I told you he hit me." Jim peered round him at Casey and came back to Kieran. "Do you see what you did? I'm lucky not to be in that bed right over there."

"What's going on in here?" the nurse who stormed into the room commanded more than her five feet of attention.

"He started it," Jim blustered.

"It doesn't matter who started it. This is a hospital and you will conduct yourself accordingly or leave." She pierced each man with a stare, waited for a response, then continued. "Good, then, we understand each other." She fussed with Casey's covers for a moment, fluffed her pillow and leaned in. "You okay?"

Kieran could barely hear the question, but spied the nod of Casey's head. The nurse spun on her heel, shot an icy glare his direction, to Jim, and left the room. He crossed behind the nurse and picked up the flowers he'd dropped on a chair.

Jim started toward Casey, but she held a hand up at him and shook her head. As he ripped his jacket from the chair back, he pulled the heavy piece of furniture a few feet across the room. Once freed, he glared at Kieran, shouldering him on his path out the door.

The flowery aroma, so pleasant in the elevator, almost sickened Kieran now as he held the bouquet at his chest. He played with the flowers in an attempt to fluff them and avoid looking at Casey.

"I can explain," he said into the flowers.

His head came up at her silence. Tears streamed down her cheeks onto her hospital gown. She turned her head away.

"Casey? Please."

He took a step up beside the bed, reached for her.

"Don't." Her voice was calm, cold. "I need you to leave, too."

Out the window, hard rain built and rippled puddles on rooftops and pavement. Kieran drew a heavy breath and placed the flowers on the foot of the bed.

"I'm sorry." He spun on his heel and walked from the room.

Flapping windshield wipers mirrored Casey's emotions, one minute clear, the next blurry. She pulled her coat tighter around her body and sniffed at the flowers in her hand.

"Why didn't you call?" Tory asked as she slipped in behind the wheel of her car.

"I did."

"I meant before now. I could have ogled some single doctor's with you." Tory shifted into gear and pulled out of the parking spot. "Oh yeah, I forgot. You have a chef."

"He's not _my_ chef."

Tory turned her head sharply at the crispness in Casey's words. "What happened?"

Casey took a few moments to relay the highlights of the previous night's events and turned her attention back out the window.

"And Kieran went out after him?"

Casey turned nodded. "Yes."

"Way to go, Kieran."

Casey lifted a brow. Not the reaction she'd expected.

"What? You're not happy about this?"

"No."

"Why not?" Tory screwed up her face. "Your ex-husband's an ass hon' and sometimes asses need to be whooped."

Casey couldn't stop the smile.

That was true, but she'd asked Kieran to leave it alone. Instead he'd left *her* alone.

"So where is he?"

"Who?"

"Kieran."

"I don't know."

"Did he bring you the flowers?"

Casey stuck her nose into the bouquet in her lap. The soft petals of the flowers tickled her skin.

"They why isn't he driving you home?"

Casey shrugged. "I told him to go away."

And he had gone. No real protest. No fight. No argument. She gazed back out the window. He just left.

What did that mean?

"Why would you do that?" Tory brought her back inside the car.

"He's just like Jim."

"He's *nothing* like Jim."

"He's a hot head who acts without thinking."

"He was defending you." Tory shook her head and gripped the steering wheel tighter. "That bastard hurt you and Kieran went to set things straight. You can't blame him."

Yes Casey could. She could blame him for turning her life upside down then abandoning her when she needed him the most. She could blame him for making her love him while all the while sneaking around burning down buildings.

Kieran an arsonist. She couldn't believe it.

She played with the head of an orange flower with long thin petals. The police obviously thought he'd done it. Charlie thought he'd done it. But he wasn't in jail.

What did that mean? Was the evidence faulty or had they just not gathered enough?

Arsonist.

"Man. I can sure pick 'em. An alcoholic, an arsonist... what's next? An—"

Exactly what her next was going to be was lost in the corner Tory took at about a hundred miles an hour. She slammed on her brakes and twisted in her seat.

"Arsonist? What are you talking about?"

Casey took a moment to swallow her stomach and loosen her grip on the dash. "Kieran."

"You think Kieran is the arsonist."

"The cops do."

"Why?"

"Charlie says there's a ton of evidence."

"So why isn't he in jail?"

"I guess there's not enough."

"But you think he did it?"

Did she?

Her mind worked in circles around this very question every time she gave it two minutes to wander. Her head told her it was possible. He was stretched to the limit in preparations for his restaurant's opening. Financially, the place had to be like a black hole, a vortex sucking money at every turn. Committee denials. Fire inspections. Construction problems. Delays. Delays. Delays. Each setback pushed the restaurant's opening further from the original plan. Did he have enough funds to weather the storm? Fire made that point moot.

Still. She couldn't picture it.

"No," she said finally.

Or was that her heart interfering?

No. It was more than that. She *knew* he was innocent.

But could she trust what she 'knew'? She'd trusted Jim once too and look where that had gotten her.

"So what's the problem then?"

"Sorry?"

"Why are you so ticked?"

Casey gazed down into the rainbow of flowers she held so tightly in her hands that her palms were turning green and a kaleidoscope of images cascaded through her mind. Her fire. His. His sparkling green eyes. The empty chair.

"He should have stayed."

Kieran twisted his cup in circles. He shouldn't have gone after Jim. He'd known it and gone anyway. He'd headed out after a fight and got what he was looking for. Now he wasn't sure if Casey would ever talk to him again.

Would he do it again?

In a heartbeat.

Why?

He glanced over at her dojo. The woman had been nothing but trouble. If it hadn't been for her and her damned committee, he might actually have had the opportunity to provide at least one service before his restaurant burned down. He might even have escaped the arsonist's flames. If the building had been bustling with activity, the chance might not have arisen.

Still, he'd walk over hot coals—had in fact walked across broken glass and other miscellaneous bits of crap—to make sure she was safe. He took a sip of his coffee and winced. Cold.

He pushed the cup aside. Why did she matter?

His own building was boarded up. Flame- and smoke-blackened streaks jutted from around windows and behind bright new plywood. Maybe he'd be able to get in today and get a few things. Dan had brought him some clothes and lent him a few dollars. And he'd managed to convince the DMV of his identity and gained a temporary license. He'd be able to get a bank card issued later today.

Not that that had helped much. He'd planned to take a small mortgage on the property to free up some cash, but...

He let the thought trail off.

Maybe he should go back to the hospital and try again. Casey might have had time to realize that he'd only been doing what he thought was right.

His sense of right and wrong blurred when it came to her. He couldn't remember setting out on such a mission ever before. He was a lover not a fighter, though 'love' might be pushing it a bit. Why was it they called guys who slept around lovers? He certainly hadn't loved any of the women he'd slept with. But what about Casey?

His gaze drifted back to the empty sidewalk in front of her building. Was she home yet?

He gave himself a mental shake. What difference did it make? She wasn't going to talk to him. Even if he hadn't gone after her ex-husband, she thought he'd tried to burn her building down. Thought he'd killed two men.

The line had dwindled and Kieran stepped up behind the two people who still waited at the coffee shop counter. He shouldn't care what Casey thought.

But he did.

When had that happened? He'd started out looking for a bit of fun, something for the here and now, something without a future. Somewhere along the way things had changed. All he could think about now was that future.

And how hard it would be to face it without her.

Chapter twenty-one

Kieran flipped the sign that read 'back in fifteen' up with his finger and stepped back from the door. He scanned the street in both directions, took in the charred remains of the bookshop next door and ground his teeth.

Exactly when had the fifteen minutes started?

The cardboard cup crumpled in his hand and he growled.

Now what? If he waited, he might not get to the rest of the places on his list this afternoon. If he didn't wait, the proprietor could return ten seconds after he left. He ran his hand through his wet hair and leaned back against the wall under the shelter of the awning. It didn't really matter. Fishing for rumors about the owners of burned out buildings gave him something to do.

He'd give them their fifteen minutes.

Cars lined the roadway as

drivers splashed their way home through the afternoon rush. The coolness from the stone building permeated his body, but calmed his frustration little. He should be making final preparations for his debut service at Tethys today. The grand opening. Instead he waited for someone who'd left his store unattended during business hours. Where was the justice in that?

Self pity had never been his style. He took a turn around the sidewalk to shake off the thoughts.

In the distance the sandwich board that alerted passersby to Casey's Karate school was conspicuously absent and he fought the urge to check on her. He would simply have to face facts. They were done. If she seriously believed he was an arsonist and murderer, she wasn't the one for him anyway.

So be it. Who needed the one when he could have the many?

A gust of wind sent him back under the awning and he tugged his collar up around his neck. Foot traffic hurried along the sidewalk in both directions. When his restaurant opened he could take advantage—he closed his eyes to derail that train.

Damn.

If the investigators would just look beyond him, they might find out what was really going on. Griffin had fixated on him from the beginning and that single vision had given the real firebug an open pass to the city.

Griffin was an idiot.

What was up with that guy anyway? Blind drunk on a city street. He was lucky that Kieran hadn't left him there. Some guys would have, some would have simply called the cops and been done with it.

Kieran smiled.

There would have been some irony in that or poetic justice—something. He leaned forward, checked the sidewalk and his watch then settled back against the wall. He shook the fresh rain from his hair and thought back to the morning. Why had Charlie been standing in the yard staring at those children? And what had been up with the lighter?

"Can I help you?" The high-pitched voice chased the firefighter out of Kieran's mind.

The short, stout woman in her fifties who struggled to unlock the door beside him didn't match the voice. He opened his mouth to speak, but had no idea of what to say. He'd intended to stroll in, look around and let the conversation come as a natural reaction to the burned-out building next door. He should have used the wait-time to firm up questions.

He hadn't even glanced at the sign outside long enough to imprint the type of business in his memory. Computers? Signs? Damn.

"Maybe I should be offering *you* the help." He smiled and reached for a bag from the overloaded woman's arms.

She hesitated then relinquished her hold and pushed into the store. The metallic taste of electrostatic touched his tongue as he inhaled the warmth of the room. The hum of equipment buzzed in his ears and the smell of ink assaulted his nostrils. A print shop.

"I wanted to check out your services." He placed the bag on the counter. If her prices appeared reasonable maybe he'd even find a local place to print his menus—

She rummaged around under the counter for a moment and handed him a pamphlet. "Look at this," she said. "I'll be back in a moment."

"Looks like a nasty fire next door," he called to her. "Guess the owner must be pretty upset."

"Ha!" The woman blustered through the curtains partitioning off the back room. Her flushed face suggested she'd sped through her business in the rear to return to him. "It's a wonder the place hasn't burned to the ground before. The thing's been a firetrap for years." She stopped, thought a second or two and handed him a different pamphlet.

"That's a more up-to-date list of services we offer. What is it you're interested in?"

"I have a restaurant down the road and—"

"Right," she blasted, interrupting him. "I know who you are, the seafood guy." Kieran smiled and nodded. "I planned to check you out this week."

"Sorry about that."

She knitted her eyebrows together and an odd expression passed across her face. "I'm sorry about your restaurant. They've got to get this guy soon."

"Yeah, I know what you mean. What I can't figure out is why he picked on my place."

"Doesn't seem to make sense down your way. I could see it here." Kieran raised his eyebrows and the woman leaned forward. "Some company owns most of this block. They proposed a casino and convention center complex, but it seems the heritage group won't let it go through." She straightened a few piles on the counter. "Something about preservation of old structures."

Interesting. Investigators seemed to think his finances were a great motivator for arson. He'd overheard something about the fires being typical of 'arson for profit' or something of the sort.

Hadn't the ex-head of the anti-heritage group had similar issues?

"So, what do you think?" the woman's bubbly voice bounced off the walls.

He brought his gaze to her and hesitated. "About what?" He followed her finger to the pamphlet in front of him and smiled. "Oh, I'll have to get back to you." He waved the paper her way before he pulled the door open. "Thanks for your help."

Slipping the folded paper into his pocket he glanced back down the street. He fought to keep his excitement at bay while he moved toward the next burned-out shell. His experience in these matters was all but nonexistent and his reasoning could be wrong. Still he couldn't keep the tingle from his limbs. Maybe he was stumbled onto something.

Casey stepped onto the dojo floor and made her way across to the front foyer and doors. Doctor's orders be damned. She was going to open the school. She'd been absent from classes for too many days. She wouldn't be able to do much, but she could at least check on things and gather some energy from her students. God knew she could use all she could get.

The cherry wood felt warm under her hand as she leaned against the doorjamb for support before continuing across the tiled entryway to the street entrance. Rain ticked at the window and practically bounced off the sidewalk. She twisted her key to release the lock and stepped to the right.

Coolness emanated as much from her mood as the window in front of her. What was she going to do? Everything was screwed up. Jim had gone off the deep end. Buildings were literally burning down all around her. Would the arsonist return at some point to finish the job he'd started with hers?

She shuddered and rubbed at the goose bumps on her arms.

And what about Kieran? She'd told Tory that she didn't believe he was the arsonist and that was true, but was she simply deluding herself? The arson investigators had their reasons for suspecting him after all. Still, he had been sleeping in her bed when she'd seen the guy outside.

She massaged her forehead, winced at the pain that bit from above the hairline. Stopped. Tears filled the corners of her eyes and she took a deep breath. She'd worked hard to condition herself, to build a reputation, to build a life. Now everything threatened to come tumbling down around her.

Casey sniffled and turned away from the street. She'd have none of those tears, none of this feeling sorry for herself. She'd made it through the turmoil of a bad marriage—and divorce as it was turning out. She could survive breaking up with a man she wasn't really even dating. All she had to do was get back into her routines. If she pretended the last couple of months hadn't happened, she'd believe it.

Eventually.

She shook the doubt away and grabbed her sandwich board advertiser and slid it toward the door. Business as usual. That was the ticket.

Suck it up and move on.

"Hi."

His voice was a mere whisper on the wind, but it took with it her new-found resolve and she let go of the hinged wooden sign. It toppled to the ground with a clatter and the river of rainwater parted around it.

"Didn't mean to startle you." Kieran bent to retrieve the sign and righted it.

His blond hair lay dark and wet against his head and his rain-soaked clothing clung to his body. He started toward her but stopped, stuffing a hand in his pocket. His green eyes pleaded with hers and she thought she might melt.

No. She straightened both physically and mentally, she couldn't—wouldn't—let him in.

So why wasn't she moving?

Breathe. Look away.

A bead of rain travelled down his nose before falling to the ground and she followed its progress. He swiped at it with the back of his hand, shrugged and looked upward as if he might duck under the drops.

"You shouldn't be out here." He slipped a hand under her elbow and escorted her inside her dojo. "You shouldn't be out of bed."

Shivers traveled the length of her at the contact. She started to lean in for more, realized it and tugged her arm away. She crossed the dojo entry. Distance was what she needed—and a solid desk between them.

He shook the rain out of his hair, ran his hands through and mussed it, releasing the curls at the back from the weight of the water. Dampness played with the natural wave to contour the hair into something out of GQ and as he slipped his fingers back into his pocket, Casey couldn't help following the movement.

She snapped herself upright. Must be the concussion.

Focus. He wasn't part of the routine.

"Don't tell me what I should and shouldn't do."

"I didn't mean—" Frustration sang on the heavy sigh and he coughed.

"Didn't mean what?" Damned concussion. She hadn't meant to say that out loud.

"Didn't mean to give a damn!" he snapped. He turned toward the door, yanked it open.

He gave a damn?

"Wait."

The scowl on his face when he looked back at her pushed all thought from her mind. She couldn't blame him for being angry.

"For what? For you to make up your mind?" He fought to control his anger, but the heat of it reddened his face. "Look lady, I've lost everything in the last week. My home, my business, my reputation." His knuckles whitened around the old fashioned door knob. "Hell, if I keep hanging out with you I'll probably end up in jail before the week is out."

"Are you saying this is my fault?"

"Well, it's all happened since I yanked you out of your building."

"Oh, right. An arsonist lights my building on fire and you rescue me and *I've* done something wrong. Of all the idiotic—"

She closed her mouth on the

statement. That's what the fire department was doing to *him*.

"The only idiotic thing I've done is get involved with you and your psychotic ex-husband. When you decide to put the past where it belongs honey, look me up." He strode through the door and into the rain.

Casey pressed the heels of both hands against her throbbing temples. What the hell had just happened?

Hell.

Kieran stormed across the sidewalk. Cold water rushed into his shoes and he stared down at the large puddle he'd stepped in.

"Figures." With the way things had gone inside, he was surprised the puddle hadn't been deeper.

All he'd tried to do was help. Well that's what he got for being a Good Samaritan. He should have just stayed in his little hovel and let everyone else—including her—figure out their own problems. From now on he'd stay out of everyone else's affairs. Let them fend for themselves.

He'd been doing fine on his own. He'd managed to get jobs under excellent chefs, worked in some of the best training kitchens in Europe and here at home. And all without emotional entanglements. Why had he broken his own rules with her?

He clenched his jaw and let out a long breath trying to chase the answer away without success.

He'd wanted an ally.

If she'd been on his side, he might have more pull with the Heritage Committee and slip his plans past. But instead he'd become so caught up in her that someone had yarded his dream right out from under him.

Had he blamed her for that? Was that why he'd yelled at her just now?

He ran his gaze up and down his building. Boards blocked most openings including the doorway that held once held the etched glass entrance doors. Rain streamed down his face and he shook his head.

Why?

What purpose could torching his building possibly serve anyone but him? He guessed that was the question investigators were asking. Water ran in streams down his face and neck, but he didn't move to stop it. He just stood and stared wondering what the hell he was going to do next.

He had no job. No money. And no destination in mind.

Was that how Charlie Griffin had felt that morning?

Kieran shook the thought away and tore the yellow caution tape in two then stepped into the alcove out of the rain. He dug his fingers in around the plywood barrier until he found a good hold and wrenched backward. A loud crack told of movement he couldn't see. Kieran propped a foot against the doorjamb for extra leverage and heaved again. The plank gave way with a bang and he pulled it away from the empty metal door frames.

The odor of wet drywall, wood, charcoal and something he couldn't quite put his finger on assaulted him as he crossed the threshold into the dining room. His lungs tightened. He spun in a circle taking in the destruction while he dug his puffer out of his jacket and drew on it.

"You okay?"

The break in the eerie silence startled him and he turned back toward the door. Casey.

"I'm fine." He took another hit of puffer. "Doc says another week of antibiotics and this thing." He shook it toward her then popped the contraption back into his pocket.

"You were lucky."

"I know, but..." He glanced round the ruins and worked his jaw. "It doesn't really feel like it."

"The sculpture survived." She dodged a few pieced of rubble on her way into the room.

"Yeah, but what good will it do now? Where will I put it?"

"You'll put it in Tethys."

He turned to her.

"When you rebuild." Her touch stopped his laughter cold and lit a fire under his skin.

"No. Tethys is done." His turn away from her broke contact and he immediately regretted.

"No, it's not."

"I'm done."

"Don't say that."

He shook his head and stared at Daniel's sculpture. The project had been plagued from the beginning. Limited approval. Construction delays. Funding problems. "It wasn't meant to be."

"Some dreams take more work. Perseverance and visualization are key."

Great. Eastern philosophy 101. Just what he needed. He smiled despite himself.

"Granted visualizing might be a little difficult right now." She righted a chair, but her pat of the seat cushion turned into more of a wet slap.

"You think?"

"Maybe just a little." Her eyes twinkled, but her hint of smile quickly vanished as her balance wavered.

He grabbed her elbow to steady her, twisted his mouth into a wry grin. So much for letting people fend for themselves.

"You really should be in bed." He braced himself for her protests.

"Your right."

He nearly fell over his jaw as they started toward the door.

"I'm sorry," she said as she let him guide her around a couple of upturned chairs. He started to wave her apology away, but stopped at her clouded expression. "No. Let me apologize." She waited to makes sure he wasn't going to interrupt. "I was so caught up in everything that was going on that I didn't take time to think about your side of things and I should have."

"You haven't exactly had an easy time."

"That's no excuse." She let out a breath.

"Let's get you upstairs," he said quietly as she sagged into him.

"Hey, Sensei." One of Casey's younger male students walked across the sidewalk in front of her toward the dojo door. "How're you feeling?"

Oh, God. Did everyone know what happened? She sighed and tried to keep the heat of embarrassment from her cheeks. "Fine, thanks. Have you been getting to class?"

"Yeah." The child beamed. "Last time, I got to spar with Sempei Aaron."

Aaron was a young black belt who helped teach the kid's classes.

Casey smiled. "You didn't go too easy on him, did you?"

He shook his head. "Nope, kicked his butt! Bye Sensei."

Before she could respond, the child was through the doors. Casey's waved at the parent, but her smile faded with the retreating taillights. The dull thud at her temples sharpened into an ache and she touched her forehead.

"You gonna make it?" Kieran's arm tightened around her waist and he shielded her from the pounding rain with his other hand.

"I can make it from here," she said as they stepped in front of her doors.

"I'll take you up."

"Really, I'm fine." But there was no energy in her protest.

"Fine? Doubtful. Going up alone? Definitely not." Mossy eyes bored into hers. "I'll see you up and inside."

Tory stormed across the sidewalk in front of them.

"Where the hell have you been?" she railed.

Casey touched a finger to her temple. "Could you yell at me a little quieter, please? My head is killing me."

"You're lucky *I* don't kill you, girl." Tory took the keys from Kieran's hand and stuffed the correct one in the door. "You promised me."

Casey hadn't—not technically, but she didn't think this was the time to mention it. "I'm okay." She touched her friend's shoulder. "Really. And I've been with Kieran practically the entire time." She looked to him for support.

He raised an eyebrow and she thought for a moment that he might abandon her, but he said, "We were just looking at the damage to my place."

Tory punched the elevator button. "I knew I shouldn't have left you. I can skip my class tonight."

"You go to class. I'll be fine. Kieran's here," Casey reassured.

"A fat lot of good that is. Traipsing a concussed woman through a ruined building. You don't have the sense God gave you." Tory's expression turned horrified. "You've done it, the two of you. My mother's words out of my mouth."

The elevator arrived and Tory blocked the closer to give Casey and Kieran enough time to get in. Kieran held Casey tightly with one arm and poked her floor button.

"You get into bed and stay there." Tory let the door go then changed her mind and jammed her hand back in. The doors retracted. "Alone." She stared daggers at Kieran.

Casey's laugh came out as a snort.

"What's so Goddamned funny?" Tory shot.

Casey shook her head and shrugged, trying to suppress her laughter.

"I mean it." Tory stormed off as the doors closed.

Kieran clicked his tongue. "Guess that means cookies are out."

Chapter twenty-two

Sirens pulled Casey from her slumber and she stumbled toward the kitchen. Kieran stood at the window already looking down toward the street. She touched his waist and he raised his arm to let her pass in front of him. Red flashes reflected off windows down the street, but no emergency vehicles were visible. Another siren grew louder as the fire truck passed on the street below.

"What's going on?" she asked and leaned back into his body for warmth.

"Looks like another fire." He draped his arms over her shoulders. "You feel better?"

The clock read two-twenty. She'd gone for a nap at four-thirty. Kieran had awoken her periodically through the evening, but she'd rolled over and gone back to sleep.

"Yes. Guess I needed some sleep." She laughed.

"You hungry," he whispered,

brushing her hair with a kiss.

Her stomach gurgled. When was the last time she'd eaten? She nodded. "There's not much around here."

"Not to worry." He glanced down at her. "Tory stopped by and I snuck out to get some supplies."

"Tory stopped by?"

"Around nine-thirty. After her class."

"Why didn't you wake me up?"

"Are you kidding me? She'd probably have kicked my ass if I tried."

He tugged her gently toward him, brushed a kiss over her hair and headed for the kitchen. Casey's smile faded as she gazed back out the window. Had the arsonist struck again? She rubbed at her arms and turned away. She didn't want to think about it now.

Casey slipped onto one of the stools at the breakfast bar and leaned her forehead against her hand. Kieran immediately stopped what he was doing.

"You all right?"

"I'm fine. *Really*." She dropped the forearm to the breakfast bar and leaned forward. "I'm just getting tired of being woken up by sirens."

Kieran glanced in direction of

the lights. "I know what you mean."

He pulled a pristine pan off its hook and inspected it. "Have you ever used this?"

She cocked her head and shrugged. "I don't think so."

"Not that I'm complaining." He put the pan on top of the stove and surveyed the kitchen. "But why go to all the expense if you don't use it."

A smile. "My grandmother insisted. She said that at some point I'd find a man I wanted to cook for—or better yet, one who'd cook for me."

"Wise woman."

"Yeah, she was."

She watched in awe while Kieran brought her kitchen to life. Once he had the oven heating, he coated the pan with olive oil, lightly seasoned a single thick steak and placed it in the pan. He grabbed another pan from rack, admired its pristine state and eyeballed her a moment before setting it over the flame of her gas stove. In this pan he added a dollop of butter, finely chopped green stuff and a clove of garlic he smashed with his knife.

"It's just you and me..."

He cocked a brow her way and she shut up. He whistled as he added something to the sizzling pan and stirred. He seemed to drink the smell then deftly slid down the counter to chop another item. Muscles flexed through the tight lines of his shirt and she battled the temptation to run her fingers along the hills. She followed the line of his tight jeans down his leg to his bare feet, then back up to settle on his bottom. He turned around and gave her an embarrassing, though outstanding, view of his package. He coughed.

"My eyes are up here." His tone dripped disgust, but the eyes she met were filled with humor. "Women! Just can't keep their minds to themselves."

She giggled. "Did Charlie call?"

He tensed slightly then shook his head. "No."

She nodded and bit her lip. Charlie hadn't been himself lately. He'd been out of touch, missing classes. He hadn't behaved like this in ages. Not since the death of his son sent him into a downward spiral. Why had the behavior resurfaced now? Why hadn't he talked to her?

The answer was standing right in front of her. She curled her bottom lip under her teeth. If she hadn't been so consumed in her own life—

No. He'd turned up the other night when she'd called for help. She held a corner of her lip between her teeth and let the rest curl out.

And he'd made it there in record time. How had he gotten there so fast?

The sputtering coffee maker drew her back to the kitchen and she crossed to pull a cup from the tree. "Coffee?"

"Please."

Casey filled two cups and she placed one on the counter beside Kieran. A few pieces of stolen veggie popped into her mouth earned her a sideways glance and Kieran pulled her close. He planted a kiss on her cheek then winked at her. She leaned back against the counter.

Was the change in Charlie a symptom of something else, something darker or simply a reaction to her dating Kieran? She had no way to know. And not knowing gnawed at her. He'd been such a good friend, helped her through her divorce and some of the toughest moments of her adult life.

"If it helps any he was alive when I left him this...uh, yesterday, morning."

Her eyebrows shot up.

His eyes nearly rolled out of their sockets. Clearly he hadn't meant to say anything.

"I took him back to his place the other night. He was tanked, nearly got himself killed by a passing car."

Her shoulders slumped. Her worst fear true. She'd let him down.

"I got him settled and fell asleep on the couch. That's why I didn't get back to the hospital."

Oh, God. She'd been angry with him and he'd simply been ensuring Charlie's safety. She chased the guilt with a swig of coffee.

"It was kind of strange though."

She looked up. "What was?"

"Well in the morning, he was just standing in the pouring rain looking at some kids playing next door." He drew his brows together as he remembered. "And then when I was leaving, he stood there flicking this lighter I gave him."

"You gave him a lighter?"

"I thought it was his, he said no..."

What the hell?

"Can I take care of that for you?"

"Hmmm?" She knit her brow in confusion.

"Your lip. You chew it every time you get worried." He stepped across and gathered her into an embrace. "I'm sure he's fine."

"You're probably right." She bit her lip again.

Kieran leaned down and brushed her lips with his once, twice and lingered longer on the third. He explored quickly and came away with her lip gently secured between his teeth. He let it go and rested his forehead against hers, careful to avoid the damage.

"Tasty. I can see why you eat it."

Something sizzled on the stove and she giggled. "Not as tasty as that."

"I don't know." He slid down the counter to tend to the stove. "We could continue our taste test."

"But you might get distracted and burn something."

"Bite your tongue." He flipped the contents of the pan with a few rapid flicks of his wrist and slid back to her. "Better yet, let me do it."

The off and on rain was off again as Kieran and Casey neared the fire scene.

"What a time for the rain to stop." She held a palm up to the sky.

Kieran pulled her closer to him, draped his arm around her shoulders to give her warmth. Coming out here at this time of night had been stupid, but she'd insisted. She needed to see Griffin.

Kieran could care less if he saw the man again, but he'd agree to almost anything to chase the worry from her face. She'd put up a good front during the meal, but he could see her concern every time she looked away from him.

Reflections of light from the streetlamps danced in her eyes and she inhaled the fresh air. Wind blew the smoke westward and she appeared energized and almost happy.

"You okay?" he asked.

"Um-hum."

Her arm tugged at his middle, to pull him closer as they moved down the street toward the gathered crowd. The murmur of voices grew louder and he could see the police barricade set in the street. As they got closer even the favorable wind couldn't keep the acrid smell of burnt material from their nostrils. Kieran's lungs tightened.

"Ugh." Casey covered her mouth with her sleeve and coughed. "My place didn't even smell this bad."

Kieran laughed. "Yes, it did. You were just too busy choking to notice."

She extracted her arm from his waist and elbowed him in the ribs. His hand shot to the point of contact. She must be feeling better.

Heat from the fire reached them before they rounded the corner and flames came into view. The three story structure was fully engulfed and it seemed the firefighters had resigned themselves to managing the flames, keeping them from neighboring structures if possible.

Water sprayed anew and steam rose from hot bricks and wood. Firefighters worked unaware, or so it appeared, of their audience, hauling hoses, barking orders, chopping away at the flames. One man moved toward Kieran and Casey, pulling his shield away. Violent coughs brought him forward, head down as he seemed to fight for air.

Her hand slipped into Kieran's and she gripped tightly. Her eyes stayed with the firefighter, but her expression remained a bland contrast to the trembles that resonated through her hand and up his arm. He stepped behind her to wrap his arms around her shoulders. Her hands sought his again as she leaned back against him. Within moments, the shaking subsided.

"Unit two?" The crackly voice came over a firefighter's radio.

"Two." An answer from another unseen party.

"Bring another hose around to Front; seven-eighty-five, we need ..." Static ate the rest of the statement.

Seven hundred block of Front Street. Something familiar about that. What was it?

Someone had mentioned a group of buildings an owner wanted to demolish to build some new complex. Where had he heard it? He wracked his memory following his path over the last few days.

The printer.

What was it she'd said exactly?

No matter. If the bookshop and printer were in the seven hundred block of Columbia, their buildings backed on this one and would make this the second structure to fall victim to the arsonists flame.

He grabbed Casey's hand.

"Come on."

Confusion rushed Casey's brain, but she followed Kieran across down the street toward the barricade. What the heck was he up to? Where was he taking her and why? Behind them the crowds and emergency personnel attended to the fire. The whoosh of all-consuming flame and sizzle of cool water as it contacted heated timbers continued behind them.

"Where are we going?"

"I have an idea." He didn't hesitate or even glance in her direction.

She tugged back, unwilling to be dragged along any farther. He stopped, looked back at her, the confusion clear in his features.

"Where are we going?" she repeated. This time her tone held more a demand than a question.

"I had a conversation with a woman who worked in a print shop around here. It was next to the bookshop." He pointed the direction they were travelling. He squinted into the distance. "I'm sure it's right around the corner."

"It is." Casey agreed. "So?"

"Do you know who owns it?"

"No." She shook her head. "But I have the title search documents back at my condo." Light danced in his eyes despite the late hour. "I see where you're going."

He nodded. "To your place."

Chapter twenty-three

Kieran squinted after the pickup truck that pulled away from the curb as he and Casey neared her front door. Where had he seen it before? He reached above Casey's head to hold the door open for her and followed the taillights into the distance. No matter. It would come to him.

"I'm pretty sure both of those buildings were on the heritage roles." Casey pushed the call button.

"And if someone wanted to develop the place, he'd need the entire block."

"Definitely." The elevator doors opened and they stepped into the box. "And if they wanted new construction—"

"They'd have to get rid of those buildings," he finished the statement with her.

Straight lines of concentration hardened her face slightly and Kieran slipped loose strands of hair behind her ear. She followed his finger around her ear with hers.

"You okay?" he asked.

She nodded and stepped of the elevator through the foyer to her door. He watched her a moment then followed. She seemed somehow taller, stronger. She moved with determination.

She glanced over her shoulder at him as she moved into the condo, flashed a smile. "I can check my computer for records of application to the committee, but if the developer didn't go that route, we'll have to back to the planning department in the morning."

Casey's athletic body swayed as her curves softened the geometric shapes of the late Victorian architecture of her hallway. He followed the lines up to her golden blond hair and back down over her curving hips then pulled his gaze away. He'd have to save that road for later.

She pulled a laptop out from under the counter and opened the lid. The screen flickered on. She clicked through a number of screens, read some pages. Stopped. Read some more. Bit her lip. He stepped up behind her to read over her shoulder.

Damn she smelled good. He gave himself a shake.

Focus.

"Anything?"

"Yes, a name. Well, numbers actually." She sent something to the printer, picked the pages up and leaned into him so that he could see.

Her shoulder brushed his lower body and the incidental contact sent a shockwave through him. He clamped his jaw. What the hell was the matter with him? He was acting like a sex-starved teenager. He shifted away and bent down beside her to focus on the document. The scent of her shampoo conspired against him and he had to fight to keep from burying his nose in her hair.

"Right here." Oblivious to his torture, she pointed to a section on the page.

He gave himself a mental slap and focused on the black text. A numbered company. Not as much help as he hoped. Still, at least it was something.

Casey whispered the numbers aloud. Hesitated and mouthed them again. She gnawed at her thumbnail a second then switched to her lip curl. She mouthed the numbers again, massaged her temples. This woman should never play poker.

"There's something familiar...I just can't place it." She grunted in frustration. "We're close. I feel it, but..."

"Don't worry. We'll figure it

out tomorrow."

He reached over her shoulders and pulled her up into his arms. She leaned into him, wrapped her arms around his waist and nestled herself into his chest. Her heavy sigh told him her mind still puzzled things and he ran his hand down her hair attempting to calm the thoughts. He planted a kiss on her head, then rested his cheek against her hair. The electricity from her touch on his hand stood his hair on end and travelled down his body.

God, but he wanted her.

She lifted her face toward him. Her eyes held a milky mix of confusion and concentration. But below that smoldered something more.

Desire?

Was it his desire reflected there?

His response to her closeness conspired to send him over the edge, but against his better judgment, he pulled her closer. Her lips parted and she shifted. Did she feel it too or was she simply responding to his hardness?

Yes, that was it.

He was transferring his desires, his hopes, his needs to her. He couldn't—wouldn't—take advantage. She'd been through too much lately. She needed to deal and to heal. Their time would come after the arsonist was taken care of and the shadow of doubt no longer hung over Kieran's head.

Once she was safe, they could explore the relationship.

If, in fact, this was a relationship.

His heart skipped a beat and his chest tightened. Where had that come from?

They'd been enemies in the beginning. Would they return there after all of this was done?

Her eyes twinkled up at him. They'd come too far.

"What's wrong?" Casey stepped back.

"Nothing." He shook his head and walked toward the window.

Lights from across the river highlighted the hilly terrain against the almost black water. Large vessels appeared like silhouettes against the glow of the Surrey Fraser Docks. Fate brought him to her, but for what purpose?

To add a new dimension to his life?

Or to play a cruel joke?

Her arms slipped up around his waist, up to caress his chest. He placed his hand over hers. Her reflection blurred by the old window glass revealed her concern. He lifted his arm and turned to pull her into an embrace. Their lips met briefly and all questions fled from his mind.

Tomorrow was a world away.

Today, they were together.

Today, he loved her.

Urgency lingered behind the tender touch of Kieran's lips against hers and heat flushed Casey's body. His feathery touch drew tingles as he moved over her shoulders, down her back and up to her sides. She inhaled when his thumbs ran along the sides of her breasts and a tiny moan escaped.

Was that her?

He pulled back, brushed her hair away from her neck and peppered it with light kisses. His eyes burned a pathway to hers and they deepened three shades. He cupped her cheek in his hand, massaging the skin just below her ear. She closed her eyes.

Shivers shook her as his hot breath met the moist trail left by his lips. He smiled into her neck as he found it again, nibbled his way back up to her mouth. His lips crushed hers and she opened to him, his hungry tongue seeking, probing. Excitement jolted through her body. Her weak knees caused her to grip him tighter and he pulled even closer. He lifted her off the floor before he broke the kiss.

Casey's heart quickened with the intensity in his eyes. Kieran spun her round, set her down onto the stool, touched his forehead to hers. His breath came in ragged spurts as if he'd run a mile. He took a few steadying breaths and shifted to the stool beside her.

He seemed to be fighting for control, but she was having none of that. She twisted on the stool, grabbed his shirt and pulled him in between her legs.

"You aren't getting off that easy."

She tangled her fingers into his hair and pulled him in for another kiss. He clasped her bottom in his hands and pulled her up against his erection.

"Honey, you make getting off very easy."

She flushed and he swallowed her giggles with his mouth. When he inched backward, she found his belt loop and pulled him back closer, pressing herself against him. He growled, steadied himself and shoved hard against her.

His T-shirt lifted easily from his waist band and heat kissed her fingertips as she explored his muscular curves, followed the lines up his back. He shivered under her touch as she tugged the shirt upward. Their lips parted long enough to shed the t-shirt and she tossed it aside. She ran her fingers along over the muscular mounds to his nipples and gave a gentle squeeze.

She replaced her fingertips with her lips then trailing her tongue across his taut skin and around his hardened nipple. He shivered, arching his back, lifting his head toward the ceiling a low noise rumbling from his throat. Breathing hard, he grabbed her shoulders and pulled back.

He lifted her from the stool and she wrapped herself around his waist, his mouth finding hers again before they tumbled onto the couch. The weight of him on top of her brought violent shudders that shook her anew with each button he unfastened. A sly smile played across his lips before he unclasped her bra, freeing her breasts. He took her breast into his mouth.

She ran her fingers through his hair and along his upper back as his tongue danced around her nipples, first one, then the other, playing with each until she thought she might lose it. He shifted, parted her legs with one knee and settled himself in her cradle. He took a moment to stare down into her eyes, before claiming her mouth once again.

Her hand found his waistband and followed it round to the button that held him in place and she freed him. She slid her hand round him and her juices flowed at the size of his hardness.

He gasped as she began massaging him and his hand quickly covered hers, stopping the motion. She flushed, almost giggled, but his hands on her waist robbed her of all breath. The button and zipper of her pants came open and fire shot behind his eyes as he pulled back to look at her.

Good God. He was getting bigger.

He found the sweet spot between her legs and smiled as he slipped a finger up inside of her. She groaned and arched upward. He claimed her mouth with renewed vigor, thrusting his tongue inside again and again, sweeping it over hers in time with his fingers. Her heart nearly pounded through her ribs as she teetered on the edge of spasms.

He stopped, pulled back to caress her hair. His gentle kisses touched her upper body and he slid off the couch to kneel on the floor. He shifted her to the front, tugged at her pants to pull them down away from her feet. Kisses teased the inside of her thighs already wet with excitement. She arched her back toward him, slid down the couch and he drew his tongue across her lower abdomen and into her wet mound.

Again, he explored, his tongue lashing along, around and into her folds. His thumb found her nub of desire and massaged until she cried out.

When she opened her eyes she gasped at the beauty of his body, backlit by the lamp across the room. He loomed above her in his nakedness, his muscular frame sported curves and lines in all the right places. As he readied himself to take her, her loins pulsed with excitement.

Had she ever wanted anything this much?

He perched himself on the edge of her, hesitated.

What the hell was he doing? She lifted her knees opening wider, hoping to entice him inward. Yet, he waited. Was he trying to drive her mental?

She shifted under him and he breached her rim and plunged into her well. He retracted and plunged again, this time she lifted her hips to meet him. That seemed to be his undoing and he thrust in again and again. He covered her mouth with his, pulled back to her edge and slammed in again. Once. Twice. Again and again until her whimpers became cries of ecstasy and he pulsed with her.

A walk signal cuckooed from below and Kieran shifted.

"Don't," Casey groaned.

He smiled. She'd kept her legs wrapped tightly round him, not letting him move hoping to prolong the contact.

He propped himself up on one elbow to look down into her eyes. Her golden blond hair jutted in every direction and he combed it back from her face. He brushed the crinkles on her forehead with his lips and pulled back.

"Are you okay?"

"Do you really have to ask that?" She lifted a brow.

"Well, you know, your concussion."

She snorted. "A little late to worry about that now."

He frowned.

"I'm fine." She cocked her head to one side, opened her mouth to say something else and stopped. Her body tensed. "What was that?"

"I didn't hear anything."

She listened a minute, frowned and shrugged. "I'm probably just paranoid."

"Little wonder." He shifted off of her and she groaned. "We had to move sometime."

Another sound preempted her response.

"I heard it too."

Another noise echoed up between her building and his.

"Sounds like...rolling glass."

Casey relaxed and Kieran rested his head against her shoulder. "Probably some idiot chucking a bottle from his car."

Breaking glass and a whoosh filled the silence and he closed his mouth, scrambled up off the couch. The strong smell of gasoline was quickly replaced by smoke as he reached the bank of windows.

"Oh my God!" His jaw dropped wide.

She rushed to his side, staring down as he was at the smoke billowing from the basement storefront of his building. The side windows glowed amber with hungry flames. Casey snatched the handset from the coffee table and dialed nine-one-one.

"Un-frickin-believable," he said and slammed the window closed..

What next?

Chapter twenty-four

Steam rose from the still-hot coals. The stench of wet burnt lumber hung on the air. Kieran stood on the sidewalk staring at the shell that was once his building. Casey's heart ached for him and she stepped forward clasping his hand in hers. He glanced her direction, lifted his arm over her shoulder and pulled her into a brief embrace. He kissed the top of her head, then let her go to walk up to the barrier erected to keep non-emergency personnel out.

Kate West, who lived on the third floor of Casey's building, placed a hand on her shoulder. "You guys need anything?"

"No, thanks Kate." Casey's smile was a feeble attempt.

Through the rubble, the wrought iron sculpture, supposed to represent heaven and bring Kieran prosperity, held fast to the one of two remaining walls. The Celtic horse seemed to laugh at their misery. If she could pull it from the wall, she would. Kieran stared in the same direction. Had he the same thought? She stepped up to his side again.

Engineers stood on the sidewalk and surveyed the structure's exterior, jotting notes on clipboards. Firefighters remained inside with the Forensic Identification Section engaged in a search for indications of cause. Early morning sky showed through a second floor window at the back of the building. Two walls and most of the floors were gone.

A hand touched Casey's shoulder and she spun around. "Charlie," she said, startled. "What's up?"

Soot blackened one side of Charlie's nose and spotted his gear. The yellow helmet showed signs of heavy use and his expression was nearly as battered. He removed a glove and extended a hand toward Kieran.

"There's nothing to salvage." Charlie's hoarse voice cracked and he glanced past Kieran into the structure. "Except maybe that sculpt—" Static cut him off as someone spoke over the radio. "I'll be back."

A flurry of activity followed and Charlie pushed past toward the entrance while he mumbled into his mike. He ducked under the tape and disappeared toward another firefighter. Two more men met them at a pile of rubble half-way to the building's rear. Charlie spoke, then pointed at an object under the pile. A white coverall clad forensics officer exited the building. The firefighters backed away.

"What is that all about?" Kieran asked.

Casey shrugged. "Don't know."

The forensics officer popped the trunk of his car and removed two cases, one silver, one black and reentered the structure. His white coveralls cut a stark contrast against fire blackened walls as he extracted a camera and flash from the silver case. The second officer joined his colleague and grabbed the black case.

"They must've found something."

"Yeah, but what?" Casey added.

She slipped into the space in front of Kieran to watch the emergency crew's actions. Flashes signaled photos from every direction. Charlie spoke into his radio, then glanced their direction, but made no move toward them. He shifted his gaze to the photographer who snapped numerous shots before Charlie stepped carefully around the rubble pile wrapping yellow caution tape around the site. The two forensics officers moved closer to him to engage in some discussion, then the camera flashed anew from a few specific angles. What were they looking at?

Kieran's body was warm behind her as she leaned into him. They'd spent most of the wee hours out on the street, watching, waiting. The fire department expended great effort controlling the blaze, but it had been too late. Over-extended by the other fire, Kieran's building had been fully engulfed by the time they got there. There'd been little hope of anything left in the morning.

Arms came around her shoulders to drape her like a cape as Kieran's chin came to rest on her head. She linked her fingers through his and he shifted his head to bring his cheek down beside hers. She leaned into the contact, ran one hand along the side of his face and neck. When her fingers found knots of tension, she gave a gentle massage. He pulled her tighter into him.

"Thanks for being here," he whispered.

"Where else would I be?"

"I don't know. Anywhere but here."

Was that defeat she heard in his voice? She bumped him with her hip. "Look on the bright side," She quipped and he frowned.

"They know you didn't do this."

He nodded. "True."

"And I don't have to deal with the Heritage Committee anymore."

"Good thing. I heard the chairperson can be quite unreasonable."

She elbowed him in the ribs and laughed.

Nothing of consequence seemed to arise from the investigation. She turned to Kieran and tugged his shirt.

"Why don't we go inside? These investigations sometimes take weeks."

The only reason the engineers arrived so quickly was the instability of the structure. With her building, they'd ensured it wouldn't fall down and then left her and the other residents hanging for another week before they'd cleared it for occupancy. Someone told her that she'd been lucky it was done that quickly.

"I wish someone would just come out and talk to us?"

Casey tugged at his arm. "When they can, they will." She pulled the copy of the title search paper from her pocket. "Maybe we should try to get this to Charlie and head back upstairs."

"Maybe you're right." He clenched his jaw. "It just makes me angry. We're right back where we started. Only this time," he paused and looked up at the façade of his building. "Everything is gone."

"Not everything."

"What's left besides a sculpture that they might not even be able to get off the wall without it toppling."

"You are."

He stopped, thought on that a

moment.

"And you have me. We'll get through this together."

She leaned next to him against the planter he used for support. She slipped her hand into the crook of his elbow and leaned her head against his shoulder. When his arm didn't come around to pull her close, chills ran down her spine. He shrugged away from the contact, turning his back on the fire scene. She bit her lip.

"Thing is, I don't even know why." His clipped words revealed his anger. "Once? It might be coincidence. But twice. The guy had it in for me."

He had a point. His was the only place to be hit twice.

There must be some reason. "It seems personal, doesn't it?"

He nodded, returned to her side.

Casey curled her lip under her teeth. "Even if some of the buildings were torched to draw attention away from the actual target, that was accomplished the first time." Concentration furrowed his brows, but she resisted the urge to caress the frown away and continued.

"Exactly." He shook his head. "So the second time was personal. But who did I get on the wrong side of and how?"

"I guess that's the million dollar question."

He yawned and rubbed his face with his hand. He cradled his forehead in his hand for a long moment before he turned his gaze toward her.

"We should get you upstairs and into bed." He leaned in to kiss her forehead then winked. "Doctor's orders and all."

"Good linc," she said. "Do you usually find it effective?"

"Usually." He cocked an eyebrow.

An unmarked police car slid to a noisy stop behind them and two men hopped out. Another car pulled up seconds later. A woman spoke into a radio, then exited. The three stopped about ten feet down the sidewalk where Charlie came out to meet them. The group conversed in low tones and glanced back toward the pile of rubble in what was Kieran's restaurant. As the huddle broke Charlie glanced toward her; held a finger up.

"Guess we better wait a minute." Kieran sat on the planter edge, letting his feet dangle.

Casey hopped up beside him and his arm came around her shoulders to pull her closer. She nuzzled herself into the crook of his shoulder.

Yawned. She leaned against Kieran and rubbed her eyes. He kissed the top of her head.

"Do you want to go up? I can wait for Charlie."

She sat up, shook her head. "I'm fine." She smiled up at him and let herself fall back against his body. His warmth enveloped her, she closed her eyes.

"I guess I owe you an apology...and my thanks."

Casey drew a sharp breath and sat up. Had she fallen asleep? She hadn't heard Charlie's approach. The firefighter's hand was extended toward Kieran who hesitated a moment before retracting his arm from around Casey and taking it.

"No problem," he said.

Charlie's eyebrows shot up. "I wouldn't blame you if you did have a problem."

"You were just doing your job." Casey gazed up at Kieran but couldn't tell if he really forgave so easily or was simply paying lip service.

"Not very well." Charlie drew his mouth into a grim line and looked at Casey. "Dina and I are splitting." He glanced around nervously. "I didn't take it very well."

Her heart sunk. They'd worked so hard and come so far.

Casey pulled him into a hug. "I'm sorry, Charlie. I thought you guys were going to make it."

"Yeah, me too." Charlie glanced away, drew a heavy breath and shuffled his feet.

That might explain the strange behavior. It certainly explained why he was sleeping in the garage apartment. "You okay now?"

He nodded. "Honest," he added when she eyeballed him.

"So how long are they going to be?" She let him off the hook for the moment.

"No telling." She yawned and he tapped her knee. "You should be in bed."

"Gotta be where the excitement is." She spoke through a second yawn.

"Excitement?" He laughed aloud. "Nothing going on here but a bunch of sampling, shifting and more sampling." He shifted his weight. "It looks like we might be able to salvage the sculpture, but the engineers aren't guaranteeing anything yet."

"You might want to take a look at this." Casey held the document out toward him.

Charlie took the sheet of paper from Casey. Read it. Looked up in question. "What am I looking at?"

She circled the area in question with her finger. "Two buildings in the same block have been destroyed by fire."

"I spoke to a tenant there and she said she wouldn't be surprised if the owner commissioned the fires," Kieran said.

Casey continued, "And I seem to remember a petition for a development—"

"'She said', 'I seem to remember'..." The firefighter looked from Kieran to her and shook his head. "We need a little more than that." He folded the paper and slipped it into his pocket. "Still, I'll check it out." He nodded at Kieran. "Where you going to be?"

"Well, I think my place is out." Kieran smirked.

Charlie touched Casey's shoulder. "Take care of her," he said as he gave Kieran's hand another shake. "She should be in bed." He turned toward the crime scene, pulled his protective gloves on, then stopped. "Resting."

A flush heated her cheeks but she laughed as Kieran pulled her up off the planter.

Rhythmic respiration fell on Kieran's ears when he emerged from sleep on the bed next to Casey. The scent of her enveloped him and he reached a hand to her hair. She stirred, shifted her position to face him, but didn't wake. He ran a finger down the impression left on her face by a crease in her pillow case. She curled her jeans-clad legs up and rested her head on her hands. Life would be good if he could stay there beside her forever.

Light filtered through the curtains into his eyes as he pulled himself up off the bed and gazed out where his building had once stood. He ran a hand through his hair, rubbed sleep from his eyes and massaged his face.

He didn't get it. Why had the arsonist struck his building twice?

The red numbers on her clock told him it was already past one in the afternoon. Casey still slept soundly and his mental fussing would only wake her. He pushed off the bed. A splash of cold water might clear his thoughts. Then again, maybe a cup of coffee would be better. He adjusted the blanket over her and headed for the door.

With the coffee brewing he wandered to the window. From this vantage, the carnage was unmistakable. Two of the walls had tumbled almost completely inward when the inner floors and supports disintegrated under the flames. Half the nearest wall and part of the back remained standing, but barely. He was sure they'd bring diggers in to finish the rest.

Coffee maker gurgles drew his attention as the machine sputtered and spat out the beverage. He grabbed a cup from the tree. What was he going to do now?

The steady hum of appliances kept him company as he downed the dark liquid. Warmth passed through his veins and a strange sense of comfort washed over him. He supposed that he should be thankful. The second go at his building had in essence cleared him of suspicion, but he'd have to get past the anger first.

He spun around at the breakfast bar, putting his back to the working part of the room. Artwork broke the warm red walls and small knickknacks brought a little of Casey's personality to the room. He picked up a tiny terracotta pot and twisted the plant in his hands. Child-like decorations spelled out Sensei. He smiled and set it back.

Her grandmother's ink-sketch of the building hung as the centerpiece flanked by two views of similar architecture. He sipped at his coffee and inspected it more closely. Charlotte Michaelson. Casey's grandmother. Above the archway, intertwined among the brick accents enclosing the door were the numbers denoting the month and day of her marriage. Curled under the signature more numbers commemorated Casey's birth. Kieran smiled and drained his cup.

He would have liked to meet the woman who had such a huge impact on Casey. She must have been a strong person. Casey never spoke of any other family member. Yet when she spoke of her grandmother, she sparkled. He smiled. Not quite the relationship he'd had with his grandfather, but in an odd way, similar. The old man had known him better than anyone else. Even in death, his grandfather had pushed him; egged him on.

He refilled his cup and leaned against the counter facing the window. If the old man only knew the trouble his building caused. Anger welled and Kieran spun away from the view. Casey's things; her knickknacks and mementos brought him back to himself. If it hadn't been for the old man, Kieran wouldn't be standing in this kitchen so near the woman he loved. He sighed and leaned on the counter, played with a pad of paper.

The woman he loved. Like a phoenix risen from the ashes.

He spun the pad absently then stopped it. Numbers. Casey had rearranged the numbers numerous times trying to find a recognizable pattern in the holding company's name. Given the wild scratches across her attempts, she'd given up. He picked up the pad, took another sip of coffee and tossed the pad back onto the counter. It skittered across and onto the floor and as he bent to retrieve it, the building sketch caught his eye once again.

What were those numbers?

He lay the framed sketch down on the counter next to the pad. All but four numbers. Huh. What did that mean? He tossed the pad back onto the counter and took another sip of coffee.

Probably nothing.

But what if...?

He set his coffee cup on the counter and headed for Casey's bedroom.

Three steps down the hallway, he stopped himself. After everything that had happened between him and Jim, Casey would never forgive him if he were wrong.

No. He grabbed his jacket off the back of his chair and headed for the door.

He had to be sure.

Chapter twenty-five

When his rap on the construction trailer's door once again went unanswered, Kieran opened the door and stepped inside. Empty. The site was bustling with activity and he cast a glance both directions outside before letting the door close behind him. It wouldn't do to have someone catch him in the act, especially Jim Taylor.

A counter ran three-quarters of the length of one wall to a desk at the far end. Unrolled plans covered the counter and top of the desk and still more peeked out from a box in the corner. Plastic and metal containers leaned this way and that between two tall filing cabinets on the opposite wall.

Rhythmic beeps and transmission clanks took his attention back outside where a construction worker flagged a delivery truck backward. Other workers looked on from the open first floor of the cement high rise under construction on the site. Kieran turned back to the room. Though the errand that brought him there was probably a fool's, the unoccupied trailer gave him the opportunity to find out for sure.

Kieran perused the desk's contents quickly, trying hard not to skew the original layout of the papers too noticeably. Bills. Permits. Purchase orders. But nothing under the holding company's name. He lifted a heavy rock paperweight and shifted a few more papers. All were addressed to Jim Taylor or Taylor Contracting. A quick search of the two desk drawers yielded similar results and he began to doubt strength of his suspicions.

But Jim was definitely in financial trouble. An increasing number of red overdue and final notice stamps decorated the paperwork the further Kieran dug into the drawers.

He glanced out the window and rubbed his chin. Money and jealousy. Two strong motivators. Still, he needed a stronger connection between Casey's ex and the holding company if he were going to take his suspicions to the authorities.

The numbers might be pure coincidence. And given his connection to the guy's ex-wife, Kieran couldn't take the chance.

He shifted his search to the filing cabinets, but found nothing out of the ordinary other than a six pack of beer and a twenty-six ounce bottle of rye. But come to think of it, he should have expected nothing less from Jim. He closed the metal drawer and turned his attention to the plans on the counter.

Everything was as it should be. Electrical. Plumbing. Engineering. Unit divisions. Every page related to the project currently under construction on the site. No connection to the holding company or some mystery project.

"Damn," the sound of his voice startled him and he glanced nervously out the window.

No sign of anyone approaching.

He frowned, dropped down into the chair behind the desk and spun away from the door.

Maybe it *was* coincidence. Maybe he'd wanted it to be Jim just so he could hate the man all the more. Not that he really needed any more reason. He should have checked with Casey before he'd come down here.

Four numbers could make a huge difference, skew the meaning entirely. They could have even been assigned and have nothing at all to do with anyone or anything in the company. Still...

Perhaps he should wait and try to bluff Jim, see what he drew out of him. Maybe the guy would even throw a punch or two and give Kieran an excuse. Kieran leaned back in the chair getting friendly with the image. Casey's face popped into his mind and he straightened in the chair.

Maybe not.

As he shifted to stand, he caught sight of a corner of paper tucked behind rolls of others. He pulled the rolls away from the wall and tilted his head sideways to get a better look.

What was this?

An artist's rendering of a large complex, complete with multilevel base and high-rise above was tucked neatly away behind everything else.

Kieran fished in the box of plans beside it, couldn't get a good look and tugged a heavy roll upward. A smaller roll slid from the middle and knocked hollowly on the trailer floor. He set the bigger one aside and unrolled the smaller one, flattening it on the desktop.

His heart sped up.

Pay dirt.

The plans showed preliminary sketches of the complex in the artist's rendering and in the corner along with the architectural information was the company name—or rather numbers. Kieran's smile was anything but happy.

He knew it.

Kieran dove into the box searching for more treasure as boot-steps thundered up the outside stairs. Jim moved in through the door.

"What are you doing here?" Jim's gaze fell on the plans across the desk.

Kieran picked up the drawings and threw them at him. "Interesting development you have in mind."

"That's . . . that's none of your business."

Jim set aside the bag he carried and straightened the crinkled plans. Kieran spied the gold-wrapped top of a bottle protruding from the paper bag. He lifted the bottle and spun it around. Champagne.

"Celebrating something?" Kieran rounded the desk. "Did you really think you'd get away with it?"

"I, uh . . . I don't know what you mean." Jim snatched the bottle and smiled hesitantly. "We just got awarded a big contract." He glanced round Kieran toward the desk. "I'm sure I have some clean cups here somewhere. If you want to join—"

Kieran blocked Jim's progress, moving right and left with him. The contractor dropped his hands to his sides; turned his gaze toward the window and Kieran readied himself for the next move.

He clenched his jaw at his own stupidity. He should have left when he'd first found the plans or at least called someone to tell them what he'd found. Now he'd have to fight his way out with the plans. Not that that was without fringe benefits. If he got another crack at Jim—

The hand with the champagne bottle rose first. Kieran ducked away from the blow but the not quickly enough and the bottle grazed the top of his head. The cork popped as the bottle continued past and bubbly liquid sprayed outward. A dull pain emanated from the point of impact, but he managed to avoid the emptying bottle as it flew past him, thudded against the wall and rolled. Kieran sidestepped, let Jim's momentum carry him past and shoved a fist into Jim's kidneys. The contractor groaned and dropped to one knee.

Kieran stepped forward to gain the upper hand but Jim's elbow came back into his groin, dropping him onto the floor. Pain ripped through him and he wondered if he'd ever breath again. Jim landed another hard blow to the side of Kieran's head. Warm liquid dribbled down the left side of his face. The coppery smell of blood bit his nostrils and a second blow came from the unseen object. He shook his head to clear the fuzz, but found only shooting stars and pain.

He blinked. He had to focus.

A flash of movement to his left. He shielded his head and

swung. The contact wasn't solid. The room spun and he struggled to stay upright. A flash of white. A T-shirt. Kieran swung again, grabbed a shoulder and followed with a knee. He staggered backwards, hit the wall and used it to steady himself.

He wiped blood away from his left eye, blinking to clear his vision. Jim fought to his feet, bobbed a moment then lunged. Kieran dodged to his left and Jim slammed into the wall. He hurled a canister at Kieran who batted it away with one hand. Unexpected weight in a second container seemed to bring Jim up short. And when he dropped his gaze to it, Kieran took advantage, landing a hard kick to Jim's middle. The man doubled over in pain, choked, then fell to the floor.

Kieran grabbed for the plans. He had to get them and get out. He fished under the desk where the plans came to rest during the struggle, grabbed a hold of an end of the roll and pull. Pain shot through the back of his skull as nausea flooded him.

"Ha!" Jim's triumphant laugh echoed in Kieran's head just before it hit the floor.

Casey stretched her hand across the pillow beside her and found it empty. She opened her eyes. Where had Kieran gone? They'd fallen asleep on her bed, huddled together; protected; safe. Now that she was alone, a hollowness filling her. She sat up and threw the blanket off.

"Kieran?" She swung her legs over the edge of the bed and stood.

The aroma of coffee greeted her as she wandered down the hall and she rounded the corner into the living area.

"Hello?"

Nothing.

Strange. Where would he have gone? She glanced at the windows. Maybe he'd just gone for a walk to clear his mind. Anyone would need it after all he'd been through.

Casey pulled a mug from the wooden tree and filled it halfway before realizing the maker's light was off. She sniffed, shrugged and sipped. Tasted fresh. So why had he turned it off?

She sighed, yawned and took another sip. Maybe he'd just gone to the store. Her stomach grumbled with anticipation. If he didn't quit cooking such delightful things, she'd have to spend all her time at the dojo just to work off the extra calories.

She smiled and touched the cup he'd left on the counter. His lips had brushed the rim. The lips that had kissed her so tenderly earlier when they'd crawled onto her bed. Falling asleep by his side, his arm draped over her middle, comfort had washed over her. No nightmares. No dreams of fire. Only warmth and security.

What would it have felt like to wake up next to him?

She ran her fingers through her hair, pulled it back from her face and wrapped it into a knot. Frowned. Her grandmother's sketch lay on the counter next to the paper she'd been figuring things on.

"What are you doing down here?"

A quick check showed nothing wrong with the frame or the wall hook, so what was it doing on the counter. She slid the pad closer. Blinked. Stopped the coffee cup halfway to her mouth and set it aside.

Good God. Why hadn't she noticed that?

She snatched her keys off the counter and hopped into the back elevator. How could she have been so blind? It had been sitting there in front of her the whole time.

A dull ache resonated outward as she hurried off the elevator and fumbled with the security gate at the back door. Why hadn't Kieran wakened her; told her what he was thinking? He should have called the police or Charlie—anyone.

Damn it.

She should have had things out with Jim months—scratch that—years ago. She hit nine-one-one on her cell and sprinted down the sidewalk toward Jim's construction site. She rounded the last corner at full speed, barely evading an approaching car as she took the last few steps. The horn that blared continued on into the distance as Casey passed through the gate into the yard. Jim's truck sat at the bottom of the stairs.

She took a few gulps of air and cast her gaze wildly around. Where were the cops?

A muffled voice filtered through the door. Kieran?

Or Jim?

The windows rattled under the weight of whatever hit the wall and Casey mounted the stairs. If she waited for the cops it might be too late. She yanked the door open as another heavy thud rattled the trailer. Movement drew her toward the desk at the end where the two men rolled back and forth in the small space.

A hand felt on the top of the desk, grabbed for the heavy paperweight that sat near the edge. Casey shot down the trailer, her panic moving back in her mind and the rhythm of her training moving forward.

Her vision narrowed as she assessed the situation and honed in on her target. Jim on top, hand raised. Kieran one arm up shielding his bloody face. She grabbed Jim's weighted hand and toppled him backward.

Jim rolled into the filing cabinet, got to his feet. His eyes, wild with adrenaline softened a moment in recognition.

"Bastard!" she cried.

He threw the rock at her, she dodged and stepped back. His hips telegraphed a kick and she closed the distance, shifting to the side out of effective range then brought a knife hand across his windpipe. She shoved him forward with his momentum. He gyrated, coughing, hand at his throat.

She clamped her jaw.

His nostrils flared.

She taught her students to walk away, to diffuse, to solve matters peacefully—whenever possible.

It was no longer possible.

Today she would stand and fight. Today she would end it once and for all.

He came at her. Anger made him sloppy and she deflected the blow and drove her knee into his stomach. He groaned and fell to the floor. She paused, waited for his next attack.

A moan from behind the desk broke her concentration, drawing her gaze away.

Kieran.

Had she been too late?

A hand closed around her ankle, pulled her leg out from under her. Instinct shot her arm out to break her fall, but she connected with a hard corner and pain stunned her. Jim straddled her, pinning her arms above her head.

His self-satisfied cackle sent shivers down Casey's spine.

"You bitch. You'll never beat me. All that training and chop suey, mojo crap won't change a thing. You will never be equal."

She hooked her foot over his right calf, pushed her hips straight up toward the ceiling and sent him into the pile of containers that lined the wall. She rolled with him, slammed an elbow into his nose.

"You're right." She stood up off of him, fisted his collar. "I'll always be better."

She released him and he rolled away, bringing an assortment of containers down on top of him. Four plastic bottles circled his head like a halo and a kitchen timer rang beside his right ear.

Sirens screeched to a halt outside the door as Kieran wrapped a hand around her shoulder. He raised an eyebrow her way then brushed her lips with his.

"Thanks," he muttered as the

first constable came through the door.

Sunlight filtered through the slight part in the curtains and into Casey's eyes. She yawned and stretched shoving her hands up under her pillow. She closed her lids and pulled the pillow back over her head.

Maybe if she ignored it, the world would go away and leave the two of them alone. They deserved a day off after everything they'd been through in the last while. Didn't they?

She yawned again, rolled toward Kieran's side of the bed.

Kieran's side.

Warmth enveloped her at the thought, but faded when she found the other side empty. Her eyes popped open and she lifted up onto her elbow at the strange noise coming from down the hall. A rhythmic...swish.

Now what?

She grabbed his pillow and tucked it up underneath her. She didn't want to know.

His scent, that wonderful mix of chocolate and spice, lingered on the pillow and she drank it in. Comfort washed over her and she snuggled back down. Her eyelids were heavy and she let them close again.

Kieran would take care of whatever it was. She was safe.

She yawned. Had it really only been two days?

Jim. The arsonist.

Hard to believe and yet, she did believe. Financial hardship and jealousy had pushed him over the edge. He'd planned to take an extra building or two then hit the ones he needed. Insurance would take care of his financial woes and the fire would clear the way for new construction, effectively killing two birds with one stone.

He claimed Al Weiss and the reporter had been accidents; the bookseller protecting his books and the reporter chasing the story. They should have gotten the hell out of their burning buildings. They'd brought it on themselves.

Casey squeezed her lids trying to stop the thoughts, but she couldn't stop the memory of her own fire. He probably would have blamed her if she'd died.

She shook her head at the stupidity

He'd rerouted the master bath vent so that smoke traveling up the electrical chase would fill her bedroom, though the rest of the building would benefit from the fire protection measures. He jammed the sash with a broken number he'd found and set the fire, planning to rush up to her rescue. If he got there in time, she'd be so grateful that she'd take him back. If not, the building would be his.

Either way he'd win.

Idiot.

She sighed and rolled onto her back. Her eyes traced the ornate pattern of the metal ceiling panels. She couldn't remember the last time she'd awoken so calm and relaxed. Even thinking about what had happened, or nearly happened, hadn't tied her in knots. She was safe. She could face whatever the day had to offer. Wanted to face it.

Albeit not at this moment.

A smile twitched at the corner of her mouth as she rolled back onto her side. Who would have believed it? Kieran Hennessy. The most crotchety man she'd ever met. Her partner. Her love. She squeezed his pillow harder, inhaled his scent again.

She hesitated. Inhaled deeper. Was his scent getting stronger?

Not possible. She flopped onto her back, let his pillow roll away. She sniffed again, sat up and grabbed her robe.

"What the—"

She cinched the terry belt round her waist and walked down the hall to the kitchen. Bowls and utensils sat neatly beside the sink and a warm spiciness permeated the space. A metal baking pan waited on the far counter and she leaned forward to spy the contents of the bowl.

Beyond the counter, plaid cotton covered Kieran's bottom and she admired the musculature of his bare back as he slid one pan into and one out of the oven. He lifted a spatula off the counter and turned toward her.

His smile turned her legs to jelly despite the white apron that hung to his knees and she leaned on the stool for support. He leaned across the counter to brush her lips with a kiss.

"What are you doing?" She asked.

He cocked an eyebrow, lowered the pan so she could see and shrugged.

"Baking cookies."

Made in the USA
San Bernardino, CA
06 September 2014